Journey to Senility

Lisa Bell

Radical Women

PO Box 782
Granbury, Texas 76048
LisaBell@bylisabell.com
www.bylisabell.com

ISBN: 978-1-7340398-9-4

In memory of my mother
and for all who watch as reality slips from
a loved one's conscious mind

Table of Contents

Acknowledgments

Many people contributed to the writing of this book. Although they provided only a tiny taste of dementia, my mother and stepfather opened my eyes to the world of those who provide care long term. I'm blessed that God spared me years or even decades of watching them decline. For that, I'm most grateful.

Melissa Griffin, thank you for allowing me to join countless Zoom and in-person meetings during the last two years. The education you and others provided through the Alzheimer's Association gave me insight from various perspectives. Listening to those in the early stages, caregivers and professionals all helped me understand dementia better. Without you all, I could never write from a patient or caregiver's perspective.

My sister and brother-in-law, Patty and Mike Smith, thank you for sharing the pain you experienced with Pat. My heart hurt for you both so many times as we watched Mike's mom decline. Your stories helped bring color to many scenes in this book.

And my sister, Wanda Strange, you provided medical background, input on writing skills, and experience from the encounters you had with Linda. You are one of my biggest encouragers, and I can't thank you enough for saying, "You have to finish this novel." Your gentle prodding kept pushing me to the end.

Kerry and Ginger Strange, thank you for lending me my sister and showing interest in all my writings. For all the dinners out and times of taking me away from work long enough to let my brain rest before getting back to it.

To Amber, Diane, Elizabeth and Angela, thank you for being daughters that assure me, if I ever take such a journey (which I pray I don't) you will either put me out of my misery or take the best care of me possible. Thank you for continuing to support my craziest ideas and always loving me.

For Living Waters Writers and Heart & Soul Writers members, without you all, I can't imagine writing this book. You kept me on task and gave me solid feedback. The words in this book run deep because of your willingness to point out both good and could-be-better passages. Pat, thank you for the extra lunches when you served as a sounding board. Chris and David, you both caught errors I missed, and helped me find spots that made no sense to anyone but me. Mary-Margaret, your sweet humor and honesty helped me hone those skills in my writing.

Mostly, I thank the Lord for giving me a mind and experiences that prepared me for writing this story. With You, all things are possible, but without You, I fall flat on my face. Your love, forgiveness, and healing touch make life not merely bearable, but extraordinary.

Death of memory

Evokes the release of emotions

Mentioning the past triggers memories or frustration

Events of the day or long-ago fade

No one can explain why

Time makes the condition worse, not better

Intimate details of life no longer matter

Anyone can fall victim—themselves or in a loved one

"Never let the brain idle. 'An idle mind is the devil's workshop.'
And the devil's name is Alzheimer's."

— George Carlin

The Fall

Oblivious to surroundings, Gertrude stared at the old shed, memories haunting her mind.

Miserable whitewash. Hid nothing. Ought to bulldoze it.

Someday.

She shook her head, averting her gaze from the wooden building. Despite the early morning coolness, the sun peeked over the back fence, hinting of the intense heat predicted later in the day. Still, her flowers bloomed, the trees blossomed. The lawn she mowed the previous day glistened, traces of dew cleansing and refreshing every inch of greenery. Gertrude breathed in the freshness scented by colorful flowerbeds bathing the yard. Birds greeted the morning, pouring peace over her soul.

Perfection.

And it all belonged to her—worth every moment she spent laboring over it. Inside the house—who cared? Too many reminders of childhood and teen years lingered there. She preferred enjoying the yard more than sitting inside, cooped up in the dreariness of the old Victorian.

Glancing at the pristine Bible on the bistro table beside her, she picked up her coffee. "I will get to that in a moment. Is it wrong for an old woman to enjoy coffee while steam still rises?"

A nearby squirrel chattered a reply.

"Oh, you pesky little thing." Gertrude detested the thieving creatures. "You leave my birdseed alone, you rat."

The squirrel vaulted to the ground, right through her rose garden. "Hmmmpf. You better run." She took another sip. "What is that?"

A revolting weed popped up its ugly head beneath the Almost Black roses, defiling the perfect bed. The rich redness of the flowers, their fragrance permeating the air—intruders did not belong beneath them.

"Oh, that will never do. A weed among roses? That is as bad as sugar in coffee. Should tend to you right now before you invite all your seedy little friends."

When did she start talking to weeds and squirrels? "I am not like my mother," she whispered to the breeze.

Oh yes, the weed. Still in silk pajamas, Gertrude sipped coffee and nibbled a bran muffin while scrutinizing the garden intruder. "Really should get the hoe out so I do not forget about that pest."

So many things to do, and forgetting the weed must not be one of them.

The key. Need the key.

Setting the cup back on its saucer, she stood and stretched. She did not like searching for things. Such a cute house plaque with neatly tucked keys. The discreet latch prevented prying eyes from discovering her secret. She tripped the hidden lock, revealing several keys. The small silver one? No, that started the mower. The one with tiny hearts—leave it alone. No one needed to know about that one. Ah, yes. The black one tinged with red roses. Perfect for the shed key. Gertrude plucked it off the minuscule hook and shut the miniature door, making sure the latch clicked in place.

Stretching again, Gertrude wandered toward the steps. Her friends kept telling her, "Sell the old place," insisting she was too frail for an old-fashioned house. Frail? Not her. True, the house reeked with unpleasant memories, but she grew up there and knew every inch of it, including those special places where she used to hide. Besides, without a mortgage from the time her mother finally passed, why should she sell it?

"Old biddies. I am not weak and decrepit like them. Jealous old women, forced to live in retirement communities, pretending they dwell in an enchanted castle instead of a place with decaying old people." Gertrude shook her head. "Not me. This is a fine, vintage house, and I shall stay here forever—at least until they cart me out."

She looked at the key in her hand, searched her mind. Gazing around, Gertrude rubbed her forehead with her fingertips. "Oh yes. I must take care of that weed."

As she shuffled toward the steps, chittering caught her attention. "So, you came back, did you? Trying to steal my breakfast now? Go on, you little rat! Get away!"

The squirrel flicked his tail, shooting icicles into Gertrude's eyes. She blinked. The creature's snout lengthened. Dropping fuzziness, the tail grew longer, thinner. Changing from a soft brown to dark gray, the animal's skin took on the pallor of death. A beady gaze bore into her own.

"Aaaaaa. A rat!" Her legs trembled as she twirled, searching for a weapon.

Nothing.

"You stay there. Let me get my hoe! I will destroy you!"

Gertrude rushed to the steps, dizziness sweeping over her. Two steps down, she caught her big toe.

Tripping.

Tumbling.

Pain searing.

Sprawled on the pathway beside the bottom step, she looked up. No rat, but the mischievous squirrel stared back, chattering while amusement spread across his face.

How dare he laugh?

The critter grabbed a seed from the bird feeder and sped away.

Fire exploded in Gertrude's hip and traveled through her entire body.

Not good.

Reaching up, a ginger touch to the forehead.

Ouch. Move. Must move.

Can't.

"Oh, what beautiful flowers."

Without warning, Gertrude's colorful world went black.

The Call

The call came at the worst possible moment.

Trudy looked at the cell phone screen, shook her head, and punched the answer button. "Irma, you know I'm at work. I'm rushing to a meeting. Can I call you back in…"

"Gertrude fell. Again. It could be bad this time."

She froze. "What do you mean bad?" Trudy's sister tended toward overreaction. Bad might mean anything. Most likely it meant Irma didn't want to deal with their great aunt.

Irma huffed. "She hit her head when she fell, but they think a stroke might be the reason she fell. They say she isn't making any sense—incoherent speech, confusion. When I talked to the nurse, she said they were taking her in for a cat scan."

Oh, Gertrude.

"That doesn't sound good, Irma. Are you at the hospital?"

"No, I'm…" her sister hesitated then gushed. "I have an appointment. Can't reschedule. It took too long to make it. Please. You go."

Trudy sighed. Not what she needed—especially on a day full of scheduled meetings.

"Seriously? You never go." Trudy inhaled, held for five seconds, and exhaled. "I can't just up and leave work. I have a meeting in five minutes. With a major presentation for the VPs. Could mean that promotion. A better future."

"Sorry. I can't go. I have far too much on my list today. Zane, the kids. They need me. Besides, you always were Gertrude's favorite niece. She doesn't even like me."

"I wonder why," Trudy mumbled.

"What?"

"I have to catch Peter. If I'm supposed to take care of Aunt Gertrude, he has to cover for me in this meeting. I'll talk to you later."

Trudy disconnected, not waiting for her sister to end the call. *So long promotion. Breathe. Deep.*

What choice did she have? Her mom had enough health issues. She didn't need the stress. Not that she cared any more than Irma did. And her sister… Too absorbed with her life and all that entailed.

Who else would take care of Aunt Gertrude? Dad used to drop everything and make sure his aunt had whatever she needed, or wanted. He never attempted putting it on anyone else. Not for Gertrude or the other people he cared about. He just did it. Whatever "it" happened to be. Oh, how she missed her daddy.

Not now, girl. Hold it together. Deal with all the emotions later.

Tilting her head back she closed her eyes for a moment, filled her lungs, dropped her head and rounded the cubicle entrance, almost flattening her boss.

"Whoa. What's your hurry? You super excited to nail this presentation?"

She looked down. "Peter, I have a situation."

He leaned in. "What's going on, Trudy?"

"Aunt Gertrude fell. Again." Tears fought for release. "They think it could be something more serious—maybe a stroke."

"Oh no, Trudy. I'm so sorry. Are you OK?"

She looked up, forcing the tears to back off.

Peter touched her arm. "Go. I got this. You know family always comes first with me."

"I know." Another breath. Deeper.

"I'm serious. It'll be OK. Go check on your aunt. Call when you know something."

Trudy didn't move.

"Go on. Get outta here." Peter gently nudged her toward the desk. "I'll talk to you later."

Packing up her laptop, Trudy silently prayed.

Let her be OK. I can't deal with this—not now.

Why did this have to happen right when her life seemed on track for a change? Trudy put so many hours on the project, and of all days, she didn't want to bail and rush off when she had a chance to prove her value to the company.

Cringing, Trudy stopped.

Poor Gertrude. She didn't mean to ruin my day. Not her fault. Irma could've gone. But…

She pushed aside the bubbling emotions, heaved the laptop bag over her shoulder, and rushed to the door. At least she could work while she waited at the hospital. If she could keep the niggling thoughts from distracting her.

At the Hospital

Trudy rushed through the emergency room door, hating the twinge of antiseptic mixed with body odor. Moans and sobs met her with a less-than-welcome vibe. Approaching the desk, she clutched her bag.

"Hello, I'm here for Gertrude Ryan."

The attendant waved her aside. "I'll be with you in a moment."

"I'll wait right here."

The woman ran her tongue over her teeth. "Suit yourself. As you can see, we're rather busy at the moment."

"Look, I just want to be with my great aunt. I know she's here, and I can help with questions." Trudy crossed her arms. "This isn't my first time, so don't push me aside to wait for hours while you don't even check her status."

The young woman huffed, clicked a few keys on her computer. "The doctor is with her now."

"Can I go back?"

"I'm afraid not. It's a new policy." She smirked. "If you take a seat, the doctor will come out momentarily."

Trudy didn't move.

"You're choice. I can't change the rules for ya. Stand there all day, but a chair might be more comfortable."

One more glare, and Trudy turned, looking for an empty seat—preferably one away from the sickest looking people and screaming children.

She slipped into a semi-secluded spot and entered the endless waiting phase of the ordeal.

An elderly man circled the room, smiling and addressing people. When he reached Trudy, he winked. "Delightful spot. It's where I hide sometimes."

Trudy shook her head and grinned. "That obvious?"

"Oh, I utterly hate sitting in a waiting room. That's why I volunteer here every day."

"What? That doesn't make sense."

He chuckled. "After my sweet wife went on to Heaven without me, I needed something to keep me busy. I spent too many days here, waiting for someone to tell me something. I figured what better place to help someone? Name's Joe." He tilted his head. "You a coffee drinker?"

"Absolutely."

"It's not great, but I can bring you a cup."

"Hmmm. That might help. I thought about working, but I can't concentrate."

"I'll be right back."

As Trudy waited for the old man's return, she checked her phone for messages.

Maybe Irma changed her mind and is on her way. Yeah right.

Startled by a blur before her, Trudy looked up.

"Your coffee, ma'am. If you need to talk, I'm a good listener."

Taking the cup, she forced a smile. "Thank you. Wish I knew what's going on. They won't let me see my great aunt. I don't know anything."

He patted her shoulder. "I'm sure the doc will come out soon. It just feels like hours."

"Thanks. You're right. Too impatient, huh?"

"Maybe. Waiting can be hard when you care about someone who's back there."

Joe gave her a smile, then spotted another person alone. "I'll be over there if you need anything."

Trudy sipped the substandard coffee. Sudden loneliness swept over her. Imagination played with her brain, filling it with pictures of Aunt Gertrude as a living vegetable, unable to care for herself.

What then?

Knots took residence in her stomach, churning, twisting.

Auntie will be fine. She's a tough old bird. All those years with her mother, Gertrude never caved. Even when Dad died, she stood like a steel tower, holding emotions together, doing what needed done. Not that Mom or Irma ever admitted it. His death shook her, though. Gertrude treated him like her son instead of a nephew.

Bits and pieces of her dad's story toyed with her memory. Only bits. Her aunt never talked about it much, blocking questions and changing the subject any time she asked.

Leaning back, Trudy wondered how her great aunt felt that night. A five-year-old left in her care while she waited for word about her sister after a head-on collision. Did fingers of fear grasp her, filling her head with unwelcome images, too? Did Gertrude know they named her as guardian? Surely, she did. All that time, she took care of Dad and her aging mother who some family members called a loon.

Never in front of Gertrude though. She never allowed them to talk bad about Grams.

Never.

Would she be as faithful and adamant about Gertrude if necessary? She tried defending her against Mom and Irma. But what could she say when they called her aunt a bitter old woman? How could she defend against icy, hard truth?

A sip of coffee.

Yuck. Nastier when cold.

She tossed the cup in a nearby trashcan. As she scooted back in the chair, a middle-aged doctor came through the door, distinguishing grey highlighting the dark hair near his temples.

"Family of Gertrude Ryan?"

Trudy slipped up her hand. The doctor ambled over and dropped into the chair beside her.

"Hi, I'm Dr. Thompson. How are you?"

"I've had better days." Shaking his hand, she introduced herself. "I'm Trudy—Gertrude's great niece."

The doctor surveyed the waiting room. "Are you here alone?"

"Yes, just me."

"OK. We're dealing with a broken hip—the nightmare of every elderly person. But I fear she may have something else going on." He paused, letting Trudy process before he continued. "I'm still trying to sort out what happened. She was home alone, apparently on the back porch. A Bible, coffee and muffin on a table there, so we think she took breakfast outside."

Trudy nodded. "She does that when weather's nice—enjoys starting her day with the birds, grumbling at the squirrels."

His smile comforted her. "So, breakfast outside—normal. But something drew her off the steps, and that's where she seems confused."

"What do you mean?"

"From what EMS reported, she may have fallen down a few steps. They found her on a pathway leading from the porch to a shed."

"Oh, shi… juice. I've been after her to get railing installed. She brushes me off and says railings are for old women. Maybe she'll listen to me now. But what do you mean confused?"

"Nothing she says makes sense. Lots of rambling about a squirrel, then a rat, back to a squirrel. Then she goes on about an intruder in her rose bed, how she needed to get the hoe and destroy him."

"A rat? Intruder?" Puzzling. "I can't imagine a rat. Gertrude hates rats—to the point of regular extermination visits. If she had an intruder… Then it makes more sense for her to head inside, lock the door and call the sheriff."

"Exactly. That's what concerns me the most."

"My sister said something about a stroke?"

"Maybe. But she doesn't have classic signs of a stroke. An obvious bump to her head, maybe hard enough to knock her out. But I think her loss of consciousness came from pain and shock rather than any head injury. Still, I am concerned."

"So, what comes next?"

"Well, we need to do surgery to repair the hip. She's stable, so I think we can do that without issues. We need someone of sound mind to sign consent forms."

"I'll take care of that. I'm her next of kin."

"Good. Out of caution, we went ahead with a CT scan. Not showing any sign of a stroke there."

"That's good, isn't it?"

"Possibly. But it doesn't account for the confusion."

"C'mon, doc. She's 80 years old."

"Have you noticed differences in her memory or behavior lately?"

"She sometimes stops mid-sentence, and several times I helped her find keys. But I have moments when I spend 30 minutes searching for my phone and keys, and I'm half her age."

They both laughed.

Trudy continued. "I guess she's been grumpier lately, but honestly…"

"What?"

"Oh, you might as well know." Trudy sighed. "Aunt Gertrude always comes across as bitter and harsh with most people. Lately though, she even barks at me, and that never used to happen. She always liked me—the favorite one."

"Hmmm. How about changes in hygiene? Clothes?"

Trudy scratched her nose. "I noticed some wrinkles in her clothes a few times."

"That's not so bad."

"For Ms. Prim of the Century? That's what my sister calls her. She doesn't go out without appearing pristine. But now that you mention it, several times she met me for lunch without fixing her hair, and I caught her in pajamas at 10:00 one morning. And before you ask, Gertrude always dresses before eating breakfast at precisely 7:30."

"Interesting. She came in wearing silk pajamas. Is there a family history of dementia?"

"What? No! At least I don't think so." Trudy traced through the stories from childhood. "Maybe? No."

"Something's giving you pause."

"Well, my dad used to talk about Grams—Gertrude's mother. She wasn't "right," but I don't know all the details. Dad said Gertrude's father was a mean man. Really mean. He used to talk about them finding Grams locked in the bedroom, thin and fragile. I remember it because Dad always flinched when he got to the part about the stench. He never went much past that part. Anytime we talked about it, he got quiet, like he didn't want to remember. He was only five or six, but the darkness that covered his face when he told the story... Disturbing."

Listening intently, the doctor tugged at his beard. "I think we should run a few tests. We already drew blood, but I want a MRI for certain, a MMSE, and maybe a mini-cog."

"MRI, I know. What's a MMSE and mini-cog?"

"The MRI will rule out a stroke, reveal one, or perhaps show signs of Alzheimer's. Blood work rules out any vitamin deficiencies that contribute to loss of mental function and confusion. The MMSE and mini-cog can help determine if she has any form of dementia."

Alzheimer's? Dementia? No.

Trembles attacked Trudy's hands. Not Gertrude. The rock-hard woman she knew couldn't lose her mind. No way. Nausea bubbled in her gut as she covered her mouth.

Gently touching her arm, the doctor continued. "It may be nothing, but prepare yourself. I've seen this before. I take it your aunt is a strong, intelligent woman."

Mild statement to describe Auntie. She nodded.

"Let's make sure nothing's wrong. At 80, it could be old age and trauma from the fall. But I don't want to assume that and be wrong. She'll have several days here and then a stint in rehab. Either way, we have time to assess her and take steps for the future."

"OK."

"I'll have the nurse get the consent forms ready. Would you like to see Gertrude before we take her to surgery?"

"Yes. Please."

Standing up, she forced her feet to move, follow the doctor through doors that blurred behind tiny droplets dancing in her eyes.

Not about whether she wanted it—she needed to see her aunt.

Gertrude Wakes

Blinking her eyes, Gertrude's heart accelerated.

Where was she?

Twinges whacked various body parts. Others ached. Sharp pain nagged at her hip.

Something happened.

If only she could remember what.

Rhythmic beeps pulsated against her brain, begging for attention. Willing thoughts to clear, she looked toward the annoying sound. A monitor.

Hospital?

I'm in…

Ah yes.

The tumble down the steps.

Pain.

Beyond that?

No clue.

She looked around the dim room until her eyes settled on a young woman reading a book. Familiar, but…

Nope. Nothing.

She should know her name. Pounding in her head. She could not think straight.

I am so tired. Sleep. Then I will be fine.

Not remembering, though. That might be a problem.

Gertrude stopped fighting and drifted back to sleep.

A flicker of light pulled Gertrude from sleep. Squinting, her gaze darted around the room and landed on the young woman.

Still there.

Ruth? Ira? No. Why don't I know her name? Do I know here?

The girl looked up. "Aunt Gertrude? Are you awake?"

"No. Maybe. I'm dreaming. Must be. Strange place, smells."

"You're still in the hospital."

"Hospital?"

"Yes. You fell and broke your hip. But they fixed it. Now you only need to recover."

"I fell?"

"Yes."

"The steps. Ground. What is that beeping? It hurts my head."

"They put monitors on you. I'll ask if they can turn the volume down a little. Are you in a lot of pain?"

"Pain? I don't know. Can't think straight."

"They gave you painkillers. Maybe you need to rest."

"Yes. Rest. "

Gertrude's vision swayed as she looked up at the kind face. "I'll wake up in a minute."

"No worries. You have nowhere to be tonight. It's alright to sleep."

"Hmmm. OK."

The woman reached up and turned off the light, while Gertrude breathed deeply, closed her eyes, and let sleep drown out the beeping.

###

Vertical blinds hung over the picture window, lights flickering through with a welcome wink. But Gertrude did not care. Those incessant beeps made her crazy. Her head ached, and her stomach growled. She peeped over at Trudy, slouched on the sofa with a book in her hand, eyes closed.

"Hmph. Sleeping. Figures."

Pushing back the covers, Gertrude swung her feet over the side of the bed. As she moved to stand, a sharp tug pulled the gown, if you could call it that. Flimsy, worn-out piece of fabric. She took a step, hoping the back showed nothing.

BEEEEP!

Gertrude jumped.

Trudy catapulted from the chair. The book hit the floor with a loud thump. "Aunt Gertrude!"

The door flung open and two nurses dashed into the room. The older of the two spoke first. "Ms. Ryan. I'm glad you're up, but you mustn't get out of bed without our help."

"I do not need help to use the restroom."

A plastic smile played with the nurse's upper lip. "You had a nasty fall, Ms. Ryan, followed by surgery on your hip. Until we know why you fell, you most certainly do need our help if you get out of bed for any reason."

The younger nurse silenced the alarm.

"Thank you," Gertrude said. "That noise makes my head hurt. Now, if you all will excuse me, I need to take care of business before you have a mess to clean up." She inched toward the open door.

Nurse Smartypants moved to her side and grabbed her arm.

Jerking back, Gertrude cut her eyes at the nurse, narrowing them. "I can walk on my own."

"I'm sure you can, but we don't want a fall on our watch. We're being safe and following protocol."

Rolling her eyes, Gertrude glanced over at her great niece.

"She's right, Auntie. They only want to make sure you don't fall again. Let them do their job."

The old woman shook her head. "If I must. But I am fine by myself." To prove it, she sped up, ignoring pain darting through her hip and daring Smartypants to keep pace.

She did.

Gertrude paused at the restroom. "I can do this part alone."

"I don't doubt that, Ms. Ryan, but protocol dictates that I stay close."

"Does that mean you plan to wipe my butt too?"

"No ma'am. I generally leave butt-wiping to the aides."

"Then maybe you can back off and let me have some privacy?"

"Let me get you beside the toilet, and then I'll turn around."

"Are you serious? You expect me to share my stink with the entire hospital?" Not that she planned to do more than pee.

"I promise you won't smell any worse than the odors we experience every day."

"But it is MY stink. I do not share that with anyone." She looked over at Trudy. "Trudy, a little help here."

Trudy shrugged.

Nurse Smartypants smiled. "Would you feel better if I held my nose?"

"No. I prefer that you shut that blasted door and let me do this in private."

"Once I know you're safely seated, I'll step out and mostly close the door. But only if you promise to tell me when you finish."

"Fine. Grrrrrr. Perhaps, while I take care of business, you can bring me some food. I believe dinnertime came and went hours ago, judging by the darkness outside."

Smartypants nodded at the younger woman. "I have this. See if you can get something for Ms. Ryan to eat. Clear liquids only." She smirked at Gertrude. "Sorry, doctor's orders."

Not what she wanted to hear. "What do doctors know about me? I suppose they think because I am "old" I need baby food."

"I can arrange that if you want. But Jell-o and broth might have a touch more flavor. I'm sure by tomorrow you can choose from the fine assortment of dishes our chef prepares."

"Ha. Chef smef."

Bad enough they trapped her in a hospital with nasty, sparse food and no doubt a bill that rivaled a five-star hotel and restaurant. And she did not like the humiliation coming from this… this… Smartypants.

Just wait until I see that doctor. He better let me go home. Tonight.

To make matters worse, Gertrude had no memory of falling, or a clue about why, and that bothered her more than anything.

Good Morning Gertrude

The gray of dawn slipped between half-opened blinds. The incessant, steady beep continued.

Annoying.

How could an old woman sleep? At least Gertrude's head ached instead of throbbing, a clearness returning to her thought processes.

"I suppose the beep means I am still alive," she muttered to herself. "Steady—a good sign, I believe."

Her bladder full, she pushed back the covers.

Don't get out of bed without a nurse.

She remembered those words from the previous day, wondering if Smartypants had the day off. One could hope. At any rate, she needed the bathroom, and her bladder had little intention of waiting.

With an enormous sigh, Gertrude reached for the call button just as the door quietly opened.

"Good morning." The young nurse exuded too much cheerfulness while the sun rested below the horizon. "How are we this morning?"

"I do not know about this *we* you speak of. However, *I* need to empty my bladder. Immediately."

"Oh, of course. Can I get your vitals first?"

"Not unless you want to embarrass an old lady and change this impossibly uncomfortable bed before the sun rises."

The nurse chuckled. "OK, OK. You got me. Let me get a bedpan."

"I think not." True, her hip felt like a truck collided with it, but surely, she could walk to the bathroom.

The nurse pursed her lips. "They do want you up if possible.

Prevents pneumonia and blood clots. But recovering from a fractured hip, it may hurt. Bad." As the nurse moved to the other side of the bed, she asked, "Can you tell me your name?"

"What a stupid question. Do you not have it on your chart?"

Wait. Fractured my hip? Not possible. Did I?

"Yes. I know your name, but I need to make sure **you** know it. Standard protocol for head injuries."

"Oh. Very well. My name is Gertrude Ann Ryan."

"Date of birth?"

"Protocol?"

The nurse nodded.

"January 10, 1939." Of all the silliness. OK, so sometimes she forgot her birth date. She did not intend to volunteer that tidbit of information.

"Very good. I'll finish when we get you back into bed. Let me just steady you."

"I am fine, thank you. Not an invalid. I can walk by myself."

"Of course, you can, Ms. Ryan, but if you fall while I'm standing right here, they'll have my hide—and my job. I got a baby to feed and clothe. Please don't make me lose my job."

Those big blue eyes reminded Gertrude of a stray puppy begging for a place to sleep and a bite of food. Such sadness did not match the cherry disposition. She shook her head and huffed, accepting the nurse's arm. Not that she admitted it, but the strength steadied her steps as she scooted to the bathroom. Pain zoomed through her hip, buttocks, and thigh. Different from the previous day. She clenched her teeth with every other step until they reached the doorway.

"Can I at least take it from here? I like my privacy."

"I understand. Hold the rail, and I'll look away." A knowing smile passed the young woman's lips.

Humph. Not all bad. At least this one does not act condescending. Not like Smartypants.

Finishing and washing her hands, Gertrude peeked out the bathroom doorway. Did she imagine seeing Trudy last night? No. She glanced across the room where her great niece sprawled over the tiny couch. Considering her nasty bed, she couldn't imagine how uncomfortable that overgrown chair felt. Poor girl. Her namesake—the only family member she tolerated.

"I suppose she stayed with me last night?"

"Yes ma'am." The nurse offered her arm again. "Let's get you back into bed so I can check your vitals. It's important."

While reattaching the clip that promised to trigger an alarm if Gertrude got up without help, the nurse continued inane questioning. "Do you know where you are and what day it is?"

"A hospital. It is… What retiree bothers with the day of the week, anyway? Unless we have an appointment. Not like I can go anywhere at the moment. I remember falling, and that happened, I believe, on Tuesday."

"Excellent. My name is Maggie, and I'll be taking care of you today." She smiled. "For the record, you didn't miss much. It's Wednesday."

About then, Trudy bolted upright. "Oh, my goodness. What time is it?"

"Long before you normally wake up, I am certain," Gertrude said.

A deep breath and Trudy leaned back. "Guess I slept hard once I drifted off. How are you, Aunt Gertrude?"

"I am fine. Better when they finish all this and send me home."

Maggie shook her head. "Not likely today. They need to run some tests, make sure you're ready to go home."

"Oh fiddle-faddle. I am perfectly fine. A little bump never stopped me before. Far too much fuss over nothing."

"Perhaps." Maggie jotted a note on the chart. "But what if we sent you home, and everything wasn't OK? I'd feel awful."

"Right. I am fairly certain you might be alone in that."

Now where did that come from?

"I am sorry. Ignore a grumpy old woman. I should not speak before I have my morning coffee. Too bad no one thought to bring my Bible and notebook."

"Actually, Auntie, I did. I retrieved them from your back porch." Trudy rummaged in a bag, pulled out the items, and placed them on the table beside Gertrude. "I'm gonna step out, use the bathroom, and grab some coffee. Shall I get you one, too?"

"Well, that would be nice." Gertrude softened a bit. Efficient little Trudy. "Thank you." No excuse for impoliteness, despite the incessant aches in her body.

Trudy slipped out.

Maggie finished noting the vital stats. "Need anything else?"

"Just a moment to myself."

"Of course, Ms. Ryan. I'll check on you later. If you need me, use your call button. Remember, don't get out of bed without me, an aide, or another nurse."

"I will try to remember. Although, I still think you make much ado of nothing."

Maggie smiled, washed her hands, and slipped through the door as Gertrude reached for her Bible.

Middle of the Night

Gertrude gazed up at the ceiling.

Stupid hospitals. So much noise and no clock. How is an old woman supposed to know the time?

Dim light filtered into the room through opened blinds.

She looked toward the window, expecting hints of daylight.

Not there.

Darkness hung in the sky, pinpricks of light coming from an unknown source.

Definitely not morning.

As she peered into the night sky, lights raced down the window.

Blue. Red. Green.

Blue.

Red.

Green.

Blue.

"That's interesting."

Was there a meteor shower expected? She never knew them to cause colored lights or fall in a straight vertical line. Could not be a meteor shower. They did not do that.

Gertrude shifted her eyes, trying to command sleep to return.

It disobeyed.

She looked at the ceiling. So many interesting patterns there. Strange how the hospital had something other than white ceiling tiles.

She watched as one tile morphed from a man's face to a little boy. He changed facial expressions.

Then the man reappeared.

Next, the little boy, and his smile turned into a grimace.

Back again to the man.

What on earth?

She clenched her eyes. Opened them. Still there. She tried turning to her side.

Ouch.

Big mistake.

She closed her eyes again, then squinted one open. Brown spots, moving, changing. She opened both eyes wide. How did they get those spots to change?

Why?

Gertrude lay awake, watching, waiting for the movement to stop or sleep to return. Neither happened. Her bladder, as awake as her, filled, insistent with a demand for emptying. She looked over at the bathroom door.

Long way.

Every move hurt, but she had to go. Pulling back the covers, she tried moving her legs. Blobs of cloth connected to tubes held her ankles in place.

Now what? Did they shackle her? Was she in a hospital or a prison?

What is the difference?

She bent forward, reaching for the restraints. At least they did not bind her arms, so she had hope. Velcro. Good. She unfastened one, then the other. Free, she gingerly swung one leg at a time to the bedside, steadying herself with the cold, metal railing. Wincing at the pain, she tried standing, felt a tug at the back of her gown, and promptly fell back on the bed.

"OUCH!"

Loud beeps screamed at her as the door flung open, the overhead light flashed on, and Nurse Smartypants barreled into the room.

"Make it stop!" Gertrude screamed.

"Hold on, Ms. Ryan. Are you OK?"

"I just need to go relieve myself."

The nurse flicked a switch. The beeps stopped. "You can't get out of bed without assistance. Remember? You'll fall again. We prefer that you use the bedpan."

"That other nurse—the nice one—said they wanted me to get up. Besides, I can make it to the bathroom. That is easier than trying to get on a bedpan." Ooohhh. She did not like Nurse Smartypants.

"OK. But not without assistance." She moved to Gertrude's side. "Let me help you."

After a laborious effort, Gertrude finished her business and let the nurse help her back to bed. Maybe she should use the bedpan next time. Exhausted, she leaned back against the pillow.

Nurse Smartypants reattached the leg bindings.

"You do not have to tie me down. I will not try to escape."

The nurse laughed. "I'm not tying you down, Ms. Ryan. The IPC inflates and compresses your legs so you don't get a blood clot. We sure don't want that."

"IP what?"

"Intermittent pneumatic compression devise. We use them all the time." She laughed again. "It's for your good, not to confine you. Although, with your stubborn, independent streak, we might need to."

"I do not find it humorous in the least."

"You're right. It isn't funny." The smile on the nurse's face said otherwise. She finished and stepped to the side of the bed, moving to take vitals. "Can you tell me your name and birth date?"

"You ought to know my name. Did you not just call me Ms. Ryan?"

"Yes ma'am. My mistake. It's protocol."

"Oh yes. I hate that word. My name is Gertrude Ann Ryan, born January 10…" She hesitated. "Yes, January 10, 1940."

"1940? Hmm. Now, I need to check your hip. Is that OK?"

"Do I have a choice?"

"Not really. I need to see if the swelling went down." The nurse moved the gown aside.

Gertrude peeked at her hip. An immense bruise covered the upper outside part of her thigh. No wonder it hurt so much.

"Nasty bruise, but it isn't as swollen as before. I'll let the doctor know. Since you're awake anyway, maybe we can go ahead with the MRI before he comes by this morning."

"I do not want a MRI." The words slipped out before Gertrude thought about it. Darnation. If they knew she did not want one, they would do it for sure—just to spite her.

"I know." Nurse Smartypants leaned over and pulled up the covers. "MRI's can seem frightening. But we need it to isolate the fracture and know whether you need additional surgery."

"Phooey. I am fine."

"Sure you are, Ms. Ryan. Sure you are." She patted her shoulder and attached a clip to the gown. "Now, if you get up, this will set off an alarm, so please be sure to press your call button if you need the bathroom again." She placed the doodad beside her. "I'll put the device here so you can control your bed—and the TV if you want it on. Do you need something for pain?"

Was she patronizing an old woman? Gertrude might question some things in her head, but she was not ready to admit anything. She sighed. "No. I think you already filled me with more than enough painkillers. Now go away, so I can try to sleep."

"Yes ma'am. I'll check on you later."

Thank you for the warning.

As Nurse Smartypants turned off the light, Gertrude glanced back at the window.

Blue.

Red.

Green.

Her head lifted and followed the flow down. She blinked, hopeful the lights stopped. She peeked back at the ceiling. The shapes continued morphing.

Must be imagining things. My brain—playing tricks on me.

She closed her eyes, and finally, sleep washed over her.

MRI

"Good morning, Ms. Ryan." The deep voice aroused Gertrude from vivid dreams of unexplained lights and morphing figures. She focused on the handsome face above her. "I'm Don, here to take you for an MRI. Are you up to riding in a wheelchair?"

Gertrude stretched. "I might need to visit the little girl's room first." She lifted her chin. "But you are not helping me with that."

Don laughed. "Ms. Ryan, trust me. I've seen it all, but I understand. I'll protect your dignity as much as I can." He flipped a switch and removed the clip from her less-than-modest nightgown. Then he detached the things squeezing her legs. What did Smartypants call them? ICE? IPI? IPAD? Oh, phooey. Who cared? Gertrude pushed up in the bed.

"Here. Let me help you."

What a nice young man. Trudy should be here to meet him.

As if reading her thoughts, her great niece came through the door, bearing a bouquet of roses and two cups of coffee in a cardboard tray. "Good morning, Auntie. How are you?"

"My Trudy. I am glorious, although they insist on these ridiculous tests. This young man thinks he will help me to the bathroom. Perhaps you can do that, dear."

He glanced at Trudy. "Sorry. Hospital policy. I have to do it."

"I understand," Trudy said. "Auntie, let him do his job, so he doesn't get in trouble with his supervisor. OK?"

"Oh alright." Gertrude allowed Don to take her arm. "Do you want a wheelchair ride to the bathroom?"

"What? No. It hurts like hell, but I can still walk. I am not old and decrepit."

"Ma'am, I bet before this accident, you ran circles around all of us."

"You better believe it young man." She smiled. "Did you see my granddaughter over there? She's pretty, isn't she?"

Don smiled. "Yes, ma'am."

"Auntie!"

"What?" Gertrude glanced at Trudy. Bright red highlighted her cheeks. "Well, you are pretty, dear."

Trudy shook her head. "He could be my son, and I'm not looking for a man, anyway."

"Hmpff. Maybe you should be. A pretty, young woman needs a husband."

"You didn't have one, and you did just fine."

"Really? You do not know everything."

Clearing his throat, Don interrupted. "Ladies, let's keep things professional here. Besides, I believe Ms. Ryan needed to empty a bladder, and we don't want to keep the MRI tech waiting."

"Very well." Gertrude took a few steps, holding her breath to keep from crying out in pain.

After settling on the toilet, she looked up at Don. "Can you be a dear and bring the wheelchair to the door while I urinate? Alone."

"I can do that. But don't try to stand without me."

"Yes, sir." Maybe. If she finished fast, she would show him. She hated giving in on the wheelchair, but walking proved more painful than she dared admit.

Before she finished, Don stood at the door, ready to embarrass her again. Such indignity. She sighed and let him assist her.

Don pushed the wheelchair closer. "Your chariot, madame."

Gertrude furrowed her brows. "Chariot? And you think my mind's slipping. I hate to break it to you, young man, but this is no chariot. It is an ugly old wheelchair."

Laughter broke free from him. "Ahhhh, but if I call it a chariot, that makes me a footman. Much more dignified than nurse's aide. Don't you think?"

"I suppose. Let's get this thing done."

"Amen." He turned to Trudy. "I'll have her back soon."

Trudy chuckled. "Have fun."

Out the door, through the halls, into an elevator, down one hall, and up another. Gertrude grew dizzy with all the turns, searching for an exit door on the way and seeing none.

Drat. I thought I might escape. I am so turned around, I could never make it back to my room, let alone find the exit.

After several minutes, they entered another room. In the middle, a long tube lingered, not intimidating, but certainly nothing that invited Gertrude either.

"Good morning." Another overly cheerful nurse. "I'm Julie, the technician who will perform your MRI. Have you ever had one before?"

"No, I never had a need for a MRI." Gertrude eyed this new person. "Why do I need one now?"

"Precautions. Your CT scan didn't show much, so we don't think you had a stroke or a brain injury from the fall, but we want to be certain. And we want to check out that hip to see whether you need another surgery. I'll take care of both views at the same time."

"Hmpff. Just a way to rack up more money out of my pocket."

"Don't worry, Ms. Ryan. Medicare will cover it for you." She placed a hand on Gertrude's arm. "It can get loud in there, so I'm gonna slip these headphones on with soft music. If you keep your eyes open, you'll see a field of flowers above you. Relax, and I'll have you out in no time."

Something in Gertrude's mind didn't feel so sure. The tube looked too small. "Are you sure this will not hurt me?"

"Absolutely. You'll be fine."

"OK." Gertrude moved to the bed, clenching her teeth and scrunching her nose, then accepted the headphones, trying to ignore the pain.

Soft violins surrounded her as the bed receded into the tube. She closed her eyes not wanting to see, but then she grew curious. Opening her eyes, the sides closed around her, swallowing her into the tube. Her breaths came faster, begging for more air.

Suffocating. They're suffocating me.

As she started to scream, a field of flowers appeared above her. Fascinated, she studied the colors moving on gentle breezes. So real she almost wanted to touch them.

Not real. They aren't real.

Gertrude sucked in a few deep breaths and exhaled slowly each time, calming herself. The music and flowers relaxed her body against her will. Relenting, she gave in. If they used this contraption to kill her, at least she would go in peace.

Before long, the bed slid back out. The technician…

What was her name?

She removed the headphones. "All done. You did fantastic."

"Done?"

"Yes, ma'am." She helped her into the wheelchair. "Don can take you back to your room now. I bet you have breakfast waiting for you."

Gertrude stared at the young woman.

Who is she? Where am I, and what did she just do to me?

Unwilling to show any fear, she pasted on a pretend smile. "Alright. Thank you."

The woman patted her shoulder. "I'll get the MRI to your doctor right away. Get some rest."

Uncertain about anything, Gertrude tensed as a young man came toward her. "Ready, Ms. Ryan?"

Looked familiar, but she didn't know him. She nodded.

"Then madame, we shall return to your quarters." He smiled, moved behind her and the chair traveled forward—to where she didn't know.

Cognitive Tests

Gertrude struggled to re-situate herself. Although her hip ached, the sharp pain no longer kept her from moving.

"Let me help you, Aunt Gertrude." Trudy moved to her side.

She should be thankful, but the woman needed to leave. "Go back to work. I am fine, dear. Why are you still here? You have a job, and I do not need a babysitter."

"I'm taking some time off. My boss insisted."

"Phooey." The assistance made sitting straighter in the bed easier. Besides, the mattress hurt her bum, so she gave up and let the young woman help her.

A soft knock, followed by the door opening revealed a handsome young man. Oh, yes. Doctor… What was his name?

"Good morning, Ms. Ryan. How are you feeling today?"

"I am stiff, sore and want to go home. I will be fine if you tell my great niece to take me home and get back to work." She paused and gazed into his deep blue eyes. "Or you could ask her out on a date. She is a beautiful woman."

The doctor chuckled.

Trudy straightened the sheets and blanket while her face turned a lovely crimson shade. "I'm sorry, Dr. Thompson. She's forever trying to play matchmaker for me."

He glanced over at the young woman and smiled. "My mother's the same way. It's embarrassing, but kinda nice to know they care." He turned to Gertrude. "You'll be sore for a while, but they'll get you up later today and let you move a little. Start working on the rehab for your hip. I need you to stay here a few more days." He hesitated. "You know I'm not sending you straight home, right?"

"What?" *Did he really say that?* "You aren't sending me home?"

"No ma'am. We need to get that hip working, and make sure you can get around well before letting you go home to trip down steps again."

"Well, I never."

"A rehab center can complete the beginnings of the healing process. You have a little work ahead until you're as good or better than before you broke that hip."

"Rehab center? You mean an old people's home."

"Some places offer both rehabilitation and long-term care. I suspect you won't need too long there. If you cooperate, and do what they say, they may release you in a couple weeks—assuming you have someone who can take care of you at home. You live alone, right?"

"I am not a decrepit, old woman. I take care of myself."

Dr. Thompson touched her hand. "We all need help sometimes, Gertrude. It isn't a shame to accept it."

"Maybe not for you. I never needed help."

He smiled knowingly. "Don't worry. I won't tell anyone your secret."

"Secret?"

How does he know I have a secret?

"That you needed help for a minute."

"Oh. That secret."

The doctor pulled a rolling stool beside the bed while Trudy retreated to her chair. "Ms. Ryan, I want to play a game with you if that's OK."

She raised her eyebrows, tilting her head to the right. "A game?"

"Yes. Just want to check your brain function—make sure you didn't mess something up when you fell and hit your head."

"Protocol, I suppose."

"We like to follow standard procedures."

"Didn't you already do all those silly tests? The kitty scanner and flower bed thingy. What do you call that?"

"The cat scan and MRI. Yes, and I conferred with a neurologist. We saw one area that concerned us a little. It may be nothing, but we need to make sure. The tests I want to give you today help us reach a better conclusion."

"Oh, alright. Let's get on with it then."

"Excellent. Thank you." He opened a notebook then locked eyes with Gertrude. "I'm going to say three unrelated words. Listen carefully. Try to remember the words. Banana, sunrise, chair." He smiled. "Repeat the words back to me."

"Banana, sunrise… chair."

Showed him.

"That's great. Now, I have this paper and pencil." He placed a drawing of a circle on the tray in front of Gertrude. "Please draw a clock for me, with all the numbers in the correct places."

"What a stupid game. Of course, I can draw a clock." Gertrude snatched the pencil and looked at the paper.

She wrote "1" at the very top.

He must think I am stupid.

The paper blurred.

What comes next? Two. Yes, two follows one.

Grasping the pencil tightly, she continued putting numbers around the top half of the circle… "2, 3, 4, 5…"

She flipped the pencil across the tray and crossed her arms. "Who pays attention to old-fashioned clocks any more?"

"That's fine, Gertrude. You did fine." He jotted down a note. "Do you remember those three words I said when we first started?"

"Of course, I do." Gertrude spewed out a breath.

"OK. Would you repeat them for me?"

"If I must. Banana, sunshine… umbrella."

Dr. Thompson nodded, jotted down another note.

"Are we done now?" She no longer wanted to play.

"I just have some questions to ask you. Answer them the best you can."

Well, this might be a better game. Gertrude knew all sorts of trivia. She prided herself on knowledge, still read many books. Although, if she admitted it, she often forgot what she read the previous day. The doctor did not need to know that, did he?

"Gertrude, what is the year?"

She rolled her eyes. "2019."

"Good. Where are we?"

"Seriously? At the stinking hospital."

He smiled. "Do you know the city, state and country?"

"I live in the United States of America. Although, we lack much united these days. Texas... I was unconscious, so I have no idea which city the ambulance chose."

"Fair enough. The three objects from before—can you recall any of them?"

"I thought we finished that game."

"We did, but humor me."

She huffed. "Banana. I love bananas. Some say instead of an apple a day, we need to eat a banana a day. Much better nutritionally."

"I've heard that. What about the other two objects?"

"Sunrays." She pondered. What was that third word? It made her think of a tropical island, the banana, sun and something else. Gertrude brightened. "Beach."

The doctor wrote another note.

Darn his notes.

"Spell world backward for me."

"I excelled at spelling. Won the spelling bee on my eighth birthday. D-L-R-W. Wait. That's not right. D-R-L-O-W."

No response. More jotting notes.

"Gertrude, I'm going to show you a couple items, and I need you to name them for me." He pointed to the watch on his wrist and the pen in his hand.

"A watch and pen." At least that one was right.

"Good. Very good." He put a check on his list. "Repeat this phrase: no ifs, ands, or buts."

"No ifs, ands, or buts."

"Excellent." Another check.

He held up a blank piece of paper. "Fold this in half and put it on the floor for me."

Gertrude took the paper, folded the corner down and pitched it beside the bed.

Perfect.

Another note on the doctor's list. Not a check. A short note.

Why didn't he check that one? She folded that paper. She glared at the doctor, catching her upper lip with her bottom teeth. Bad habit. Why didn't she let go and call him on his mistake?

Better to maintain control. Don't give him another reason to keep her imprisoned.

The doctor held up a note card. "Read this and follow the instructions."

Gertrude squinted. "I don't have my reading glasses."

Trudy bounced to the bed. "Here, Auntie." She retrieved glasses from the nightstand and offered them.

Gertrude's eyes widened as she leaned forward in the bed. Snatching the glasses, she batted Trudy's hand.

So that's it. They're conspiring to put me away.

Her gaze shifted between the man and the woman. Nice young couple.

NOT.

Her Trudy and this slick young doctor had it in for her. If they locked her up, the two of them could take over her house and money, living together outside of marriage, sleeping in her bed.

How could they take advantage of an old woman?

How dare they!

She shrieked, "I don't want to read it. I won't let the two of you lock me away in some facility. I know what you're trying to do."

The doctor patted her hand. "Ms. Ryan, I assure you, we both want what's best for you."

"No, you don't." She jerked away from his touch. "You want my money, my home. Well, you can't have it!"

Trudy placed a hand on her shoulder. "Aunt Gertrude, calm down. Dr. Thompson and I barely know each other. I have a house. Why would I try to take your house from you?"

"Liars! Both of you! Get out. Get out of my house. NOW!"

Dr. Thompson closed his notebook and motioned for Trudy to follow him.

I knew it. They're in cahoots. I'll show them.

Diagnosis

Trudy followed Dr. Thompson into the hallway and closed the door behind her, trembling, holding back tears.

What just happened in there?

The doctor touched her shoulder. "Let's get a cup of coffee."

She nodded, swallowing the golf-ball sized mass in her throat. She dared not speak, terrified that one uttered word might morph into sobs.

That wasn't her aunt. Gertrude never treated her that way.

In a cozy, enclosed alcove, Dr. Thompson poured two cups of coffee and placed them on a table. "I'm sorry about what happened back there. I can tell it shook you."

Easing into a chair, Trudy sighed. "I don't understand. Aunt Gertrude's an intelligent woman. She should have aced that test. And the thing at the end? Where the heck did that come from? My aunt has her moments, but never toward me."

Dr. Thompson sipped his coffee. "It verified my concerns."

Trudy waited, leaning forward. Her attention focused on the doctor, willing him to continue, yet fearing his words.

"I suspected dementia," he said. "We ruled out stroke and damage from the fall. Unfortunately, I saw something suspicious on the CT scan, which is why I ordered the MRI."

"Suspicious? Like what?"

"CTs don't always show everything, but it looked like some atrophy of the medial temporal lobe."

Trudy furrowed her eyebrows. "And?"

"Well, the MRI captured definite atrophy of the hippocampus."

She tilted her head to one side. "Sorry, I'm totally confused."

Dr. Thompson chuckled. "I know. Medical speak. I need to

work on that." He relaxed into the chair. "Let me explain."

"Please do." Trudy pushed back into her chair, crossed her legs, and sipped coffee.

"I'll make it simple. With the confusion, I had to rule out the possibility of a stroke or severe head injury. The atrophy on the CT indicated a possibility of Alzheimer's. The MRI confirmed it as much as possible. Unfortunately, only an autopsy proves the disease exists in someone. While we can't know for sure, Gertrude shows powerful indicators."

The room tilted as Trudy's grip on her cup tightened. She shook her head. "Alzheimer's? No way. Not Gertrude."

"I'm sorry. With what I saw on the MRI plus her responses to the mini-cog and MMSE..." He shook his head. "It's always the most difficult for well-educated people, and I sense Gertrude didn't miss out on intelligence, independence, or perseverance."

"You got that right. I just can't believe it. Is there any chance you're wrong? Maybe... Maybe it's just something from the fall."

"Not any detectable injuries. I wish it was that simple. Dementia can come from a TBI."

Trudy bit her bottom lip, searching her brain for a meaning of the acronym.

"Traumatic brain injury. While we can only do a little to reverse the dementia in those cases, it remains constant. If this came from the fall, we might have hope for her brain to reroute. Even with a stroke, that happens. Unfortunately, with Alzheimer's, the disease progresses. It gets worse."

Trudy leaned forward. "Can't we do anything?"

"We can try medications to slow the progress, but we have no guarantees. Sometimes they work. Sometimes they don't. Eventually, the disease wins."

Trudy looked at the ceiling, willing tears to stay put. It didn't work.

Dr. Thompson touched her hand. "They make new inroads

every day. Perhaps someone will discover a cure before it steals your aunt. I can see how much you care for her."

That did it.

Tiny splashes dripped from Trudy's eyes, creating a steady stream down her cheeks. One she couldn't possibly control. Struggling to regain composure, she pulled a napkin from the holder and dabbed at her cheeks, willing the dam to close. After several minutes, she inhaled, held her breath, and slowly released it.

"So, what next?"

The doctor looked at his notes. "She scored mild to moderate. Hard to tell since we couldn't finish. That means she still has a sense of reality at times, but she may need supervision. I plan on sending her to rehab for a couple of weeks because of the hip. She needs physical therapy to recover from the break. They can observe her and get a better idea of where she falls on the spectrum. That also gives your family time to decide on the future for Gertrude. If she doesn't have medical and legal power of attorney already, that may cause some difficulties."

Nodding, Trudy tried to absorb everything the doctor said. "Thank you. I have no idea about all that. I'll have to search through her papers—see what I can find. She won't like it."

"I know this isn't easy." He handed her a card. "Call my office. They can connect you to resources that will help you through the initial crisis and moving forward."

"Thanks."

"I'm truly sorry I can't give you more hope right now." He smiled. "We keep praying for a cure and better treatment, and sometimes, we see tiny answers to those prayers."

Trudy tried to smile, although she sensed her face didn't belie her deepest feelings. She learned long ago God didn't answer *her* prayers. She tried. Believed. None of it worked—at least not since childhood. He answered back then. Maybe she had more faith before life destroyed it. Or maybe God answered, but these days He only gave her solid nos.

I have no intentions of praying for Auntie. What's the point?

Tears begged for release, but she kept them at bay.

A soft touch snapped her back to the moment. "Keep hoping, Trudy. Anything is possible."

"Yeah. Miracles, right?"

Not holding out much hope for Gertrude, she thanked Dr. Thompson again, and stumbled from the room, wondering how to face this mountain.

Denial

Gertrude glanced at the door as the doctor and Trudy slipped out.

Where did that come from? She always trusted her niece. Why would she accuse her of such an outlandish idea?

"This blasted hospital," she mumbled to herself. "No sleep. Got me seeing things and imagining all sorts of hogwash."

She knew better. Her memory suffered, but everyone had problems with remembering little things as they aged. Visions of her friends searching for glasses perched on their heads flooded her thoughts. At least she did not do anything that silly.

But questions on those tests Dr… what was his name again? Did not matter.

But it did.

She got the answers wrong. She knew by the look on his face and those incessant notes he wrote. Even worse, because of her outburst, she failed to finish the test he tried to disguise as a game. Tests to assess her mental state, no doubt.

Her friend Martha told her about a test her son made her take. When she failed to button her shirt correctly and missed the name of the president, they called her demented. Before long, they put her in "assisted" living.

Assisted, bah.

They assisted her straight to the loony bin. Put a sane person in a place with nothing but half-dead people. What did they think happened? They went berserk, of course. She visited Martha once. Only once. Most of the people in that facility muttered to themselves—meaningless dribble. No actual conversations. Martha said little during that visit, although she tried to converse. Every few words, though, she got a blank stare and hesitated before continuing, sometimes with a phrase that made no sense.

"I will not end up like Martha."

And I certainly will not end up like Mother. I am not losing my mind.

Picking up the bed control, she pushed the television button. Maybe she could find a game show—something to challenge her brain, get her thinking straight. She no longer wanted to consider the possibilities of what the doctor might say—if he dared come back.

A soft knock sounded at the door.

What now? With my luck, probably Nurse Smartypants.

Wanting to ignore the knock, Gertrude started to say, "Come in." But before the words broke free, the door opened slowly.

Ahhhh. The doctor. Returning to the scene of his crime.

At least he had guts. Maybe she could play his game. Get him to release her to go home.

She put on her best smile. "Doctor, I am so sorry about earlier. This place… They wake me up every few hours. I cannot get an ounce of good sleep. You know, that can make people say and do things they never do."

He smiled and approached the bed. "You're right Ms. Ryan. A lack of sleep can cause issues." His smile faded. "Do you sleep well at home?"

"Like a baby."

Yeah. Waking every two to three hours.

"You never wake up in the night?"

"I'm an old woman. Sometimes, I have to get up in the night—if I drink too much after dinner."

"That's true for most of us." The hint of a grin played at the corner of his mouth. "Do you go right back to sleep?"

"Of course."

If my mind does not drift off to strange places. If shadows fail to grow and make me think someone came into my room.

"Hmmm." The doctor pressed his bottom lip between his thumb and index finger. "Ms. Ryan, I see too many indications to ignore this."

"Ignore what?"

"Signs of dementia."

"Dementia?"

There. He said it. Now he will tell me I need to be in a facility.

"I'm not sure what level—since we didn't complete the tests. Time will tell, but I…" He paused, holding back.

"Just shoot straight with me, Dr. Thomas."

Was that the right name? Crud. What if that proved his case?

He chuckled. "Dr. Thompson. Close." He breathed deeply and stepped back. "I suspect Alzheimer's. I'm sorry. No one wants to hear that word, but I must be honest with you."

"**You** are crazy. Sure, I forget things sometimes, but I do not have old-timers. We can leave that for those people who know nothing and cannot recognize their families. That does not fit me."

"Not yet, but if I'm right, you'll reach that point in the future."

"Well, you are not right. I am not some senile old woman. I refuse to accept that. Besides, they brought me in here because I messed up my hip, not because of memory problems."

The doctor scratched his head. "True enough." He shrugged. "Sometimes an unexpected fall or illness gets a person where they need to be, so we can help them with other problems. You could count that fall as a blessing."

"A blessing? I am trapped in this God-forsaken hospital where I cannot get a decent cup of coffee. And you plan to send me to some facility where it may be worse. You want me to call that a blessing? I think **you** are the one who needs brain work."

A smile flashed across his face.

He would make a nice addition to the family. I should introduce him to Trudy.

"I'm with you on the coffee, Ms. Ryan. I think they make it terrible on purpose. And you can disagree with me all day, but that won't change my diagnosis."

"Well, thank you for permission to disagree. Not that I needed it. You can say what you want, but I refuse to end up in some old people's home. I can take care of myself. As soon as this hip heals, you will see."

"I hope so, Ms. Ryan. I'd love for you to prove me wrong. It wouldn't bother me if I misdiagnosed this one."

"That has to be a first. A doctor admitting he might be wrong."

"I didn't say that."

"Ha. Now you backtrack."

"I'll make a deal with you. If I'm wrong, I'll be more than happy to admit it." He wrote a note on the chart. "In the meantime, do you mind if we proceed as if I'm right?"

"And what, pray tell, will that include?"

"You need rehab anyway, for your hip. Right?"

"I suppose." Gertrude sighed.

"While they take care of that over the next week or two, I want the nurses to monitor your cognitive ability, behaviors, that sort of thing. If they can't confirm my diagnosis, then I'll recant. If they do, let me help you the best we can. Alzheimer's doesn't have a cure, but we can possibly slow the progress and maybe alleviate some symptoms."

"Possibly. Maybe. Not very promising words. Maybe I am better off taking chances with believing you are profoundly incorrect."

He laughed. "Maybe. Are you willing to give it a shot?"

"Perhaps. I will give it some thought."

"With your permission, I want to give your great-niece some

information."

Gertrude bristled. "Information? On what? The best—or worst—old folks' homes?"

"No." He shook his head. "Not at all. If we can get you through rehab and back home, that's the best place for you. We want you to live at home as long as possible. It's preferred. But in the future, you'll need some serious help."

"Oh. OK then. Make sure Trudy has it, but none of the others. I trust her, but the rest of them… They will not be able to find a home fast enough. Trudy though—she is a good girl. Did I mention she is single?"

"I believe you did."

"And pretty."

"Yes ma'am."

"You single?"

"Ms. Ryan, they should be here soon to do some rehab at the hospital. I'll get the paperwork ready to transition you for in-patient rehabilitation. Listen and do what they tell you, and we can get you home much faster."

"Of course. Maybe Trudy will come stay with me, and you could visit us. Do you make house calls?"

Dr. Thompson laughed. "Not very often. I'm afraid I don't have much free time these days."

"Pity. You seem like a nice young man."

"Thank you. Maybe I'll consider making you an exception—because I like you too." He placed a warm hand on her arm. "I'll see you later, Ms. Ryan. Get some rest until they come in for PT."

He patted her arm and left the room.

Now, why did they all think they needed to pat her? She shook her head. Bless their hearts. Dementia—Alzheimer's. What a foolish diagnosis. She might be getting old and forgetful, but she did not buy it. No way, no how.

Not going insane.

Impossible.

Next that crazy young doctor will tell me I need a host of pills to make me feel better. I know how they play that game. Take a pill that makes me sick, and then I need another. And another. And more. We shall see who wins at that game. It will not be the doctors or those drug companies.

Gertrude sank back in her bed, only then realizing the tenseness in her body. She closed her eyes and rested—just for a minute.

Accepting the Diagnosis

Gertrude pushed herself up, considering whether to call for a nurse. She almost wanted to stay in bed and see what happened.

Nope. She could not do it. The thought of a warm gush filling the bed and her having to lie in it flitted across her mind and promptly left.

As she reached for the call button, a soft knock came at the door a second before it opened. The happier-than-a-bluebird nurse entered.

"Good afternoon. I don't know if you remember me. It's been a few days."

"Of course, I remember you. You are the sunshine one. At least you are not that smarty-pants nurse." Gertrude lowered her voice. "I do not like her much."

The nurse chuckled. "Your secret is safe with me. I'm Maggie."

"Yes. Of course, you are Maggie. And because you stick like a bandage to protocol, I am Gertrude Ryan."

"Excellent. And where are we?"

"Still in this pitiful hospital where they serve the most god-awful food I ever tasted. I swear they do not put a dash of salt or pepper on anything they cook."

"Well, I can always bring you an extra packet or two."

Gertrude brightened.

Maggie.

She needed to remember that name. Maybe when the nurse slipped out, she could write it on the inside of her forearm. That helped sometimes.

"Thank you, Maggie. Not sure how much flavor that will add, but I am willing to try."

The nurse smiled as she continued taking her blood pressure. "Do you know what month we are in?"

"Hmm. I believe I came in here back in April, and it seems I cannot get the doctor to release me, even though it must be August by now. At least it feels like months since I last sat on my back porch."

"You haven't been here that long, Ms. Ryan." The nurse narrowed her eyes. "Do you really believe it's August?"

"No, silly. I know we are still in April."

"Good. You had me worried for a second there." Maggie patted her hand.

Again, with the patting. Really? Am I a dog?

"Have you been out of bed today, Ms. Ryan?"

"I went to the bathroom and took a shower, but that was hours ago."

Maggie entered information on a tablet. "I bet you could use it again, then."

"Yes. I could."

"After that, maybe you can sit in the chair for a while. Would you like that?"

"I guess. Too bad I cannot go outside and get some fresh air."

The nurse glanced over at the window. "The windows don't open, but maybe I can pull the chair over where you can at least see out. Let me unhook your alarm and help you to the restroom. While you take care of business, I'll move the chair—if you wait for me to help you off the toilet."

Gertrude shook her head and sighed. "Very well."

Settled into the chair, Gertrude gazed out the window. The trees swayed as clouds danced across blue skies. Nice view anyway. At least she could enjoy seeing outside. Oh, to be home sitting on her back porch. She might even welcome the thieving squirrels.

Or not.

Maggie tucked a blanket across her lap. "All good now?"

"Much better. Thank you, dear." She closed her eyes, drinking in the warmth of the sun shining through the glass.

"Are you alright, Ms. Ryan?"

Gertrude opened her eyes. "Yes. Not too much pain." She sucked in a breath and held it for a moment before blowing it out again.

"Are you sure?"

"What if they are right? What if I am losing my mind?"

Maggie placed a gentle hand on Gertrude's shoulder. "I can't imagine how you feel right now, but it must be scary. My Mimi has Alzheimer's. It isn't fun to watch her memory failing." She grinned. "Although, I must admit, she comes up with some crazy stories at times. I'm never sure if they're real or if she purposely makes them up to fool us. She's a hot mess."

Gertrude glanced at the young woman. "Why would she do that?"

"Sometimes, she regains a sense of reality—for a moment. Maybe it's her way of coping with the disease. She always had a quirky sense of humor."

"Oh. I never had much humor. I found little in life to laugh about."

"I'm sorry, Ms. Ryan. We all need to laugh at times." She patted her shoulder. "I hope they are wrong about you. I hope you don't have Alzheimer's. But if you do, I also know your Trudy will take good care of you. I can tell she loves you."

"I treated her so mean the other day. I doubt if she can ever forgive me." A tear trickled down her cheek. "I have no idea why I did it either. Trudy sticks by me—always did. No one else in the family even likes me. Not since my son died. Not that I blame them. I am not a nice person to most people."

"You're nice to me, Ms. Ryan."

"I have to be. Otherwise, you might not take me to the bathroom. Then what am I left with? Nurse Smartypants?"

Laughter burst from Maggie. "I can't believe you call her that. Can you keep a secret?"

"Well, if that handsome doctor got it right, I will not remember what you said anyway." A smile played at Gertrude's lips. "So?"

"Oh. So you do have a sense of humor after all." Maggie pursed her lips. "We all call her Nurse Ratched. Not to her face of course. One of the older nurses started it, and then the rest of us got together and watched *One Flew Over the Cuckoo's Nest*. It stuck from that time forward. She can be a tough old bird." She shook her head. "But she's a good nurse and knows her stuff better than most. Sometimes, she reaches a diagnosis before the doctors."

"She still seems too bossy, and so… con…" Gertrude's brow furrowed. "I hate when I forget what word I want."

"I know." Maggie put her hands on her hips. "It stinks when it slips right out your brain. And you don't have to be old or have any disease for that to happen."

Gertrude nodded. "I suppose you are right." She smoothed the blanket. "You should get back to work. I kept you long enough."

Maggie pulled the call button over to the chair. "Please remember to use this. I still have the alarm attached, so if you try to stand, it will go off. I'll be here until after you go to sleep tonight. If you need anything, call."

"I will. Thank you."

As she leaned her head back against the chair, unbidden thoughts flooded Gertrude's mind.

What will I do if I lose the ability to think straight? I knew, though. I knew something was off. Too many times forgetting tiny tasks like paying bills. But dementia? Alzheimer's? No.

Is that what plagued Mama?

Maybe losing her mind had advantages. Maybe she could forget some of the past—pieces she wanted to ignore, but never seemed able to push from her mind.

As she stared out the window, her mind drifted back to the day she took Ben to visit for the first time after her sister and brother-in-law died in that terrible accident. So small and lost without his parents, she thought a visit with his grandmother might help. Her mama did not fare well at the funeral, so despondent, and time made no difference. Mama needed the visit more than Gertrude's nephew did.

Irene's and Fred's unexpected death hit all of them with the force of a train, as if they rode in the car with the couple. She still remembered the police officer coming to their home, giving her the awful news while little Ben slept peacefully in his bed. After that night, he insisted on sleeping with her for years.

She pushed aside the sorrow that mounted. After so long, the memory seared her mind like a million hot coals.

When they entered the house that afternoon, she called to her mother.

No answer.

She took Ben's hand as they climbed the long flight of stairs, searching. Finally, Gertrude heard a whimper coming from the tiny attic room they used for storage. She turned the knob and pushed, but it did not budge.

"Mama?" The sound of her voice echoed through her brain, queasiness flooding her stomach.

Met by sobs behind the door, Gertrude reached up to find the key. She unlocked the door and stepped inside.

The stench drove her back. Urine, feces, filth. She glanced down as Ben gasped.

"Quick, baby." She handed him a handkerchief from her pocket. "Cover your mouth and nose."

She bent down where her mother leaned over in a chair, both wrists strapped to the arms. "Mama. What on earth happened? Where's Father?"

Her mother shook her head. "He. Tied. Me. Here." Tears flooded the woman's cheeks.

"Oh, Mama." Words stuck in her throat. She shoved down her emotions. "Let me untie you and find Father. Then I'll get you cleaned up. Have you eaten anything?"

Mama nodded, then shook her head.

Gertrude looked around the room, shivering in the cold air. A half-eaten bowl of soup rested on a nearby table. She touched it, hoping for warmth. Instead, the icy liquid filled her veins with rage that raced past her heart to her mind.

How long has Mama been sitting here like this? Hours? Days? Weeks?

A guttural roar climbed into Gertrude's throat, but she suppressed it.

If her father did this...

After untying her mother, she said, "Wait here. I'll be right back."

Taking Ben's little hand, she led him to her old bedroom and gave him some toys. "Stay here, honey, and play until I come back." She slipped out the door, quietly closing it behind her.

Fury taking control, she flew down the staircase and peeked outside. The shed door stood wide open. No doubt Father left Mama tied up while he went out to work with his wood, but from the odor, it wasn't just that day.

How dare he leave Mama like that? She clenched her teeth, hands shaking. How could he be so cruel?

Every memory of times he whipped her, locked her in her room, that one night in the shed—none of it compared to this.

She slipped through the back screen, resolving to have it out with him. She survived everything he did to her, but Mama? She never hurt anyone. She did nothing but wait on him like a slave, and he repaid her by leaving her in filth, bound and starving.

Heat rushed through her, the pounding of her heart beating against her eardrums.

She stomped to the shed. "You better have an explanation."

He looked up. "What's your problem?"

"I just found Mama."

"Well, good for you."

Gertrude planted her feet wide, adrenaline drowning any fear of this man she hated. "You tied her up and left her in that freezing room alone. For how long? Don't you lie and tell me just today. She stinks to high heaven. How could you do that? She never did anything but obey your every demand. Never. Not even when she saw the whelps you left on mine and Irene's legs and butts. How could you be so... so... evil?"

He shrugged. "She's lost her mind. I can't control her, and I'm sick of her pissing all over the floor and crapping all over herself. I ain't taking care of no full-grown toddler. She can sit in the mess for all I care." He turned his back. "Besides, she gets into everything, making a mess for me to clean, and she almost burned down the house. Don't judge what you don't know." He picked up a hammer. "Yeah, I tied her up and locked the door— had to for her sake. If I didn't, she'd kill us both."

Gertrude glared at the back of his head.

Pick up something and smash his skull. No jury would convict me.

She looked around. Nothing within her grasp. Nothing— except the padlock and keys hanging on the hook beside the door.

"You ass!" Without thinking past the moment, she grabbed the keys and lock. "Maybe you need to see how it feels being locked up."

With those words, she slammed the door and threw the padlock in place, cramming it to the locked position. The pounding of his boots against the wooden floor inside reverberated, rattling the tiny window pane. The knob twisted.

"Open this damn door."

His fists beat against the wood, shaking the entire shed. "You little whore. Unlock this—NOW!"

The lock held tight.

She knew it would.

"I wanted to do that for years. Maybe a night in the shed will change *your* behavior."

Reaching the porch steps, Gertrude's knees buckled.

Did she just do that?

Her father's pounding and shouting shook her to the core. She could not let him out. Too much anger seeping beneath that shed door.

Let him rot in there with the rats. He deserves it.

In the morning, she might remove the padlock and let him bust out, but not before she rescued her mother and disappeared somewhere safe from that monster.

A soft knock broke Gertrude's concentration, her hands quivering.

Oh, to forget that dreadful memory. If she had to forget, why not start with that one?

She swiped away a tear as Trudy's voice sliced through the silence. "Hi, Auntie." She moved in front of the window, concern flooding her face. "Are you alright?"

"Of course, dear. Just re… remembering something."

Confronting Rehab

Trudy breathed deeply, uttering a silent prayer. *Lord, let it be a peaceful visit. Give me a moment of senility with Aunt Gertrude. Just this once, give us back the old relationship we used to enjoy.*

She knocked softly and pushed the door open.

Gertrude faced the window, sitting in the hospital room's straight-back chair. As Trudy watched, her great aunt brushed aside a tear.

"Hi, Auntie." Trudy moved between the window and Gertrude. Red-rimmed dullness tainted her aunt's eyes. "Are you alright?" Trudy squatted and touched Gertrude's hand.

"Of course, dear. Just re… remembering something."

"What's that?"

"An old memory." Her eyes glistened. "If I must forget things, why do I remember the ones I prefer not to recall?" She shook her head.

"I don't know, Auntie. Our brains don't always act the way we wish. Do you want to talk about this memory?"

"No. I prefer leaving the past where it belongs."

"OK. If you change your mind, I'm willing to listen." Trudy sighed. So far, she faced the old Gertrude—crusty and cool, but not raging.

The older woman shifted in the chair. "You should be at work. What are you doing here, tending to a helpless old woman?"

Trudy chuckled. "At least you know you're helpless right now. I took some time off work. Remember? I want to get you settled where someone can watch out for you and get you back to your old self. Then I can focus on work instead of worrying about you falling again."

"As soon as this hip heals, I will be fine. You do not need to concern yourself with me."

"But that's my job. Someone has to watch out for you."

Gertrude caressed Trudy's hand. "You have done that well over the years since your daddy died. I may not always say it, but I appreciate the way you treat me. I doubt anyone thinks I deserve it. You have that way of caring for the most unlovable people—probably get it from your dad. He always did that, too."

"Everyone deserves a little love, Aunt Gertrude. Everyone. None of us really deserve mercy, but thank God, we sometimes get it anyway."

"True."

Trudy moved to the sofa across from her aunt, knees cracking as she stood. "I really need to get more exercise." She ran her fingers over her bottom lip, then dropped her hand. "Aunt Gertrude, we need to talk about something."

Gertrude wrinkled her eyebrows, her jaw tightening. "Like what?"

"I know you want to get home. I understand. Hospitals stink, and I'm sure you want to sleep in your bed." Trudy bit her lower lip and rushed through the thoughts tripping over each other. "Right now, you need people to help you heal from the fall and surgery. Although you don't want to go to rehab, it really is the best thing for you. I can't take off work forever, and you may need me more later."

There. She said what needed saying. With eyes shut tight, she waited for angry words to slap her.

A quiet voice responded. "I know."

Trudy opened her eyes. They widened as she took in the sheepish look on her aunt's face. "You agree?"

"Do I have a choice? I can barely make it to the bathroom, even when Nurse Smartypants helps me. At least she will not go with me." Gertrude drew back as her eyebrows furrowed. "Will she?"

Trudy laughed. "No, Auntie. She stays here."

"Well, that is a relief. Hopefully, she does not have a twin at the rehab place. You will check that for me?"

"Of course. I looked at a few different places Dr. Thompson's office recommended. One of them has so many fun things you can do while you're there."

"Such as?"

"Well, I know you used to paint some. They have an art room, full of supplies. Maybe you can try painting a little. And they have a beautiful garden. Some residents help care for it. And I saw a few of them gathered, singing hymns and enjoying a Bible study."

"I will not be a *resident*—only a visitor. For a short time."

"The doctor said only a few weeks. Less if you cooperate and work hard at physical therapy."

"I need you to promise me this is not a permanent situation, Trudy."

"Auntie, I promise."

"I want to believe you, but I know how these things work. Some of my dear friends went for a so-called visit and still live in those places—or they died there. They sit alone, waiting for their families to take them home. They say, 'One day...' but that day never comes." She pursed her lips. "I will not be one of those people."

"Auntie, of course not. That isn't my intention at all. I promised Daddy I would always take care of you, and I won't go back on that promise—no matter what."

Gertrude studied her face, staring straight into her eyes. She focused on her aunt, hoping the direct eye contact reassured the older woman of her sincerity.

Suddenly, Gertrude grabbed Trudy's hand. "You loved your father more than anything." Her face softened. "So did I." Gertrude squeezed with unexpected strength. "But I promise you one thing. You leave me in that place longer than necessary, and I will bust out of there. I will find you and make your life miserable."

Trudy sucked in her cheeks, demanding the laugh building inside remain there.

"Do not laugh at me, little girl. You know I can do it."

"Yes, Auntie. I know." She smiled. "Trust me. As soon as you are ready, I will take you to your house. In the meantime, I plan to talk with my boss. How would you feel if I came to stay with you for a while? Just until you get back on your feet 100%. I can do most of my work remotely anyway."

Shadows covered Gertrude's face. "Is that necessary?"

"I feel better about you not being alone until I'm certain you're really OK."

Gertrude slowly nodded. "Maybe for a while. But I am not easy to live with, you know."

"At least you admit it." The laugh burst out, no longer containable. "We could end up having fun, like when I was a kid."

"Ha. You were a pain in the derriere." A chuckle broke out of the old woman. "But I suppose we enjoyed some good times."

"Whew. I'm relieved we got that settled. Now, I need to pop into the office and have that talk with my boss. Do you need anything before I head out?"

"Well, if I am to spend time away from home, I need some clothes. I will not be caught trying to do physical therapy while mooning everyone near me. If I moon someone, it will not result from an accidental flash of my derrière. Mooning should always have a purpose."

Trudy giggled. "You are so right, Auntie."

"Oh, and I need my favorite sweater—the soft, blue one. It should be hanging on the hook at the front of my closet. Bring that one."

"Done." Trudy rose and bent to kiss her aunt's forehead. "I

love you, Aunt Gertrude."

"Yeah, whatever. Get out of here. And have that young nurse come help me back to bed. I need a nap. These serious conversations exhaust me."

Trudy chuckled. "Yes ma'am. I'll see you tomorrow."

Gertrude's Mess

As Trudy trudged through the house toward Gertrude's bedroom, something felt off. Pillows on the floor instead of neatly placed on the sofa caught her attention. She paused at the doorway to the office. The desk. Cluttered, filled with stacks of paper. Envelopes dotted the carpet beneath the over-sized rolling chair. Books cluttered a small table, a cup perched near the edge.

No saucer? What on Earth? Gertrude never leaves things in disarray, and she always places a saucer beneath her cup.

She slipped into the room, scrunching her nose against a musty stench. Not a Gertrude smell. Flipping on the fan and light switches, she approached the cup first. Odor from the half cup of creamy liquid gagged her. Tiny dots of black stared up. More than a few days old.

When did her aunt leave coffee in the office? Why? She never left a cup of anything—not even in the kitchen. Trudy feared checking that room. The aunt she knew emptied leftover drinks and promptly washed the dishes.

A sign of dementia?

Trudy didn't like this behavioral change. Best search the entire house for other unwashed dishes. She shuddered as mental images of half-consumed sandwiches, full bowls of soup, or plates with unknown crusties inched into her brain.

Yuck. Not in this house. No way.

She pushed the cup back and straightened the books. After a moment, she made a mental note of the titles and placed them on the bookcase, making certain she alphabetized each one.

Next, she approached the desk. Dare she look at the papers? Yes. She dared.

Address the scattered pens first. Easiest.

She picked up the half-dozen writing utensils, depositing them in the round leather holder. Authentic leather, not the cheap faux stuff.

Bright red "PAST DUE" glared from several bills. Gathered and set aside, she vowed to take care of them. An American Express statement fluttered, begging her to view it. Not past due. Good. Amount due—what? $5,000 credit?

She overpaid her credit card by $5,000 and ignored the other bills?

Nimble fingers flew over her phone, searching for "signs of dementia."

There in black and white. "Inability to complete day-to-day tasks."

While surveying the desk, she couldn't ignore the subtle details. A letter opener stuck through a water bill, like a sword thrust into a body. The checkbook—top check illegible.

I always adored Gertrude's beautiful handwriting.

Tears welled up. Trudy shoved them down.

A stack of envelopes teetered on the edge of a half-open drawer. Stamps dotted various places on each one. Some held two, one three, and others had no stamp at all. Most had the intended company's name on the envelope.

At least she got that right. Maybe. Did she even put a check inside?

Squatting down, she rifled through envelopes, most of them empty, some torn in half.

Was that before or after she removed contents? Who knew?

She deposited them in the trashcan and stood.

As she gathered the bills into a neat stack, reality hit. Trudy sank into the chair and covered her face, willing the flood to stay behind her eyes. She lost the battle, tiny drops joining and cascading down her cheeks, dripping from her chin onto the desk.

Surely Gertrude knew. How could she not suspect something? Why didn't she tell me?

Anger bubbled, closing Trudy's throat. Shove it down. Deal

later. Focus on the task at hand—retrieving Gertrude's favorite blue sweater.

She gathered the coffee cup, turned off the light and fan, and deposited the stack of bills and checkbook beside her bag on the way to the kitchen. Mustiness wafted to greet her, slowing forward progress.

Must I?

Holding her breath, she slapped the light switch. Stumbling backward, pulses swooshed through her ears. Trudy caught hold of the door frame. Her head shook back and forth, disbelief screaming.

Pots and pans covered the stove, except for the one in the middle of the floor. Unknown remains surrounded that one. Plates, cups, saucers tottered on the counter. Bowls and glasses filled both sinks. Spills dotted the once pristine floor.

"Oh, Lord. So not my auntie. So not her."

Her knees buckled. Trudy sank to the one clean spot on the floor, hugging her knees. Burying her face in her arms, sobs convulsed her body.

Gertrude's Closet

Hours later, every tear in her body spent but the kitchen spotless as usual, Trudy ventured toward the master bedroom again.

Lord, please don't let it be a mess. Please. I can't take another surprise. Not today.

At the door, she hesitated, squeezing her eyes shut for a moment. She opened one eye. The bed, although wrinkled, had the spread pulled up. Pillows scattered instead of their normal perfect placement. Trudy released a pent-up exhale.

I can handle less than perfection.

After crossing the room, peaking around for dirty dishes, she inhaled, relaxed, exhaled. She opened the closet, expecting a waft of mothballs. Not that her current nemesis ever smelled that way. Given the state of the office and kitchen, though, she imagined an uncooked whole chicken, rotting in the cavernous walk-in.

Instead, a faint whiff of musk met her nostrils.

Yep. That smelled like Auntie.

Why did she expect a stale, pungent odor? Gertrude—anything but a common old woman. She hoarded nothing, kept her clothes and home tidy—usually—worked in the garden every day, and at 80 she still loved doing word puzzles and watching educational shows.

At least Trudy thought so until the office and kitchen debacle. She questioned the reality of that thought, peering inside.

Yet there, in the closet, order remained. She stepped through the door into the forbidden world.

With eyes closed, she let her mind drift back to childhood.

###

She and Irma loved playing hide-and-seek in the old house. Gertrude seldom joined their game, but she forbade them entrance into two rooms. This one and the locked door leading to the attic room.

No one went there.

One day, Irma dared defy their aunt. She sneaked to the front room, slipping into the closet. When Trudy didn't find her, Gertrude joined the hunt. A stifled giggle filled the front hallway. They knew. Memories of that moment chased across Trudy's brain as she reminisced, standing there still and alone.

Gertrude flung open that door and yanked Irma from her hiding spot.

"I told you never go in my closet. Never!"

Irma shook before their great aunt, her eyes wide.

The old woman ripped a belt from the holder near the door. The only time she struck either of the girls, Trudy watched, her belly tumbling as Irma endured repeated lashes. Welts appeared on her legs as she twisted, trying to free herself.

"I'm sorry. Please stop. Please!" The wails filled the room.

Trudy's hands flew to cover her ears. "Please stop, Auntie. You'll kill her!"

The whispers somehow caught Gertrude's attention. How, Trudy didn't know. The slap of leather stopped.

The old woman gathered Irma into her arms. "I lost my temper, Irma. I didn't mean to hurt you. I'm sorry." She wiped away tears on both her cheeks and those of both little girls. "This closet harbors unsafe items for small children. You must never come in here again."

I glanced up at a shelf and saw the handgun. Even then, I wondered why my great aunt hid a gun in her closet. I didn't ask. Not with the belt still in her hand.

We never spoke of it again—neither Irma nor me. Daddy would've spanked her for disobeying Aunt Gertrude, too. After that day, Irma never wanted to play hide-and-seek at Gertrude's again.

Pulled from the memory, Trudy glanced at the door. The holder remained, but not a single belt hung from it. She traced her mind, digging for a time when Gertrude wore a belt. She didn't remember one. The shelf with the gun? Empty.

Does she still have it? Locked away somewhere else? Better find out.

Her fingers brushed gently over first blacks, then moved to navy, royal blues, a few reds and browns. Every suit, dress, slacks and shirt in perfect array. Predictable.

A smattering of brighter colors hung in the back. Did Gertrude ever wear them? Trudy searched her brain, desperately pleading for a single memory of her aunt decked in fun, festive outfits.

Nope. Not there.

The staunch, simple, sophisticated style stomped across years of memories. Holidays, work days, school performances. Aunt Gertrude always appeared impeccable. Never a wrinkle nor a single strand of hair out of place.

Never. At least not until those few recent times.

She rifled through the clothes. "No jeans? How can she not own a single pair of jeans?"

Tucked behind a barrage of winter coats, a few khaki pants and casual shirts filled a small area. A wide-brimmed straw hat peeked over them from the top shelf. Ahhhh. Gardening clothes.

A sigh escaped. "She's human after all. I'm glad to know she doesn't plant flowers and vegetables in her best suits."

A sudden vision of her petite aunt bent over dirt, spade in

hand, doing her best not to soil a pristine outfit flashed in Trudy's mind. A giggle bubbled up. She covered her mouth, trying to focus on finding that sweater. The image lingered, growing deeper and wider. The giggle resurfaced. Her imagination expanded, filling in minute details of the fictitious tale playing with her reality. A sudden laugh caught her by surprise, but Trudy couldn't stop it. The more she tried, the harder she laughed.

Her brain begged her to stop.

Gertrude was in terrible shape, and she stood there laughing? What kind of person was she?

Deep breath, then she exhaled, and instantly, the thought of Aunt Gertrude in her best suit digging sent Trudy into spasms until she snorted.

She wiped her cheek and regained control.

Oh, that felt so good after such a rough day.

Pushing aside coats and clothes, a soft blue caught her eye. "Ah, there you are."

She pulled the soft fluffiness from the hangar, which dropped to the closet floor. Stooping, she retrieved it, bonking her head on the way back up and dislodging a shoe box. The contents spilled, making a mess.

"Ouch. Great. Now I have to pick all that up."

Not a stoop or crouch for this one. She sat on the floor and pulled the box and contents toward herself, prepared to pile everything back and return the box to the shelf.

A photo, letters…

Wait.

The photo. Gertrude?

In the picture, the young woman wore a light-colored suit, maybe white, with a matching pillbox hat. An elegant corsage hinted at a special occasion. The woman looked like… herself? Dad always said she looked like Aunt Gertrude.

Had to be her great aunt. But who was the young man beside

that youthful version? Handsome. Wearing a uniform.

Hmm. Boyfriend? The girl looked like a teen, despite the coiffed hair. Typical mid-50s style.

Trudy flipped through more photos. The two appeared in every picture, smiling, joy and excitement flashing across both faces. It shined in their eyes. In the last one of the stack, the couple held a certificate, grinning bigger than imaginable.

She pulled it closer, studying the faded image.

Heartbeats pummeled her chest, filling her ears again with the whoosh of shock.

Aunt Gertrude—married?

No way!

Secrets

The initial shock subsided, Trudy tilted her head back. Why had Gertrude not talked about this marriage? They all believed she never married—never wanted to. Any time someone brought it up, she changed the subject.

But this? It changed everything. How could she approach this subject with Gertrude's current state of mind?

Trudy pulled the letters back out of the box. Tied with a yellow ribbon, she did her best not to disturb them. With a partial return address, each envelope bearing her name showed signs of wear. Tiny, round drops splashed across most, leaving a trail of blotched ink stains.

Toward the bottom, a handful of letters held a local address. Unopened, they all had a "return to sender" stamp across the front. Beneath those, another group, same return address, but opened, stained and obviously read. The addressee read William Dade.

Who's William Dade? Her husband?

Gently placing the letters back in the box, Trudy scooped a handful of papers. A yellow slip peeked from one corner.

She pulled the telegram free and read the words.

October 30, 1957

Mrs. Dade. The US Army regrets to inform you that William Dade died today of infection and complications from injuries sustained on October 22, 1957. Please contact...

Trudy froze.

Gertrude. Married young, but her husband died?

She flipped over the apparent wedding photos. Date stamp. Jun 15 1956.

Poor Gertrude.

No wonder she avoided talk of marriage and boyfriends.

Tears pooled.

Not again.

She blinked, refusing to cry more.

Tempted to read the letters, she refused to invade Gertrude's privacy more than she already did. She gently tucked the telegram back into the stack of papers and laid them in the box.

A card fluttered to the floor. She leaned over and retrieved it, trying to avert her eyes. Already seeing more than she intended, Trudy didn't want to know what it revealed. Too painful. Too private. As she slipped the card back into the box, she noticed pink and blue baby booties in one corner.

"Baby Dade."

Baby Dade? Gertrude had a child? That can't be true. She never had a baby. Yes, she raised Dad, but…

No. He was her nephew. He talked about his mom and dad. They died not long after his fifth birthday. Gertrude took him in and raised him as her son then. He had vague memories of his parents. Photos as a baby in his mother's arms. A toddler on his dad's shoulders. A little boy, smiling between the two. He always thanked Gertrude for loving him and becoming his mother after their sudden deaths.

She looked back at the card. Dated one day before Dad's birthday. Maybe Gertrude and her sister got pregnant around the same time. It happened, didn't it? How many friends of hers had children close together. They joked about something in the water. How crazy, though, that two sisters gave birth one day apart.

Possible.

She'd have to investigate, do some online research.

But what happened to Gertrude's baby? Was it a boy or girl? The card didn't say. Did she give it up for adoption? Did the baby survive? Why would she not tell the family about this child?

So many questions.

With the dementia diagnosis, could Gertrude tell her the truth?

Would she?

Trudy slipped the card into the box and turned to retrieve the lid.

What was that? There in the back of the closet? She pushed aside a long coat.

Tucked in the back corner, a small fire-safe box, complete with an old-fashioned key lock.

Answers. She felt it.

"I gotta get into that box. I have to find the documents that prove the truth—whatever it is."

Trudy replaced the shoe box, picked up the sweater, and closed the closet door behind her.

Time to go check on Gertrude.

Welcome to Rehab—Roommate and All

Gertrude eyed the room as an aide wheeled her through the doorway. "Who is that old woman?" She glared across the room.

"Oh, that's Martha. She's been here a while now." The aide parked Gertrude and walked toward the woman who sat facing the window. "Martha." She touched her shoulder. "Dear, you have a new roommate."

The elderly woman turned to face the aide. "What?"

"This is Gertrude. She'll be your roommate for a few weeks."

"Oh." The woman brightened as she turned toward the doorway. "Hello. I love having a roommate. Will you be staying long?"

"Not if I can help it. Stupid doctor refused to let me go home straight from the hospital."

Martha pushed against the arms of her recliner, as if to stand, then sunk back into it. "But it's very nice here. We have a personal chef you know. I enjoy mealtime. And we have movies and crafts…"

Gertrude snorted. "I do not intend to stay any longer than needed. As soon as they finish working with me and get this hip going, I will go home." She gazed over at the bed. "I can already tell I will not sleep a wink in that uncomfortable bed."

Martha looked at the bed nearest her. "I sleep wonderfully." She smiled. "Of course, I've been here about a month."

The aide shook her head and looked over at Gertrude. "Martha gets a bit confused, but she's kind and will help you get used to our daily routine."

"Oh, yes." Martha pointed to a white-board above a small chest. "I have Missy here write the week's activities for me every Sunday night. That way, I don't miss a thing."

The aide smiled. "Yes, ma'am." She turned back to Gertrude. "Well, I expect your family to come soon with your clothes and such. I'll watch, but if I miss them, and you need help, just press the call button."

Rolling her eyes, Gertrude forced a tiny smile. "Sure."

As the aide left and closed the door behind her, she looked over at Martha. "A month, huh? Why are you here?"

Martha shrugged her shoulders. "I can't remember exactly. I forget things sometimes. My children live far away, and I burned myself cooking. Now someone else cooks for me, and I kinda like that. Our chef does a much better job, anyway. Besides, cooking for one isn't all that fun." She giggled like a preteen. "I just rhymed. How about that?" Her face clouded. "I used to write poetry—so they tell me. Not any more, though. Most days, I can't focus long enough to make sense in a poem."

"Great." *What did they get me into?* "I never cared much for poetry. Too sappy."

"What's your name?"

"Gertrude Ryan."

"What a lovely name. Will you be staying long?"

"What? No. I told you—just until my hip heals."

Martha frowned. "Oh."

Somewhere down the hall a clock chimed five times.

Martha smiled. "It's dinnertime. We have a personal chef you know."

"So you said."

"Yes. He makes the most delightful meals."

"I am not hungry."

"That's because you haven't tried his desserts yet. They are… umm… good. They're good. Shall we go?"

"You go ahead, Martha. I will come along later."

Martha headed out the door.

Great. They put me in a room with a loon. Did they think I would not notice?

She blew air between her lips. ***Ppfft.***

What a funny sound. ***Ppfft.***

She grinned. ***Ppfft.***

Never paid much attention to that before.

Ppfft. A chuckled escaped. ***Ppfft.***

Laughter surrounded her.

Why's that so funny?

Ppfft. She laughed again.

Gertrude shook her shoulders, straightening in the wheelchair. "I am cracking up here. Maybe I should get some food." Probably nasty like the hospital, but to get home she needed to keep her strength up. Besides, what else could she do in this God-forsaken place?

As she tried to maneuver her chair toward the door, wondering how to open it, a soft knock sounded.

"Come in."

Trudy peeked through the door with a small suitcase in hand. "Hi, Auntie. I'm sorry it took so long, but I brought some clothes like you asked."

"Good. They put me in this old thing."

"Well, it isn't your usual style, but you look nice." Trudy sat the suitcase on the end of the bed. "I noticed people going down for dinner. Shall I push you to the dining room so you can eat?"

"Hmpff. I can push myself, but if you insist." No need to let her know she needed any help. "I am a bit hungry."

"OK. Let's go then."

Trudy pushed the chair to the door, opened it up and wheeled her through.

The door did not automatically shut, which meant Gertrude could get through it without help. If she could make the chair work right. The sooner she got busy with physical therapy, the better.

Lose the wheelchair, make progress, and then go home.
Good plan.

As they neared the dining area, a mixture of aromas met Gertrude's nose. She inhaled, trying to pick out the offerings before seeing them. Tables scattered around the room held fresh flowers and votive candles, inviting residents and guests to enter and make themselves comfortable. Several young men and women flitted between tables, carrying single-page menus.

Martha waved at Gertrude, then motioned for them to join her.

Trudy leaned forward. "Gertrude, do you know that woman?"

"What woman?"

"The one over there waving wildly at us."

"Never saw her in my life." She refused to share a room and table with the crazy woman.

"Apparently, she knows you. Shall we join her."

"I prefer a table alone."

"Oh, Auntie. You might as well make the best of being here. Maybe make a new friend or two."

"I like the friends I have already. Why do I need a new one?"

"You never know. Maybe she has a vault of secret treasure, or a safe hidden in her closet, filled with money or diamonds."

"You always had a vivid imagination, child. Too many of those silly novels you adored reading. Besides, I have quite enough money to last the rest of my life you know."

"I didn't know, but that's good information." Trudy laughed. "Honestly, Aunt Gertrude, you always had things together. I figured you planned for retirement. Insurance should cover this stay in rehab, so it won't eat up your savings."

Gertrude looked up at the young woman. "Better not."

Wait. Safe? Did she find that old safe in my closet? Why would she snoop in that closet? Why even enter my closet? "What do you know about safes in closets?"

Red splotches covered Trudy's face.

She was snooping in my closet.

Fighting the urge to yell, Gertrude took a deep breath. "Were you in my closet?"

Trudy's eyes widened. "Yes. I had to get your clothes and favorite sweater. Remember?"

"Oh."

"Do you have a safe in your closet, Auntie?"

"If I do, it is my secret. None of your business."

"No problem. Unless I need paperwork or something from it. Insurance or something."

"They already have all that on file." She hoped they did. "You have nothing to concern yourself with."

Shift the conversation. Shift it.

"Oh look. My roommate wants us to join her for dinner."

"Where?"

"That woman over there. The one waving like a madwoman. She has issues—with her mind."

"OK."

Trudy maneuvered the chair between tables until they reached the old woman.

What was her name? Didn't matter. She had no plans to stick around long enough to care, and based on the earlier conversation, she doubted Macy would remember her name either. At least they had that in common.

Gertrude picked up the paper menu and looked over the options. Maybe she could survive the place for a day or two, until she figured out a way to convince the powers-in-charge to release her.

Or escape.

Trudy Visits Rehab

Trudy approached the door to Gertrude's room, cautious. Who knew which Gertrude she might find today? The final day in the hospital and the transfer both proceeded without issues. But they warned her. Sometimes the change of location brought on episodes of confusion. She hoped not. After all the discoveries in the closet, she had too many questions for her great aunt to check out mentally.

She clutched the overnight bag and blue sweater, breathing a silent prayer for patience. Why, she had no clue. Praying for patience might meet with an answer—along with the rough road to obtain it.

She changed her prayer. "Just help me through this, Lord. Whichever Aunt Gertrude I get today."

She knocked gently and pushed open the door without waiting for a response, peeking inside. Gertrude hovered near the door, as if she expected her and moved to greet her.

Wishful thinking.

The determined look on the old woman's face dumped goosebumps on Trudy's arms. She shuddered.

"Hi, Auntie. I'm sorry it took so long, but I brought some clothes like you asked."

"Good. They put me in this old thing."

"Well, it isn't your usual style, but you look nice." Trudy sat the suitcase on the end of the bed. "I noticed people going down for dinner. Shall I push you to the dining room so you can eat?"

"Hmpff. I can push myself, but if you insist. I am a bit hungry."

"OK. Let's go then."

Trudy pushed the chair to the door, opened it, and wheeled

Gertrude through.

In the dining room, a white-haired, pleasant looking woman waved wildly at them. At first Gertrude didn't recognize her, or maybe she did but pretended not to. In her typical style, Gertrude preferred dining alone, although the woman obviously wanted them to sit with her.

"Oh, Auntie. You might as well make the best of being here. Maybe make a new friend or two."

"I like the friends I have already. Why do I need a new one?"

"You never know. Maybe she has a vault of secret treasure, or a safe hidden in her closet, filled with money or diamonds."

Gertrude snapped her head around, daggers shooting from her eyes.

Oh crap. Not the right time to bring up a closet or safes.

Her great aunt turned around. "I have quite enough money to last the rest of my life, you know."

Maybe she dodged a bullet. The anticipated barrage of accusations didn't assault her.

Make it better. Compliment her. Change the subject. Quick.

"I didn't know, but that's good information." Trudy dared a laugh to lighten the mood. "Honestly, Aunt Gertrude, you always had things together. I figured you planned for retirement. Insurance should cover this stay in rehab, so it won't eat up your savings."

"Better not." Gertrude tilted her head. "What do you know about safes in closets?"

There it was. Trudy braced herself to repel the accusations, then reminded Gertrude she had to be in the closet to get the clothes. She dared not mention the fireproof safety box. And she certainly wasn't bringing up any of her discoveries.

Before she could say anything else, Gertrude cut off the conversation, waving across the room. "Oh look. My roommate wants us to join her for dinner."

"Where?"

"That woman over there. The one waving like a madwoman. She has issues—with her mind."

Trudy clenched her teeth to keep from laughing and reminding Gertrude that was the woman she'd never seen in her life. She shook her head. Was that the disease, or was Gertrude playing with her mind?

She weaved the chair between tables until they reached the roommate. "Hi, I'm Trudy, Gertrude's great niece."

"Hello, dear. I'm Martha. At least, I think that's my name. Sometimes I forget my own name. How sill is that?" She looked at the menu. "Yep. Martha. Right there. See?"

Trudy raised her eyebrows, looking at Gertrude. "It's nice to meet you, Martha."

"And your name, again?" She motioned at Gertrude.

"Gertrude. I arrived today. We share a room."

"Oh, how nice. I live here now. For months. I just love the chef. He makes such tasty meals." She glanced at the other tables. "And the desserts. Umm. Brownies tonight. I sneaked one earlier today. But don't tell."

Trudy smiled. "Your secret's safe with us."

The three women settled in for dinner.

When an aide came over to ask for their selections, Gertrude snapped at her. "What must I do to get a glass of wine."

"I'm sorry, we don't serve wine here. It doesn't always mix well with medications. Besides, we don't have a liquor license."

Touché. Obviously not the first rude old woman she dealt with. Don't like this version of Gertrude. Snobby—yeah. But outright rude?

"Aunt Gertrude, maybe you can have a nice cup of tea."

"Oh, alright." She huffed out a breath of air. "Is anything on this menu worth eating?"

Martha piped up. "Oh, all the food here tastes delicious, just like going to a fine restaurant."

"I am so sure." Gertrude's sarcasm dribbled over the table. "Just give me the beef whatever."

The aide smiled. "You're new here, aren't you?"

"Is it obvious?"

"A little. You get used to it, and we try to make the food taste good. It usually needs a little extra salt and pepper. They watch it for those with high blood pressure. I think you will like the chopped steak."

"I would rather have a T-bone."

Who's this rude woman I call Auntie? Didn't she always tell me to be nice to your servers, so they didn't spit in your food?

Trudy rested a hand on her sleeve. "It'll be fine, Auntie."

The daggers returned to Gertrude's eyes, then dissipated. She shook her head, as if trying to clear it. "Trudy, dear, what do you want for dinner?"

Trudy cleared her throat. "I'll have the same as my auntie, but I want iced tea instead of hot."

"I'll have that right out." The aide flitted away.

Martha grinned. "I already ordered my chicken salad sandwich. It's my favorite. I think they went out back to wring the chicken's neck, though. I've been waiting for hours."

Gertrude pinched her lips. "No, you have not. You came down her five minutes before we did."

"No. It was much longer than that." She vehemently shook her head. "I'm sure it's been at least…" She counted on her fingers. "Fifteen minutes. But they didn't feed me any lunch. I'm starving."

Gertrude leaned over. "I told you she had mind issues."

Trudy smiled, nodding.

Surely Gertrude wouldn't become like that, would she? Dr. Thompson had to be wrong. But deep inside, Trudy knew. And she feared the demented Gertrude wouldn't be half as pleasant as her roommate.

Dinner with Mom

The scent of sizzling fajitas from a nearby table tantalized Trudy's nose. Her stomach rumbled in protest over yet another missed lunch, trying to catch up at work. The time she spent finding a suitable place for Gertrude, then getting her settled, left unfinished project tasks begging for attention. At least for a short time, someone else got to deal with her great aunt, and she could resume a somewhat normal life.

She filled a tortilla chip with salsa and popped the entire thing into her mouth at the precise moment her mother stepped through the door. Seeing her, she waved and dotted her mouth with a napkin. The pressed slacks and silk blouse gave her mother a feminine yet intimidating look.

She and Irma, the opposite of my thrown-together self. Always perfect and beautiful.

"Hi, Mom."

Her mother planted a quick kiss on her cheek before sitting next to her. Never across from a person, Mom always sat at tables, never booths, and always in the nearest chair. In the crowded restaurant, Trudy didn't mind. That night, she had questions and hoped her mom had answers. But that didn't mean she wanted everyone around them in on the conversation.

"Trudy, you look exhausted. Are you sleeping at home or still at the hospital?"

"Actually, we transferred Gertrude to rehab a few days ago. I go by to visit most every day, but then I go home." She took a sip of water. "I probably have stayed up too late, though. I'm so behind at work, having taken time to get her settled."

"Don't you dare let that old woman cause you to lose your job. She doesn't deserve that much attention."

"Mom, she's old and scared. What would you have me do? Leave her alone, confused and clueless about how to maneuver the system?"

"You ought to put her in a permanent facility and say good riddance."

Trudy clenched her teeth and counted to five. "Dad would never do that."

"Well, your father never saw Gertrude's mean streak." Her mother snatched the menu. "What tastes good here? I don't know why you chose this place."

"I found it while checking out the rehab center and wanted to try it. Besides, it gave me time to run by and check on Gertrude after work."

"Oh. I see." Her mother studied the menu, sniffed, and set it on the table. "So, how is she doing?"

Swallowing the desire to ask why her mom never showed up at the hospital, Trudy shrugged. "Physically, she embraces the therapy, determined to improve and go home in a day." She chuckled. "Gotta admire that spunk."

Mom planted a plastic smile across her lips. "She always took good care of herself physically. I admit that."

Tears tickled Trudy's eyelids. She forced them down, unwilling to share emotions with her mother. "Her mind though… I never know which Gertrude to expect."

"What do you mean?"

"Dr. Thompson suspects Alzheimer's, Mom. He tried assessing her, but halfway through the tests, she went bonkers. Accused us of all sorts of junk and threw us both out of the room. This sudden switch of the aunt I always loved to a mean, old accusing woman—scary."

"That sounds exactly like the Gertrude I know." Mom shook her head. "You and your father never saw that side of her. Irma and I caught it all the time."

"I know she can be harsh, but not like that day. It rocked me to the core."

"I'm sorry, honey. I wish you didn't have to deal with **that** Gertrude, but welcome to my world. She never liked me and constantly accused me of using your dad to get her money. As if she has so much money."

Do I tell her about the house? The mess? The unpaid bills and massive credit? The fireproof lock-box? No. Best not to share all that.

"She prepared well enough for retirement, and I suppose, to her, it's a lot of money."

"Good. Those memory-care places cost a fortune."

"Let's hope it doesn't come to that."

"Oh, Trudy, be realistic. If she has Alzheimer's, you won't have a choice but to put her in a facility. Maybe not right away—but eventually."

Trudy dismissed her mother's words. She didn't want to fight about any of this. So far, their conversation leaned too far in that direction.

"Mom, did Aunt Gertrude ever marry—that you know of?"

"No. She devoted her life to your dad after his parents died. Your dad and her mother. Now that was a loony old woman, from what I understand."

Trudy ignored the "loony" comment. "Are you sure?"

Mom shrugged. "If she did, I never knew about it. Your dad said she never married. Why do you ask?"

"I found some old pictures. They made me wonder if something happened. I mean, maybe something awful happened and led to this bitterness in Gertrude."

The waiter finally appeared with fresh glasses of water, and the two women ordered food.

Her mom took a slow drink before looking at Trudy. "Honey, some people don't need a reason to act mean. They just do it. In her defense, I understand her father abused both her and his wife.

He died not long after the sister's car accident, so your daddy didn't have to deal with that. But his parents never took him around if the dad was home either. He remembered a few times of seeing the old man, but he never really knew him."

Sighing, Trudy circled back around. "Wait. Did you say something about Gertrude's mom being loony? As in crazy or demented?"

"Oh, yes. Your dad talked about finding her tied up and stinking to high heaven, locked up in a spare bedroom."

"I remember dad talking about finding the old woman."

"I don't think Gertrude ever got over it. One time, I dared to go into that room. She never locked the door, but she kept it closed and refused to use it. Sad because it had some amazing furniture in it. Authentic antiques. Probably worth a fortune."

"Did her father tie her up—his wife?"

"Apparently. Maybe he needed to control the old woman because she was off her rocker."

"That's so cruel. No wonder Gertrude fears being locked away somewhere."

"Maybe." Mom shrugged, selected a chip and loaded it with salsa. "But I believe her father died right after that. I'm not sure, but Gertrude might have found him in the shed."

"Hmmm. I wonder if I can get her to talk about it. Maybe gain some insight into the root of her attitude."

"Ha. Good luck with that. She never talked about her past. I learned early in my marriage not to ask questions. Anytime someone brought up the past, her eyes darkened like a massive thundercloud, a storm brewing behind them. I don't have a clue what really happened." She dipped another chip. "Frankly, I think you should leave it alone. She'll bite your head off if you ask."

"Maybe. But it might be worth it if I can help her find some peace. Who knows? Maybe it will make life more bearable for me and everyone around her."

"I'm telling you, Trudy, keep her in the facility for **her** good and **your** peace of mind. You don't need that kind of stress."

"Dad wouldn't."

Mom stopped chewing mid-chip. She flinched and looked down, her cheeks turning pale. After a moment, she swallowed, staring at the basket of chips. "Well, Dad isn't here, is he? Besides, he might change his mind." She looked up. "I have friends dealing with parents who have Alzheimer's. Honey, it gets worse, not better. You don't know what you're getting into."

Trudy slumped back in the chair. "I need to take care of her, Mom. I promised Daddy."

"Your daddy loved Gertrude, although I never saw why. He said I didn't understand her. I didn't. Wanting to honor him is virtuous, but I don't think he expected her to go off the deep end." She gently touched Trudy's hand. "Most people can't deal with Alzheimer's patients long-term. You'll see. She'll wear you down, beat you up, and make you want to check **yourself** into a facility. Trust me on this."

"Oh, she's not **that** bad, Mom."

"Not yet, but she'll get there."

Trudy bit her bottom lip. "Thanks for the support, Mom. I'm trying to do what Daddy wanted."

"I know. Commendable. But don't be stupid, girl. Gertrude doesn't deserve your devotion. No more than she deserved your father's."

"Why do you dislike Gertrude so much?"

"I don't want to discuss it. Let's just say we had a parting of ways decades ago. I tolerated her because of your dad, but she and I had an unspoken agreement. We acted civil for his sake, both knowing we'd never be friends. Truth is, I wouldn't have anything to do with her if it hadn't been for him."

"That must've been some fight you two had. What about?"

"It doesn't matter. I don't remember details, but I know how she left me feeling. And I swore she'd never do it to me again. I agreed to disagree rather than argue with the old witch. Her holier-than-thou attitude made me want to puke. Always 'so blessed,' but inside she seethed with a poison no one could endure. Your father… He somehow saw past that part of her, and you do the same thing."

Trudy settled back into her thoughts as the waiter placed steaming platters before them. As they fell into a tentative silence, she let the uncertainties tumble through her brain.

So many questions. I only want to find the truth and help her release the pain before it's too late. Maybe she hasn't lived in peace, but I don't want her to die that way.

Mom doesn't understand. I'm on my own in this one.

The women continued with small talk over their food, and Trudy knew the conversation wouldn't return to her great aunt, other than another admonition to forget about her.

And that Trudy couldn't do. Ever.

Kit

Discouraged by her mother's assessment of the situation, Trudy left the restaurant and headed home. Thoughts of the lock-box captured her attention as she drove.

How hard could it be to pick the lock?

The tidbits she found in the closet left so many unanswered questions. Mom did not know about a marriage or a baby, but she saw the pictures, the memories of a child. Surely that old safety box held documents that detailed it all. She needed to find the truth.

Why? It's none of your business. You'll only make Gertrude mad at you.

She's already mad at me.

True enough. But what if she found out?

How's she gonna find out?

Trudy carried on the argument in her head. "I never win these arguments," she said to herself.

As she approached the intersection that led to her house, suddenly Trudy switched lanes and made a U-turn. Why, she didn't know. Maybe if she discovered the truth of what happened all those years ago, she could understand her great aunt better. Maybe she could help her overcome the pain and anger that left an embittered old woman in their wake. And maybe, just maybe, she'd find peace in her own life.

She had to try. Not like the box had high-end security. Simple little lock on it. Gertrude probably hid the key nearby. And if not, it couldn't be that difficult. Could it?

Trudy knew if she went home, she'd toss and turn, thinking about those pictures, wondering if the lock-box held the answers. She'd never get to sleep. If ever she had an open opportunity to find the key or pick the lock, that night was it. Besides, who wanted to go home and sit alone on a Friday night?

Pulling into Gertrude's driveway, she sighed. The house loomed before her, daring her to come in and find more secrets.

Did she really want to do this?

Yes. She did.

Opening the door, she slid from behind the steering wheel and almost tiptoed up the sidewalk.

"Hello!" The shrill voice made her jump.

Trudy's heart danced on her ribcage as she turned toward the woman. "Hello."

Act innocent. Act innocent.

"Hi there. Aren't you Gertrude's great niece?" The woman flashed a warm, welcoming smile. "I've been so worried about my neighbor. Is she OK?"

Trudy breathed, willing her heartbeat to slow. "Hi. Yes, I'm Trudy."

"Oh, Trudy. How lovely to meet you. Gertrude talks about you all the time."

"She does?"

"Oh, sure. She tells me you check on her every day." She reached out a hand and touched Trudy's arm. "I'm so glad. I worry about her living all alone in this big, old house. Don't know why she doesn't just sell it and move on."

"Well, her mother left it to her. I suppose she has fond memories of childhood here."

"I doubt that. I'm in my old homestead too, and I remember Gertrude's father." Kit shuddered. "Not a nice man. Not nice at all."

She pulled Trudy toward the door. "Now, tell me. How is our poor Gertrude? I called the ambulance after I heard her squeal that morning and saw her on the ground, not moving. I couldn't do anything else to help."

Resisting the urge to push the woman away, Trudy had an

idea. Maybe she could answer some questions.

"Why don't you come inside… I'm sorry. I didn't catch your name."

"Kit. Well, my name is Katherine, but Daddy always called me Kit Kat, and the Kit stuck."

"Nice. I came to pick up some things for Auntie, but I'm sure she wouldn't mind if we had some coffee or tea."

"I'd love that. You can tell me all about what's going on. The entire neighborhood wants to know."

Kit followed Trudy to the door chattering about the plants along the sidewalk, neighbors and a host of other things. Trudy unlocked the door, pushed it open and motioned for Kit to come in as she continued talking without coming up for air.

When Kit finally took a deep breath, Trudy rushed in. "Kit, do you want tea or coffee?"

"Probably better go with a nice herbal. Too late for caffeine you know. I'd never get to sleep if I had coffee this late."

"Of course."

Trudy busied herself in the kitchen, trying to figure out how much she could ask Kit without raising suspicion. Maybe take the direct route—straight to the past. And maybe she should resist telling her too much about Gertrude. She had a feeling Kit liked to share gossip.

Returning to the living room with the tea, Trudy served the neighbor and settled into a nearby chair.

Kit took a sip. "Lovely. Now, how is our Gertrude?"

"They released her from the hospital, but she needs a couple weeks at rehab. She broke her hip."

"No. That's terrible. No older person wants to hear those words. You are bringing her home eventually? Please say you aren't leaving her in some home. It'll kill Gerd."

"Gerd?"

"Sorry. When we first moved here, I couldn't say Gertrude,

so it came out Gerd. I'm the only one who can call her that."

"Gotcha. So, you live next door?"

"Yes. We moved in before I started school. I chose a college in another state, finished, got married. After Russ passed—God rest his soul—I came back. Of course, by that time, Mother needed me to look after her."

"Your mother's still living?"

"Heavens yes. I believe she'll outlive us all." Kit chuckled. "At 92, she stays inside most of the time. The thought of a broken hip terrifies her. She won't like hearing this news about Gerd." Kit shook her head. "Such a shame. Of all the old neighbors, Gertrude's the one who stays most active, always out in her garden and taking walks in the neighborhood. She checks on all the old ones who live alone. Few of them anymore, though."

That could prove problematic. Gertrude might go visiting and forget her way home. From her research, that happened frequently with Alzheimer's patients. Something to consider for later.

Kit's voice drew Trudy back to the conversation. "So, when is she coming home?"

"Oh, sorry. I got distracted for a second. I'm not sure. If she responds well, a couple weeks. It depends on how stubborn she gets with the physical therapists."

"She can be stubborn, for sure."

Trudy snickered. "That could work in her favor. Her stubbornness might drive her to show them how soon she can get out of there. And she already told me if I don't come get her, she'll bust out."

Kit laughed. "That sounds like the Gerd I know."

Opening. Take it. "So you know Gertrude well?"

"Oh, goodness yes. She used to babysit me sometimes. I think she liked it more at my house than at home."

"Really? From what I heard, she adored her mother."

"Absolutely. But her father? I didn't blame her. What a cruel man."

"I never knew him. Daddy and Gertrude never said much about him either."

"I don't doubt that. He scared me."

"Why?"

"He yelled all the time, especially at Gerd. She came to our house crying so many times." Kit settled back into her chair. A glaze covered her eyes. "I remember one day in particular."

Trudy leaned forward. "What happened?"

"I was on my swing in the back yard. Our fence had boards missing, so I could see everything. He came out their back door with his big hand wrapped around Gertrude's wrist. Her screams stopped me cold. I didn't know whether to stay put or run inside. I stayed, frozen to my swing."

She sipped her tea, a slight tremble in her hand.

"He dragged Gertrude across the yard to the shed and shoved her inside. She begged him to let her out, but he cackled and slammed the padlock shut. His words echoed across the fence, so loud I thought he was coming after me."

"What did he say?"

"He called her a slut and told her a night in the shed would change her behavior." She rubbed her arms. "Poor Gerd. She pounded on that shed door, yelling for help. When her father lumbered inside the house, I ran to my mom."

"Didn't your mother try to help Aunt Gertrude?"

"No. She said we should mind our own business and that Gertrude should have known better than to bring that young man around."

"A young man? Gertrude had a boyfriend?"

"Hmmm. I don't know for sure. I vaguely remember a handsome young man coming over once, maybe twice. Her father threw him out of the house, I remember. And I don't think he came back again. That happened not long before the shed night. Gerd left the day after the old man locked her up. She sneaked out the back door with a beat-up old suitcase before he came home from work."

"She didn't come back?"

"No. I saw her occasionally, mostly during the day. Then the old man lost his job, and she quit coming to the house. Then one day, I saw her there with Ben. I started to go over, but my mama stopped me, and then Gerd's car was gone. Her father died that night."

"Ben was my daddy."

"Oh. I loved that little guy. Such a sweet boy."

Trudy didn't want to think, much less talk, about her dad. "How did Gertrude's father die?"

"Mom said he had a heart attack out in the shed and couldn't get to the house for help."

"He died in that old shed?"

"Yep. Apparently, Gertrude took her mom with her. No one answered when I went over right before supper to sell candy for school. I never thought to look out back, but then again, I didn't go anywhere near the grump. They say he stayed out there all night, and the rats got to him before Trudy found him the next afternoon."

"Rats?"

"Yes. They had some monstrous rodents in that shed. Gerd had it fumigated after her father died. Man, you should've seen those critters scurrying away. I had nightmares for weeks, terrified they'd come to our house. They didn't, of course. Most of them keeled over, right there in the yard. The pest control guys hauled 'em off."

"You said they got to the old man?"

"Yeah. At least, some kids said they saw the body, and it had tiny teeth marks all over it." She shook herself. "Of course, Billy

Don shared that story, but you never knew if that kid told the truth. He lied a lot."

"Wow."

"Yeah. Mom said if the rats chewed on him, he deserved it. She didn't like that old man much either, but she never said bad things about people. She still doesn't, you know."

"I'll have to come over and meet your mother sometime."

"Oh, yes. You should. She loves having visitors." Kit looked at her watch. "Oh, my. I must go so I can get Mama ready for bed." She set her cup and saucer on the side table. "Please give Gertrude my regards, and tell her when she gets home, I'll bring over a big chocolate cake."

"She'll love that. Thank you."

Trudy closed the door behind Kit.

What a monster. Poor Gertrude.

Closing her eyes, Trudy leaned against the door as she struggled against imaginations drifting across her brain. What did Gertrude endure that no one knew anything about?

Not sure I want to know, but if it can help her find peace, I need to know the truth.

Back at Rehab

Trudy ventured into the rehab and wandered toward Gertrude's room. As always, she held her breath, wondering which great aunt to expect. The beloved woman who made her feel loved and special, or the one that shot daggers from her eyes? The one who trusted her or accused her of unimaginable acts of betrayal?

When she reached the room, the door stood open.

Gertrude looked up from her Bible and smiled. "You are here early today."

Trudy released a breath she didn't know she held. "Yes. I have a busy day and late afternoon meeting. I wanted to come by before work, since it may be too late when I get off."

"You work too hard, child."

"So I hear—a lot." Trudy chuckled, thankful her great aunt didn't seem irritable. At least not at the moment.

"You ought to be out having dinner with a nice young man instead of staying at the office late. That is no way to find a husband."

"Maybe someday. I don't have time for a man right now." Trudy took a breath. "I went by your house to check on everything last night. Your neighbor, Kit, came over."

"Oh heavens. I hope you did not tell her all my gory details. The whole neighborhood will know before I ever make it back home."

"Not everything. Only about breaking your hip. She seemed genuinely concerned. Did you know she called the ambulance after hearing you scream that morning?"

"I do not remember screaming."

Trudy tapped her lips. "She might have used the term squeal."

"Well, I suppose a squeal might have slipped out when I fell. Unfortunately, or fortunately, I have no recollection of those events."

"Probably just as well."

Trudy cleared her throat. Did she dare bring up the things Kit told her?

Eying Gertrude, she sat on the end of the bed and took a chance.

"Auntie, Kit said she lived next door to you as a child."

"Yes, she did. I babysat her sometimes. Even as a little girl, she always wanted to know everyone's business. Her mama kept her in line though." Gertrude shrugged. "She did come back to take care of her aging mama, though. I must give her credit for that."

"Umhmm. She said when you come home, she'll bring over a chocolate cake."

"Oh, Lord. I hope not. That women cannot bake worth a flip. She always wants to make it 'healthy,' but everything ends up tasting like chalk."

They laughed together.

"She did say some interesting things."

Gertrude's brow furrowed. "Like what?"

"Memories from childhood. She said your daddy was mean."

"Well, he was, and I do not want to discuss that." She shifted in her chair. "When you come back, will you bring that new hairbrush I bought? It should be in the top right-hand drawer in my bathroom."

"I'll check into it." Trudy hesitated, then rushed forward. "Can I ask a question?"

"I suppose you can. You certainly *may* ask a question."

Trudy grinned. At least that part of Gertrude remained. "Kit mentioned a young man when you were much younger. Did you have a boyfriend?"

Gertrude stared across the room. "Did you bring that new brush I bought?"

"The hairbrush?"

"Yes, a hairbrush. It is in the bathroom. Still in the package."

"I didn't see a new one, but I brought one out of your bathroom."

"Well, I want that new one."

"OK. I'll bring it next time." Trudy breathed deeply. "But what about that young man? I'm curious, Auntie."

"Kit should keep her nose out of my business." She crossed her arms. "Father did not like him. End of story."

"Oh. I'm sorry. Kit mentioned your father didn't treat him nice."

"My father did not treat anyone nice. And I told you, I do not want to talk about my childhood."

"I remember photos of you in your early 20s. Stunningly beautiful, Aunt Gertrude. I always thought so."

The old woman stared at the wall. "Sometimes, beauty is a curse."

"I understand. It's just… I never knew you had a beau. Tell me about him, please. I found a photo in your closet—with a young man in uniform."

Gertrude's eyes smoldered. "My closet? Why were you in my closet?"

"Remember? I went to get clothes. You asked me to bring your blue sweater." Trudy's heart quickened. She needed answers, not this brusqueness. She couldn't risk angering the old woman. Reaching back, she pulled the sweater off the end of the bed.

Eyeing it, Gertrude softened. "That's mine?"

"Yes, of course. You wanted it for the chilly evenings while your hip heals."

"I do not remember asking you to explore my closet."

"I know, dear." Trudy looked down at her hands, scolded like a small child caught hiding in that closet while playing. "The brilliant organization mesmerized me. I never saw such beautiful order in a closet. Mine is pure chaos." She looked up, meeting black holes where her aunt's eyes used to sparkle. "I'm sorry," she whispered.

Gertrude huffed. "Do not go snooping in my things. Ever."

"Yes, ma'am."

So much for getting answers. One more try, then she had to let go. "It's too bad things didn't work out with that young soldier. He looked kind and quite handsome."

"Will. William—his given name. He loved me, but not enough."

"What do you mean?"

"He joined the military. After Korea and before Vietnam—should be safe. Serve six years and walk away with benefits and money saved." For a moment, Gertrude's eyes sparkled, but the darkness returned much too quickly, anger smoldering across her face. "What kind of man dies in the army without a war? He should have loved me more—stayed home instead of going off to pursue a career. Instead, he joined up and promptly left—forever."

"Oh, Auntie, I'm so terribly sorry that happened. But do you really think he planned that? Surely, he intended to come back to you."

Gertrude's face didn't shift. "Perhaps. But his intentions meant squat."

She looked at the window for several moments, then back at Trudy. "Did you bring my hairbrush? The new one?"

Trudy shook her head. "I'm sorry, Auntie. I'll stop by the house, pick it up and bring it by tomorrow after work. Can I bring you anything else?"

"I'd love one of those old-fashioned chocolate malts. You know the ones at Cherry's?"

"Cherry's closed years ago."

"No, they didn't. I went there just last week."

"Last week?" Trudy rubbed the back of her neck.

Dementia kicking in?

"Oh yeah. That Cherry's. I'll see what I can do. Maybe I'll pick up chocolate malts for both of us."

The old woman smiled and patted Trudy's hand. "Thank you, dear. They don't feed us much around here. I definitely can't get a malt."

"Of course not, Auntie. I'll make sure to get one." She stood. "I should get going if I'm gonna stop by your house and get that hairbrush."

"Hairbrush?"

"Yes, the one you wanted."

"Why would you bring a hairbrush? I already have one in the bathroom here."

"My bad. I'll see you tomorrow then."

In the hallway, Trudy pushed down tears. Today wouldn't yield answers to the many questions flitting through her mind, but at least she confirmed the name.

William.

She wondered if a new hairbrush existed, but maybe she should check to be safe. And maybe she'd try to open that lock-box. With Alzheimer's progressing and Gertrude's hip improving, she might not have much time left to search the house—or her aunt's mind. After work, she had every intention of breaking into that box, but none of admitting it to her great aunt.

No reason to rouse an angry bear.

Keeping Secrets Hidden

Pretending to sleep, Gertrude didn't stir when the door opened. Sunlight burst through the window as an aide opened the blinds. "Good morning, sleepyheads. Gotta get the two of you up and dressed for breakfast. Rise and shine."

Gertrude rolled over—slowly. Her hip still ached. But at least she could move better. "You are much too cheery. Why do you people need to be so happy all the time?"

Her roommate stretched and yawned from the neighboring bed. "I love the happy ones. Much better than that weekend crew who come in all grumpy or not at all." She pushed herself out of bed and took hold of her walker. "I'm hungry. What's for breakfast?"

The aide smiled and approached the roommate. "Ms. Martha, you can have whatever you want for breakfast. Do you want help with dressing?"

"I prefer wearing my pretty robe with roses for breakfast today. I'll dress after I eat."

"It is shower day, so that's fine." She handed Martha the robe.

Gertrude grunted, maneuvering out of bed rather than jumping up to greet the day. "Blasted hip. I used to enjoy getting up in the mornings, taking my breakfast out to the back porch and feasting with the birds, coffee, and my Bible."

The nurse brightened. "Ms. Ryan, would you like to have breakfast on the back patio today? It's lovely outside."

"Can I do that?"

"Sure. We have a few tables out there. Several people enjoy meals there when weather permits."

Energized by the option, Gertrude grasped her walker. She

liked it better than the wheelchair. Moving to the closet, she selected a simple dress. While classy slacks fit her style better, putting them on wore her out, and most of her physical therapy required walking, anyway. They kept saying she might surprise them all and go home sooner. One could hope.

Martha piped up. "Well, you can go outside if you want, but I'm not waiting on you. I gotta get some food in this old body."

"You go ahead, Martha." Good thing she paid attention earlier. Half the time she forgot the old biddy's name. Not that she disliked her roommate, but the woman never ceased talking, and she always smiled. It bothered Gertrude. No sane person could smile all day, every day. Then again, she doubted Martha's sanity.

"Do you need help, Ms. Ryan?" The aide waited by the door.

"No, I am fine. I just want to slip on my dress."

"I'll wait here. They want me to accompany you—just for a few more days, I think. You're doing great with your PT. We all thought you'd still be in a wheelchair, but you surprised us."

"None of you know my tenacity. I worked hard all my life, and a little hip injury will not keep me down for long."

As Gertrude dressed in the bathroom, she assessed the situation. True, her memory lapsed momentarily. The less time she spent in this place, the less chance they had to determine how often that happened. Of course, with a roommate like Marcia, she didn't have to worry too much about that. If she kept quiet, the extent of her memory issues remained hidden. Once she got home, it didn't matter.

As she stepped from the bathroom, Gertrude motioned to her nightstand. "Can you carry my Bible and journal? I have difficulty maneuvering this thing and carrying anything at the same time."

"Of course." The aide picked up the Bible and notebook.

"Let's go."

In the hallway, Gertrude did her best to out-walk the aide. While she did well, she still moved like a turtle. Give her another week, and she would race them all down the hallway.

After an uneventful, bland breakfast, Gertrude sipped coffee and opened her Bible. Too long since she had a chance to read, let alone pray without interruptions. The words blurred before her.

At home, she talked to God aloud. Here, they might think her crazy.

Who am I kidding? They think I am crazy, anyway.

A drop trickled down her cheek.

You sissy. Get a grip. Crying never helps.

She drew in a deep breath and released it. Time for a reality check—while she still could check reality.

Wanting not to believe the doctors, she searched her mind. Too many things pointed to them being right, although she hated admitting it. Her roommate's name escaped her most days. Half the time when Trudy came by, she caught herself thinking, "Who's that?" Only for a moment, of course, but it happened. And all that ugliness she kept spewing all over her only ally? Definite sign of the brain slipping.

Settling back in her chair, she let her mind drift to the days after her father died. She detested going there, but moving in with her mother, she understood what he meant. Not that it excused what he did. Never could she excuse that. But she had to face the issues he endured—perhaps for years. She always thought he caused Mama's memory issues, locking her up in a room, starving her.

But what if he didn't? What if that all happened like he said? What if she became her mother? Wandering in and out of the house, turning on a burner and walking away. Looking at the one she loved most with a blank stare, unable to communicate well.

The rush of her heartbeat pulsated in her ears as she wrapped her arms around herself.

"Please, Lord. Don't let me end up like Mama was at the end. Take me before I reach that point. Spare me that trauma. Spare Trudy that pain." Gertrude paused, dabbed her eyes with a napkin. "And, Lord, if it isn't too much to ask, please make that girl quit asking so many questions. I don't want to remember those things. If you must erase the past, I choose those memories to go first."

She tried going back to her Bible passage, but a tiny bird landed nearby, mesmerizing her with its beauty.

Why did life look so ugly when nature held pure wonder?

Distracted, she watched the bird fly to the top of a tree. A sweet fragrance drew her attention to honeysuckle on the fence. Gentle drafts fluttered her hair, easing tension, while the sun peeped through branches, inviting closed eyelids and her entire being to drink in the peace surrounding her.

If she could only stay in that moment.

Maybe this Alzher thing had benefits.

Suddenly, her eyes shot open. It could work. When Trudy brought on the questions, she could feign forgetfulness.

"If I must be demented, I can use it to my advantage. Avoid the past by refusing to remember—even if I can never forget the nastiest parts." She took a furtive look around, not believing she said that out loud.

Cannot risk someone overhearing my plan. Why does Trudy care about my past, anyway? She never asked about any of this before.

Another thought surfaced, bringing with it uncontrollable quivers in her hands.

Am I dying soon, and they want to hide it from me? I'm awfully tired of this world. Lord, I don't like the Gertrude I see in the mirror these days. Can I forget her too?

The door opened, another aide busting through. "Ms. Ryan, what are you doing out here all alone?"

"I like alone."

"I get that, but didn't you notice the storm coming?"

Gertrude looked up. Menacing clouds roiled above them. Not sure when that happened, she wondered if she dozed off for a minute. How long did she sit with her eyes closed? "Oh goodness. I got so entrenched in my thoughts… Yes, we must get inside."

She pushed herself up, grabbing the walker, and moving faster than normal.

The aide held the door.

"Oh, no! My Bible and notebook."

"I'll get it. You wait here."

She ran to the table, grabbed Gertrude's belongings and dashed back to the door, closing it seconds before large splashes hit. "Let's move away from these massive windows—maybe head to the theater. Much safer there."

Gertrude looked back outside, nodding. "Yes." Thunder boomed as a stroke of lightning split the tree where the bird lived.

And the storminess invaded her soul, stealing the peace from minutes earlier. "Well, what are you waiting for? The lightning to hit the glass?" She yanked the aide's arm and pushed her toward the hallway. "Go."

The aide following close behind, they rushed to the hall, trying to outrun the storm.

If only I could escape the raging in my mind, too.

Progress

Another day, another round of PT. The never-ending, daily round of PT. Gertrude wanted to vomit.

She tried her brain.

"Date?" She tapped her upper lip. "I have no clue. Not good."

A quiet voice said, "It's May 5, silly. That's why they have all the Mexican stuff everywhere. Although, I don't know why on earth we celebrate a holiday for Mexico."

She looked across the room. Not Martha. She left, but Gertrude couldn't remember why. Just gone. The new roommate. What was her name? E... Ethel. Yes. Like the old super gasoline. And Ethel often expelled fumes from her rear end, like a broken-down jalopy.

Gertrude shook her head. "Hmph. Are you kidding? Any reason to drink alcohol, eat a lot of food, and shoot off fireworks becomes a holiday."

I should keep my thoughts in my head.

"I never thought of it that way." Ethel giggled. "You think they'll have margaritas at lunch?"

"I doubt it, E. Margaritas and meds seldom work well together."

"You know, I like it when you call me E. It's like a special name, a secret between you and me."

Did she dare admit the truth? Who cared? Ethel forgot more than she remembered.

"Honestly, Ethel, sometimes your name slips from my brain."

Ethel laughed. "I thought that only happened to me. When they come in asking my name, I sometimes shift the conversation and hope they don't catch on to my game."

"Does that work?"

"Not usually. I can remember E, though. So much shorter and easier." A shadow crossed her face. "I often wonder what happens when I can't remember even that much anymore."

"I hope I die before that day."

Ethel nodded. "I know what you mean." She slipped into her rocking chair and fell into uncharacteristic silence.

Gertrude returned to her morning brain check, keeping it to herself.

Day of the week? Thursday. No, not Thursday. Tuesday?

She glanced at the calendar.

Tuesday. If today really is May 5.

She had little confidence in E's assessment of the date.

Name? Ha. I know that one. Gertrude Ann Ryan.

Whew. At least she knew her name. She looked over at the rocking chair where Ethel rocked gently, her eyes closed and tiny streams flowing down the cheeks.

Poor old woman. Really? I feel bad for her? She makes me crazy. I gotta get out of this place.

As she watched her roommate, sorrow washed over Gertrude. Fighting back tears, she stood and eyed her walker. She hated that contraption. Several steps from her chair, she crept toward it. Leaving it in the room seemed like a good idea—until she took a few steps. The hip still hurt, but less every day. Dare she go down the hall without the extra legs?

In answer to the silent question, the therapist sauntered into the room.

E and she really should close and lock the door. Keep riffraff out.

With his broad shoulders and ever-present grin, Mr. PT pointed at her. She never could remember his name. "Were you anxious to get going today or trying to escape from me?" He snickered. "I can still outrun you, Ms. Ryan, but you keep going like you are, and that may not always be the case." He motioned at her. "C'mon. Let's go see what you got today."

Gertrude huffed. "When will you say I can go home?"

"When you're ready. And that's not today, slowpoke."

"Slowpoke? I'll show you slowpoke."

"Whoa. Don't do something ridiculous. We don't want to restart this entire program. Nice and easy."

"Whatever." Gertrude retrieved her walker. "Can I at least get one of these gadgets that has wheels?"

Mr. PT rubbed his beard. "Maybe. We'll see how you do today, then I'll talk to your doctor."

Gertrude stuck out her bottom lip. "It will make life easier—help me heal faster."

PT laughed. "Not sure about that. More likely it would leave you open to another hard fall when you get going too fast."

"You are scared if you give me wheels, I will escape this torture chamber and hitchhike home."

"Oh man. You nailed me." He flashed his best smile at her. "Now, Ms. Ryan, Put away that pouty face and let's go get to work. The sooner we get you back in shape, the sooner you go home."

She drew her lips into a pucker, relaxed them and replaced the pout with a grin. Clenching her teeth, she moved behind the walker and headed to the doorway. Every step created a twinge, but PT did not have to know that. She worked to hide the pain as they ventured through the facility to the torture room.

Over the next hour, Gertrude focused on the exercises, pushing harder than she should. Mr. PT held the key to her release, so if she impressed him, she could persuade him to side with her against the doctor.

Good plan.

"Well, I am impressed today, Ms. Ryan. You exceeded my expectations." PT jotted notes on her chart.

"Does that mean I get to go home now?"

"Not quite. But it might get those wheels you want. If you promise not to escape."

"I have no idea where we are. I certainly do not want to get lost trying to get home. If you give me wheels, I will use them to make my hip even better."

"Hold on there. You pushed harder than normal. I want you to rest for the remainder of the day—don't overdo it. The last thing I want is to drag you out of bed tomorrow morning and you slough through PT." He patted her shoulder as he walked toward the back room. "I have a wheeled walker in here. If I catch you on it other than going to the cafe, I will take it back. Understand?"

"Yes sir."

Progress. I love getting what I want.

Mr. PT disappeared for a few minutes and reappeared with a shiny blue walker, loaded with wheels and a fold-down seat. "How's this?"

"No basket?" She reapplied her pout. "I need a place to carry my Bible in the mornings."

He shook his head. "You are a piece of work, Ms. Ryan. Put away the pout, and I'll see if I have something that will work."

She smiled. "Thank you."

After waiting a few more minutes, he resurfaced from the stock room and held up a white woven basket with bright flowers painted on it. He raised his eyebrows. "Yeah?"

Running fingers through her hair, she surveyed it. "It could work. How will you attach it?"

Without a word, PT pulled two zip-ties from his pocket.

Gertrude nodded. "That will do it."

With basket attached, she turned from Mr. PT and strutted from the room. Rounding the corner she sighed and slowed her pace, praying she made it to her bed before collapsing in pain.

The Pain of Insanity

Trudy set an extra-large to-go coffee cup on her desk, breathing a deep sigh. Back in the office for a full day, the first in what seemed like a lifetime. She opened her laptop, signed in, and accessed the calendar. Multiple meetings. The things she dreaded before enthralled her. Interaction with people—people who knew everyone's name, didn't scream at her for no reason, and in place of demands, asked for help or assigned tasks.

Rolling her shoulders, she settled into a rhythm, working through emails and preparing notes. Over the past few weeks, she attended meetings—some in person, but many online as she waited for returned calls, met with doctors, rehab administrators and groups of people to explain the world of dementia.

With anticipation, she sipped the coffee and smiled to herself.

"Good morning." Peter's voice pulled her attention from the computer. "I was gonna ask if you wanted coffee, but I see you're already set."

"Yeah. I treated myself on the way in."

"I haven't seen you this early for a while. Everything OK?"

"For the moment." Leaning back, she smiled. "For once, I have no appointments, no follow up calls, no rushing to make sure Gertrude has what she needs. Freedom!"

Peter chuckled. "And you spend that day of freedom at work?"

An easy laugh broke from Trudy. "Right? Maybe insanity's contagious. Who in their right mind defines a day in the office as freedom?"

"A crazy person like you." He relaxed into the extra chair in her cubicle. "Seriously, Trudy, it's nice to see you here and smiling. The last few times you popped in for a meeting, I worried when you left. The stress shows in your face."

"Busted, huh? I tried to hide it. Guess I failed."

He shrugged. "Not with most, but I know you. You can't hide anything from me."

"I never could." She took a drink before continuing. "I appreciate it, but I'm good. Processing things."

"Sure you are." Peter lifted his eyebrows.

Trudy shook her head. "Dang, you're good."

"I read you like a novel. What's really going on?"

"I spent some time at my aunt's house." She shuddered. "You wouldn't believe the mess she left. So not my fastidious aunt. When I finally finished cleaning, I went to get clothes from her closet." She paused for a few seconds. "I found some things that raised a ton of questions."

His forehead crinkled. "Like what?"

"Letters, photos… And a card that said baby Dade."

"Wait. Your aunt never married or had kids, did she?"

"Not that any of us know about. But the photos look like a wedding with her and this William Dade holding a marriage certificate. I don't have a clue about the baby."

"Did you ask her about it?"

"Yeah. She didn't want to discuss her past at all, but she finally talked about Will—for maybe 30 seconds. All I got from that conversation—Will apparently went into the military and never made it home."

"So maybe she had his baby, but he died? When?"

"Based on a telegram, 1957. Apparently, he somehow sustained injuries but died of an infection."

"Weird. Between Korea and Vietnam, but injured. A training accident?"

"Could be. When I got Gertrude to talk about it, she lashed out at me."

"What about the baby?"

"I didn't ask. Sometimes she gets agitated, and her demeanor and actions slide faster than a downhill racer."

"You thinking it could have been your dad?"

Trudy shook her head. "No. The date's wrong. But I wonder if she and her sister both got pregnant around the same time. When Dad's parents died, Gertrude raised him as her own. I don't know if this was a boy or a girl, if it survived or died. Maybe she put the child up for adoption."

As if on cue, her phone buzzed.

Gertrude.

"Sounds like an intriguing mystery. Talk to your aunt. I'm sure she has a logical explanation. I'll see you at the nine o'clock meeting."

Trudy answered her phone as Peter took off.

"Aunt Gertrude, how are you today?"

"Terrible. I'm starving. They haven't brought breakfast, and I don't remember the last time I had a bath."

Rolling her eyes, Trudy responded. "Aunt Gertrude, you just came back from a shower when I dropped by yesterday. Why don't you just walk down to the dining room? It isn't too late to get breakfast."

"I don't want to walk down there. It's too far, and my hip hurts today. I want to stay in bed."

"Well, push the call button. They'll bring you a tray of food."

"I did. Hours ago. They won't come. I'm starving—wasting away to nothing."

Trudy held the phone away from her ear, cringing at the volume coming from her aunt.

"Auntie, please calm down. I'll call the nurses' station and get someone down there."

"Well, you best hurry. I'll die before they come to see about me."

"I'll call now. I have a few minutes before a meeting."

"You need to come up here and set them straight. Don't call. They won't answer. I need you to come. NOW!"

Taking a deep breath, knots took root in Trudy's shoulders. She exhaled. "Gertrude, I'm at work. I have several meetings today. I can't just get up and walk out. I will call as soon as we hang up."

"You don't love me. Don't bother. I'll just die here. All alone. Then you'll be sorry."

"You'll be fine, dear. I'll take care of everything."

"Oh, whatever." Gertrude hung up.

Trudy took another sip of coffee, heat building around her eyes.

Don't cry. Don't cry. Don't cry.

She looked up the rehab center in her cell phone.

"Country Club Rehab, Nurse Taylor speaking. How may I help you today?"

"Nurse Taylor, thank goodness." She liked this one. "Gertrude just called me, saying she hasn't eaten, that y'all won't bring breakfast to her. I'm sure that isn't right—mostly because she doesn't remember having a bath yesterday."

"I'm sorry she called you, hon. Your aunt isn't herself today."

"She sounded so upset."

"I know. Dr. Thompson wanted us to assess her disease. From my experience, she's at least in the moderate stage. You may see more of these days, where what she thinks differs drastically from truth."

"So, are you saying she ate this morning?"

"Oh, yes. She came down early. When I came on at 7:00, I saw her coming out of the cafe, even commented on how well she's doing with walking."

"Then why did she say she didn't eat?"

"She probably went back to her room and dozed off. After waking up, she may think it's another day."

Trudy's breath caught. "Now what do we do?"

"I'll go down with a light breakfast tray. More than likely, she'll refuse it, but if she's hungry, she can eat again."

"Thank you so much. I'm at work, but if you need me to come in, I'll see what I can do."

"That's not necessary. Drop by after work, and she probably won't remember even talking to you this morning."

Trudy doubted that, but she couldn't leave yet. "OK. Thank you again."

"No problem, hon."

With minutes left before her meeting, Trudy disconnected, gathered her laptop, pen and pad, and headed down the hall. She silenced her phone—just in case.

Peter greeted her, and a teammate rushed in behind her. During the next hour, the normalcy of work soothed tense muscles. Back in the middle of coworkers, thoughts of Gertrude dissipated.

Until her phone screen lit up, and "Aunt Gertrude" appeared as the caller.

She ignored the call, focusing on Peter's comments.

Two minutes later, the phone screen again distracted her.

"Trudy?"

She froze, heat rushing to her face. "I'm sorry, what was the question?"

"Results from your research last week."

"Right." She hurried to the front where her slides waited for explanations.

Ten minutes later, she returned to her seat, breathed deeply and exhaled, her lips parting to a slow smile. Around the room, thumbs up, smiles, and nods lifted her spirit.

Her screen brightened as she reached for a final slug of her coffee.

Gertrude. Again?

Trudy brushed her screen down.

Seriously? Ten calls?

She pushed the phone away as Peter wrapped up the meeting, and she closed her laptop.

"Good job, Trudy."

"Thanks, Peter. Sorry about that moment of distraction."

Her phone lit up again. Repelled by the name, she snatched the phone and dropped it in her pocket.

"Let's talk in my office." The steadiness in his voice unnerved her.

"Yes sir."

Great, Gertrude. You probably just cost me my job.

Understanding

Trudy trudged into Peter's office.

"Close the door."

Crud. Here it comes. Whatever he says, don't cry. I won't come across as trying to manipulate with tears.

She closed the door, took a seat, and breathed deeply.

Peter stood up. "On second thought, I need more coffee. You?"

She nodded, not trusting her voice to remain even.

"Why don't you call Gertrude back while I step out? I'll give you a few minutes."

"Thank you." She blinked away the sting.

As Peter closed the door behind him, Trudy whipped out her phone. The call count showed 40. Pressing the call button, she gritted her teeth, trying to calm the hoof beats of her heart.

"Oh, hi Trudy." Gertrude's sunny disposition rattled her.

"Gertrude, what is the matter?"

"Nothing. I just wondered when you were coming by today."

"You called me 40 times in the last hour. And you're telling me nothing is wrong?"

"Don't get all bent out of shape little girl."

Trudy inhaled, counting to ten, then released the breath slowly.

"I'm sorry, Auntie. I'm at work. All those times you called, I was in a meeting—presenting part of the time. Now I'm sitting in my boss's office—probably about to get fired."

"Why on earth would they fire you?"

"Never mind. Nothing for you to worry about."

"Well, you can come live with me. If they ever let me out of this place. I can take care of you."

Trudy softened. "Thank you. I'll be fine. Did you need anything when I come by after work?"

"No. I just haven't seen you in weeks."

"What? Gertrude, I was there yesterday!"

"No, I don't think so. I asked E, and she agreed."

"E?"

"My roommate. A new one. I miss you."

Trudy raised her eyes to the ceiling, closed them, and shook her head. "I need to work today, but I'll come by as soon as I get off."

"Good. It's been too long."

The door opened quietly as Peter returned, two cups in tow.

"I have to go now, Gertrude. I'll see you later." She disconnected before her aunt could say anything else and slipped the phone back into her jacket pocket.

Peter handed her a cup. "Everything alright?"

She blinked back the tears trying to creep out. "I don't know if it will ever be alright again. I truly am so sorry about my aunt calling and letting it distract me." She sipped the hot liquid, letting the sweetness soothe her throat and mind. "The worst part—she just wanted to know when I planned to come by there today."

"And she called how many times?"

"A hundred. Well, maybe only 40."

Peter laughed. "She must really miss you."

"Oh, yeah. And it's only been…" she looked at her watch. "Yep. About 14 hours, but she thinks I haven't been there in weeks."

"I'm sorry. I shouldn't laugh, but you gotta admit, 40 calls in less than an hour for nothing? Kinda comical."

Trudy grinned. "I guess. More like kinda frustrating."

"I can see that, Trudy. It can't be easy. How's the rest of your family?"

"Carrying on with life as if nothing happened. They don't

have quite the compassion for Gertrude I seem to have inherited."

"Ouch. That stinks. You're carrying the full load of all this?"

"Mostly." She looked down at her hands, waiting for the dismissal.

"Is she still in rehab?"

"For now. I expect the doctor to call this week with an update. Although, from a physical standpoint, I suspect they could release her soon, maybe days."

Peter stared out the window for a moment, then returned his gaze to Trudy. "Then what?"

"I hope she can go home. It could get tricky. I'm not sure she can take good care of herself. When I first went by her house…" A knot took root in her throat, forcing her to stop. Her mind demanded the tears remain unshed. "Gertrude never left a dish in the sink overnight, but it took me hours to clean her kitchen. She left dishes all over the house, and my aunt never does that."

Why was she spilling her gut to Peter? She didn't want his sympathy, but maybe he'd cut her some slack under the circumstances. Losing her job—not an option.

"Alzheimer's changes people. She'll only get worse as it progresses."

"I know. It scares me a little. And her hip still needs to heal. I hope they release her with home health care lined up." She took another sip. "I think they will. So I can focus on work, knowing someone checks on her during the day. I can stay at her house, be there at night."

"Sounds like you have a good plan—at least an initial one."

"Umm hmm."

"Have you considered assisted living? Big expense, but if she can afford it…"

"No. Before he died, my dad asked us to watch over her. I promised."

Peter nodded. "I'm sure he didn't expect this to happen." He laced his fingers together, putting thumbs on his chin. "That complicates things, doesn't it?"

"Yes. And no one understands. Family, friends—they all say put her away somewhere. I can't."

He dropped his hands to the desk. "I understand. You honor your dad well, Trudy. I admire you for that." He took a deep breath.

Here it comes.

"You can probably manage for now, like you plan. Eventually, this disease will ravish your aunt, and she won't be able to stay alone for any amount of time. You know that, right?"

Trudy nodded.

"I value you as a team member, and I'll do all I can to help. When it gets bad, let me know. I'll go to bat for you, insisting they let you work from home. And if it gets too bad, you can take FMLA. But you must keep me updated. I need to know where we are in the process."

"You aren't firing me?"

"No way. Even distracted you work harder and give more than anyone on this team. We'll make it work."

The dam holding back the tears exploded, uncontrolled rivulets destroying her make-up. She had no words.

Peter moved to the chair beside her, offering a box of tissues. "Trudy, you know the time may come when you have no choice about admitting her to a facility. I hope not, but you can't do this all alone long-term. Just don't rule out the possibility."

Although the stream lessened, she didn't trust herself to speak. Instead, she nodded.

"Good. If you need to hang here for a few more minutes, feel free to stay. I have another meeting, so pull yourself together and do what you can today. If you need to leave early, go." He stood and gathered his laptop and notebook. "I am glad you came in, though. You make this place brighter." He brushed her shoulder and headed out.

Floodgates reopened, releasing a torrent of fresh tears mingled with relief and sorrow. Minutes trickled by as Trudy sat alone in the office, thankful for a boss who cared, who showed compassion and spoke the truth with understanding. She hated the idea of institutionalizing Gertrude, but Peter had a point. Unlike others, though, he understood her need to wait until she had no other choice.

Maybe God heard some of her prayers.

After dabbing at her eyes, she ventured from the office toward the ladies' room to check her face. As she rounded the corner, her phone vibrated.

Gertrude. Again.

Nasty Memories

Hours later, Trudy responded to one last email, logged out and shut off her computer. She glanced at her phone and shook her head. Far too many missed calls from Gertrude. Rather than trying to call her back, she dragged herself from the chair, much too exhausted to deal with her aunt.

Despite a wonderful beginning, she dealt with multiple fires throughout the day, tending to her job as if Gertrude didn't exist. For a change, 5:00 p.m. arrived with a sense of accomplishment yet mental fatigue.

Trudy rolled her neck, gathered her things and sauntered out the door, smiling to herself. Coming to the office? An excellent decision. It removed Gertrude from her thoughts—at least for most of the day.

Maybe if she stopped and picked up a chocolate malt, Gertrude might like her again. It might even loosen up her lips a little. Trudy obsessed about the safety box and how to get inside for a peek.

Not sure a malt had enough power to do the job. For a moment, Trudy considered picking up a little whiskey to lace the malt.

Only for a moment.

No idea how Aunt Gertrude might react to alcohol. And with her current track record, Trudy dared not risk it.

Gertrude getting tipsy might backfire. As far as Trudy knew, Gertrude seldom drank—possibly an occasional glass of wine. And if she never drank, who knew what whiskey might do? She might simply fall asleep—hopefully answering questions from her subconscious thoughts. But what if she morphed into a mean drunk? Lately, her belligerent attitude came through at the least expected moments.

A vision of the old woman chasing her down the hall, yelling, threatening… A wave of dread washed over her.

Yeah. No. Maybe I'll get the whiskey and save it for myself afterward.

Since when did she take to drinking whiskey, or even thinking about it? Could insanity be contagious? Trudy chuckled. She sometimes thought she might be catching Gertrude's dementia.

Best leave the alcohol out of the equation all together.

Thoughts of the hidden secrets resurfaced as she headed toward the rehab facility. If she could only get all the facts, coerce Gertrude into talking about the past, maybe it could help. From the pieces she had, the repressed anger made sense.

A father who abused her—to what level Trudy had no idea. Finding love and marrying, only to have that man ripped from her life. And what about the baby? The questions toyed with her.

At a drive through, Trudy ordered three chocolate malts. Might as well indulge herself, and she didn't want to leave out the roommate—Martha. Just her luck, they didn't have malts. She should have gone to Gertrude's old haunting grounds. But Cherry's no longer existed, and she didn't know of any other classic diners in the area. Chocolate malt, chocolate shake.

What's the difference? It's chocolate.

Balancing the drinks, Trudy took her time getting to her great aunt's room, wondering again which woman waited for her there.

At the room, she paused, shifting her delectable cargo and tenaciously pushing the door open.

"Aunt Gertrude?"

Her aunt looked up from the chair, eyes wild with a grimace covering her lips. "Who are you and what do you want?"

"It's me, Auntie. Trudy?"

Gertrude switched on a table lamp, studying the cups in Trudy's hand. "What's that? Did you come to poison me?"

Trudy forced out a nervous laugh. "Well, who knows what

they put in these things? Too much sugar, so I suppose we could consider that poison. I brought one for your roommate and one for myself, though."

"I don't have a roommate." Gertrude spit the words out like venom.

"What happened to Martha?"

"She died. Good riddance, too. What a loony toon."

"Oh, Gertrude. I'm truly sorry."

"Why? It isn't like she was my friend or anything."

Tears pooled. Trudy stuffed them. "I know." She eeked out a smile. "How about a chocolate malt?"

She crossed the room and handed a cup to Gertrude. "You can have two if you want them."

"You are trying to kill me. Two malts? I'll have to sit on the toilet all night." She took the cup, straw, and spoon Trudy offered and poked the straw in without unwrapping it. Taking a sip, she curled her upper lip. "That tastes nasty. Like paper."

"You forgot to remove the wrapper."

"Stupid idea. Covering a perfectly good straw." Gertrude yanked out the straw, flinging frosty chocolate across the floor.

"Would you like some help?"

"I don't need any help. You think I'm a child?"

"No. Of course, not. I… Sometimes those wrappers don't come off easily."

Gertrude threw the straw on the floor.

In an effort to avoid more conflict, Trudy thrust her drink in Gertrude's free hand and retrieved the one her aunt held. "Here. Mine's ready to go. That way you know it isn't poisoned either."

"Yeah, right. You probably did that on purpose so I'd think you gave me the one without poison."

Trudy sighed. "Take whichever you want."

"Doesn't matter. I'm gonna die soon, anyway." Gertrude sucked hard until the liquid reached her mouth. Another grimace.

"That isn't a chocolate malt. And it isn't from Cherry's."

"I know, Gertrude. Cherry's closed a long time ago."

"No, they didn't. You just didn't want to drive over there."

The truth of her aunt's statement bit hard. "You're right. I had a long day at work, but I wanted to come by and bring you a treat. My bad." Trudy gritted her teeth, trying to stay calm.

Gertrude sucked down more shake and softened. "It isn't awful. Did you bring my hairbrush?"

"Oh curmudgeon. I forgot."

Wait a minute. Didn't she say she had a hairbrush?

"Well, I suppose it doesn't matter whether I brush my hair. Who cares?"

"I think you have one here." Trudy stepped into the bathroom and retrieved the brush. "I found it. Would you like it if I brushed your hair? I used to do that when I was young."

"I don't remember that. It isn't my brush."

"Yes. Look. It has your name written on it."

"I want my new one. Where's my new one?"

"You said it was in the drawer in your bathroom at home. I'll go by there when I leave here tonight and bring it back tomorrow. OK?"

Gertrude heaved a sigh. "Oh alright. That one will do for now."

Trudy crossed over, removed the clip, and gently brushed. "You have such soft hair." Maybe she could relax her aunt a little. "Is that too hard?"

"It's fine."

"While I'm at your house, I might need to get some papers for the rehab center. Do you have documents locked in a safe?"

"Who said I have a safe?" Gertrude sat up and looked back at Trudy. "Have you been snooping again?"

Trudy shook her head.

Stupid. You should not have gone there.

"No ma'am. It's just… Well, I keep my important documents in a small fireproof box. I… I… I call it my safe."

Gertrude squinted and grabbed the brush from Trudy.

A gentle knock broke the conversation. Irma pushed her way into the room.

"Hi. I had a few minutes before picking up the kids. Thought I'd drop in."

Trudy took a deep breath and released it. "Good. We have an extra chocolate shake. Gertrude no longer has a roommate."

"Yum." Irma turned to Gertrude. "How are you, Aunt Gertrude? I can only stay a few minutes."

With lips pursed and eyes narrowed, Gertrude looked over Irma. "And I suppose you came to gang up on me with your sister! I will not give either of you the combination."

Irma stepped back. "I'm sorry. What are you talking about?"

Gertrude's nose flared. "Yes, you are sorry. Trudy tried buttering me up with this crappy excuse for a chocolate malt, and now she wants the combination. Isn't that right? DEAR?"

Trudy looked down. "I can't get in your lock-box without a key."

"You don't need the combination. Why do you need it?"

"Aunt Gertrude, I need your papers for insurance."

"No, you don't. They have my card. You just want my money. What makes you think there's money in my little safe, anyway?" Her volume increased.

"I don't care about your money. I have plenty of my own." Trudy rubbed her forehead. "Please, Auntie. I'm only trying to help."

"Like hell you are!" Daggers shot from the old woman's darkened eyes. "You thieving little bitch. You keep your hands off my money!"

Gertrude never hit Trudy, but the words slapped harder than a hand ever could.

Trudy had no response. Just as well. The lump building in her throat didn't leave room for speech. The glare coming from her aunt blurred as she fought back tears.

Don't let her see you cry. Don't let her see you cry.

Irma lashed out at their aunt. "I can't believe you'd say such a spiteful thing. Trudy's done nothing but take care of you. All her life, she made excuses for your meanness. But this? How dare you?" Irma reached out, as if she might push the old woman.

"Irma, stop. Don't hurt her." Trudy grabbed her sister's hand.

Using a trick she learned in the corporate world, Trudy shot her gaze to the ceiling for a moment and then brought it slowly back down to meet her aunt's stare.

"We should go now. C'mon, Irma." Trudy turned to the door, her sister following with an arm wrapped around her shoulders.

"Good. Stay away from me, you b…"

The door closed behind them.

In the parking lot, the tears broke free from Trudy. "It's just the dementia."

"No, it's not!" Irma fumed. "She's always been this way. Face it, big sister. You're finally getting what the rest of us always did." She stopped. "I'm sorry, Tru. I know it hurts. She should never talk to you like that. And you don't have to take it. Walk away and leave her there to rot."

"I can't, Irma. I can't do that to Daddy." She sniffled. "Besides, I think we don't know a lot of things about Gertrude."

"Like what?"

"Stuff from her past."

"Is that what this safe is about?"

"Yeah." Trudy hung her head. "If I could get in the lock-box I found, maybe it holds some answers, and I can help her work through the junk. Can't you see the pain in her eyes?"

"You're a better woman than I am then—especially after what you just got in there." Irma shook her head. "No pain can excuse that behavior, and it isn't new. You know that—you just don't want to admit it."

"Maybe."

"Walk away, big sister. Before it consumes you, too. You don't have to let her drag you down into her cesspool of bitterness."

Trudy looked up, gazing deep into her sister's eyes. For once, she almost agreed.

Almost.

A Moment of Repentance

Gertrude gazed across the patio. Birds fluttered around several feeders hanging in trees rimming the enclosed yard.

Something seemed off—her heart heavy. But she had no clue why.

This place. It makes me crazy and sad.

She knew better. Her brain failed, but her spirit whispered loudly. She did something the day before, but what? As she sipped coffee, Gertrude searched her memory.

Nothing.

Fuzziness coated her mind.

An empty plate sat before her. Breakfast? Yes. But what?

An aide appeared with a pot of coffee. "Ms. Ryan, do you want more coffee?"

"Yes, please. And can I have my breakfast now?"

"Well, you ate an omelet." The aide's brows dipped and quickly lifted. "But I can bring you something else. What do you want?"

"I hate omelets. Just a nice bran muffin. They keep me regular."

"No problem. I believe they just took out a fresh batch. Do you want butter for it?"

"Of course."

She patted Gertrude's shoulder. "I'll be right back with that. Do you need anything else?"

"No, I am fine, thank you."

Omelet? I do not remember eating an omelet. That silly aide must be confused. Someone else had an omelet. I always eat a muffin for breakfast.

Gertrude took a deep breath, believing herself. She watched the birds, wishing for freedom to fly away. One of the Psalms.

136

"Oh, to be a bird and fly away." Something like that.

The aide reappeared, steam rising from a muffin, butter melting on top. "Here you go." She set the plate in front of Gertrude.

Did I ask for a muffin? How could I forget asking? Didn't I already eat?

Without a word, she smiled. "Thank you, dear."

"You're welcome. Are you feeling better today?"

"I'm fine."

"Good. You seemed quite upset when your niece came by last night."

"My niece?"

"Yes. Trudy."

"Oh. She's not my niece. She's my granddaughter."

"Oh, that's right. I always forget."

"I was upset with her?"

"Heard you all the way down the hall, yelling at her. She walked out with her sister, crying."

"No. Not Trudy."

"Yes, I'm afraid so." She frowned. "I'm sorry. I shouldn't have said anything."

"Was I mean to her?"

"I wasn't in the room, so I don't know what happened." The aide smiled. "You know, I'm sure you were upset about Martha getting to go home and you being stuck here with us."

"Martha. The woman who invaded my room. She went home? I thought she died."

"No. Her son plans to stay with her for a while." The young woman glanced around. "Between us, I have a feeling she'll be back before too long. I don't think he knows how far her mind has diminished."

"I always said she might be loony. And then E took her place. She talks more than the first one did. Never shuts up. Even talks in her sleep, and her mind is no better."

The aide smiled. "Well, hopefully, they release you soon, too."

"I am certain they will." Gertrude glanced at the muffin. "Thank you for the… cup… bread… muffin. Sometimes those ·words get tangled."

"They do for us all." She stood. "I'll be back in a while to check on you."

Alone again, Gertrude stiffened in her chair. A fight with Trudy. No wonder her heart felt like a bowling ball. Why did she get upset with Trudy. And she yelled at her? Not possible.

Irma maybe.

But Trudy? No.

Her spirit said different. Besides, why would the aide lie to her?

She bowed her head, droplets forming and trickling down her cheeks.

Lord, I do not understand. I love Trudy. Why would I fight with her?

She searched her mind, a memory lingering at the tip of recollection but evading her senses. Her eyes squeezed tighter until her head ached. If she could only remember.

Nothing. A blank slate from the previous night.

How could she make things right with Trudy if she had no clue why they argued or what she said? What either of them said? Maybe she had a reason for the anger.

Gertrude shook her head. Not at Trudy. Responsible, respectful, compliant Trudy. No one got mad at her. Why did they fight? And yelling? She never lost control of anger like that.

Never.

Blowing out a breath, she looked toward the garden. A furry ball scampered across the ground. A squirrel? She trembled.

Wrong color.

A rat.

She hated rats.

Her mind drifted back. Ever since the shed.

Images drowned her reasoning, flashing across her mind. Relentless, they drew her back in time as her mind battled to regain a sense of control. Clinching her jaw, Gertrude struggled against the thoughts raging for attention.

"No! I won't let my mind go there."

But what if she lost control? What if, one day, she awoke with only the horrid memories remaining? Her hands shook as the possibility took hold.

I'm scared, Lord. Take this from me. If you must take me home, do so.

In that moment, she faced a terrifying truth. The fear caused her anger toward Trudy. Facing the unknown, the one who loved her most made a soft place to land her uncontrolled blows. Trudy—always the one who stood by her—would never stop loving her. Would she?

What if she does? What if I cross that line one too many times? Will she walk away, give up on me like everyone else?

With moist eyes, Gertrude pictured herself locked in that upstairs room in her house. Tied up, the door locked, left alone like her father did her mother.

No! Even if Trudy left her to die alone in some facility, she could never show that kind of cruelty. Tears slid down her cheeks, unbidden and unyielding to her determination to hold them inside.

Could she trust Trudy? Maybe…

No. Not ready to tell her everything. Not yet.

She still had time. Letting Trudy get that close gave her too much power. Power Gertrude would not concede.

She glanced back at the garden, wondering about the furry beast. The rats of her life would not win. She reached for her walker, leaving the muffin untouched and the coffee growing cold.

Humor in Insanity

Trudy pulled into a parking spot. Of course, the only open space left her as far from the door as possible. Plenty of time for dread to encompass her mind as she strode toward the building. No rush.

After the rough beginning of her week, Gertrude settled down and quit calling every two minutes. A week of work left Trudy feeling human again. She even went to lunch with friends and took herself to a movie in the middle of the week. Earlier that day, Peter praised her and presented an award to her during a team meeting.

A perfect day.

She hoped Gertrude had a pleasant one too, but a phone call minutes earlier dashed that dream against a stone wall. Trying to ignore negative thoughts, they pestered her brain, begging for admission to consciousness.

No. I won't indulge those nasty memories.

Suddenly, they flooded her like a tsunami, massive waves sweeping away every ounce of joy she experienced earlier.

She wanted to keep loving Aunt Gertrude, but the hateful words from the last visit bit deep, wounding all over again as they replayed in her mind.

"You just want my money. What makes you think there's money in my little safe, anyway?"

"Please, Auntie. I'm only trying to help."

"Like hell you are! You thieving little bitch. You keep your hands off my money!"

"We should go now."

"Good. Stay away from me you b…"

A car door slammed, dragging Trudy back to the present. She

pushed through the front door, signed in at the desk, and trudged down the front hallway. Filled with dread, she uttered a prayer. "Lord, please get me through this."

She knocked and pushed open the door slowly.

Wait. That's not Gertrude.

A bright smile greeted Trudy. "Hello, dear. Can I help you?"

"I thought this was my aunt's room. I'm so sorry. I must've chosen the wrong door. So sorry to interrupt you."

"Not at all. Are you looking for Gertrude?"

"Yes, ma'am. I'm her great niece, Trudy."

"Oh. You're Trudy—her namesake. She told me so much about you." The woman eased from her chair. "I'm Ethel. I just moved in here after the other woman went home."

"Home?"

"Yes. I think family came to take care of her. Anyway, we're roomies now and fast becoming best friends. Gertrude's in the bathroom." She knocked on the inner door before shouting. "Gertrude. Gertrude. Your Trudy is here."

The door opened. "I'm not deaf, you know. I heard her, but I had to pull up my britches."

Britches? Gertrude never said britches before.

Trudy raised her eyebrows, still praying her aunt wouldn't lash out again. Maybe a roommate offered a modicum of protection.

Maybe.

She could hope.

Probably not.

Gertrude hobbled across the room with her walker and dropped into a chair. "Now. That's better." A brightness crossed her face as she sighed. "It's so hard getting around. I can't wait to come home."

"Hopefully, that's soon, Auntie." If only that were true. Trudy really hoped her aunt stayed in rehab for a long time. The house was nowhere near ready for her, but she dared not say that.

Instead, she mustered up a false enthusiasm. "You seem to get around better. The rehab's working, yes?"

"I suppose so. Of course, Ethel and I don't get much sleep."

"Oh, that's so true," Ethel jumped in, returning to her chair. "It's those little men coming up out of the floor at night."

"What?"

Little men? This woman was crazier than her aunt.

"Oh, yes," Gertrude agreed. "Every night. The floor opens, and they move us to new places. They've taken us to facilities all over the place."

Trudy tried to hide her surprise. "Really?" Was Gertrude simply going along with this story, or did she believe it, too?

Ethel responded first. "All over the country, I think. We've moved so many times, and I've only been here three days."

"It has been three weeks," Gertrude corrected.

Trudy shook her head. She saw Martha less than three weeks earlier. Ten days before, Gertrude said she had no roommate, that Martha died. A knot formed in Trudy's stomach. That visit made her never want to come again. But she honored her obligations. Listening to the two women, she wondered if she might need to check in a little more often. Either way, both women had their days off kilter, but she had no intentions of arguing with them—especially about the passage of time.

She looked at Ethel and then at Gertrude. "So, these little men move you?"

Both women nodded.

"Wow. That's interesting."

"You do not know the half of it," Gertrude insisted. "They enter the room, pleasantly enough, dressed in tiny uniforms, almost like the doormen in… in… that big city I used to visit." She paused. "New York. Yes, in New York. Rather handsome, most of them."

"How many little men come?" Maybe she shouldn't feed their

fantasy, but Trudy couldn't help it.

"Ten." Ethel chimed in.

"Maybe. Sometimes more, sometimes less. One night, I swear 30 men hurried through the opening. That night left me exhausted." Gertrude sank back into her chair.

Trudy pursed her lips and nodded, praying her aunt didn't share details. "I bet. Well, hopefully, they will stay away tonight so both of you get some sleep."

"I sure hope so." Gertrude laughed. "But they are rather entertaining, singing and dancing sometimes."

Ethel quipped, "Oh, especially Tobias. He's my favorite. I think he fancies me." She picked up a book and started reading as if the other two women didn't exist.

Gertrude pointed at Ethel and circled both temples with her index fingers.

Trying desperately not to laugh, Trudy raised her eyebrows and smiled knowingly. Likely neither woman knew the extent of their personal battles with dementia.

The visit continued for another 30 minutes with one or both women throwing out a comment here and there, always returning to their subterranean visitors at some point. Trudy listened intently until she could no longer stand the ludicrousness of it all.

"Well, it's getting late. I need to get going."

"So soon?" Gertrude seemed almost her old self. "You really should stay. Ethel will have our servants prepare dinner. We have the most wonderful personal chef."

"Yes, of course, my dear. Please stay and dine with us." Ethel started to get up from her chair.

"No, no. I can't tonight. I already have plans."

"A date?" Aunt Gertrude—always playing matchmaker. "Do I know him?"

Trudy laughed. "No, Auntie. Just one of my friends—not even a man."

"Oh." Disappointment skipped across her aunt's face and then disappeared behind a broad grin. "Well, maybe we shall have one of our visitors stay behind so you can meet him."

"Not Tobias. He's mine." Ethel staked her claim.

"Of course not. He is ancient—much too old for my lovely young granddaughter."

Oh no. She is losing it. Then again, Gertrude raised Dad, so she might think of me as a granddaughter.

"I'm good, Auntie. But thank you for caring." At least the visit didn't end with a battle, and for that Trudy thanked God. "I'll come back in a couple of days." She leaned over and kissed the old woman's forehead.

"OK, love. Be careful."

"Always."

Trudy exited before one of the women picked up where they left off. Of all the crazy tales. Little men coming up from the floor? Dancing? Singing?

Suddenly, a vision of Oompa Loompas filled her thoughts. OK, they didn't say anything about orange skin, but still… Trudy chuckled. She pictured little men coming through a smoky opening, red, double-breasted jackets with gold buttons and trim, giving them an air of official doormen. How many times had Gertrude described the ones from Fifth Avenue?

In Trudy's mind, the little men waltzed the old women across the room, lifting them and filling their nights with wonder and excitement. Thoughts of Gertrude's old Sinatra vinyl records hummed in her brain. She knew none of it was real, but she couldn't stop the images.

As she imagined the ludicrous scene, laughter bubbled up and spilled over.

Oh, that felt so good.

Still, the images traveled across her imagination, and she laughed harder. By the time she burst through the facility's front door, Trudy couldn't suppress it.

She barely got inside her car when the phone rang.

Her sister's harsh voice broke the moment. "Well, how did it go? Do I need to come deck the old biddy for you?"

"Actually, you won't believe it. Gertrude has a roomie, named Ethel."

"Did you convey your deepest sympathies to her?"

"Oh, Irma. C'mon." Trudy chuckled. "You won't believe the story they told me. I think Ethel might be more off her rocker than Gertrude."

"Is that possible?"

"Um, yeah. Apparently, they have little men visiting them in the night?"

"What?"

"Yeah. Coming up through the floor."

For the next 20 minutes, Trudy sat in her car and relayed the story to Irma, embellishing it with her imaginative visions. The sisters laughed hysterically. Trudy dared not drive at that point, tears streaming down her cheeks.

"That's quite a tale," Irma said, still laughing.

Trudy wiped her eyes with the back of her hands. "I know it isn't funny. I shouldn't laugh, but I couldn't help it. And the more I thought about this story they both so obviously believed as rock solid truth..." Suddenly, the laughter overtook her again.

"Trudy, you're right. We shouldn't laugh, but it is hilarious. At least the way you told it to me. You have such a great imagination."

"I haven't laughed so hard in such a long time. Not even before Gertrude got sick." Trudy sighed. "I hate seeing Gertrude like this, but perhaps I needed to see some humor so I didn't dissolve into tears."

"I think you're right. Maybe we both needed a little humor tonight."

"Yeah. I'm glad I made you laugh, too. But now, I need to get going."

"Goodnight my favorite sister."

"Hey. I'm your only sister."

"Technicality. You're still my favorite."

As she started the car, the tension drained. A brief respite from the darkness that surrounded Trudy's life. Good medicine indeed. For the first time since the call about Gertrude's fall, she breathed deeply and released it without a sigh.

Next time might bring tears, but tonight, she planned to rest well.

Cracking the Fireproof Box

Trudy sipped coffee on her back porch. Far too early on a Saturday morning. After a night filled with strange dreams, the first light drew her from the bed. More accurately, her bladder demanded she push aside the covers and force herself up. Oh, to crawl back in bed for a little longer—snoozing and pretending the world didn't exist.

Once up, she poked her head out the back door, deciding what to wear for the day. The surprising early morning coolness beckoned her to enjoy a moment outdoors—something she missed in all the recent turmoil.

Friday evening's encounter with Gertrude, although strange by all counts, went by rather uneventful—a definite improvement. The new roommate and utter ridiculousness of their joint story still put a smile on Trudy's face. Her conversation with Irma tugged at the corners of her mind, pulling her back to fresh memories of the laughter they shared.

How they could laugh in the middle of such craziness made her question whether she might be losing *her* mind.

It wasn't funny. Not really.

A giggle popped from Trudy. She shook her head, trying to chase away the strange pictures from her brain.

Little men. Dancing. Singing.

She laughed. Who said dementia couldn't have a funny side? Maybe she could hold on to this memory for those moments when Gertrude did anything *but* make her laugh.

Despite the continued fuzziness of Gertrude's mind, Trudy knew rehab couldn't last forever. Physically, the woman surpassed every expectation. In a matter of days, she expected a call, insisting she come retrieve her aunt. If she had any chance of cracking the code on the lock-box, today might be her best option. She needed to check the mail anyway for any past-due bills.

How to broach that subject…

Leave it for another day.

Why spoil this delicious moment of peace?

She drank in the warm sunshine and uncharacteristically cool breeze. If she tried, it felt like gentle caresses—something she hadn't known for years. Did she even still want a husband? One awful marriage didn't spoil her taste for men, but years of dating losers left her wondering why she bothered. With all the Gertrude mess, she didn't have time or energy for a relationship. Maybe that was a bonus.

She considered the advantages of singlehood.

House. No man wanted a cute little cottage, but she loved it. Small, easy and quick to clean, decorated in a feminine yet practical style she adored.

Travel. The trips she took for work left her hungering for more and gave her confidence that she could travel alone. Not that she had much, but she could. Not worrying about whether someone else liked her choice of destinations, she booked a few random weekends and enjoyed a change of atmosphere. Nothing major or overseas. Not *that* confident.

Maybe she should ask Gertrude if she wanted to go somewhere.

Trudy shook her head.

At least not until some of the craziness subsided. Surely it would—when she got her back home. Better idea, get someone to stay with her great-aunt while she flitted off on a relaxing weekend.

Still, if Gertrude had as much money as she swore, maybe she wanted to take a vacation somewhere. She might even pay for both of them to go on an extravagant getaway.

Yeah, right.

Without warning, thoughts of the fireproof lock-box intruded on her morning reflections. The rabbit trail ran right after Gertrude, and Trudy didn't fight following. Needed to get over there and break into the box.

Part of her wanted to listen to Mom and Irma. Run away with whatever money she found and leave Gertrude at the rehab center. Let her be someone else's problem.

Crazy idea. I'm not a thief. No matter what Gertrude accuses me of doing. And I could never abandon her.

"Daddy wouldn't." The spoken words escaped, strengthening her resolve. "But he would treat himself to breakfast before tackling undesirable tasks."

She smiled, remembering the many early mornings the two of them sneaked out to get breakfast before anyone else in the house woke up. She pushed the memories back to dark corners of her mind, headed inside, placed her mug in the dishwasher and hummed while she dressed.

Breakfast at Del's Diner sounded perfect for a lazy Saturday morning.

Getting the House Ready

As Trudy pulled into Gertrude's drive, Kit waved from her porch.

No. I can't deal with her today. I need to prepare for Gertrude to come home. Please keep Kit at home.

Stepping from the car, she breathed a sigh of relief as Kit shouted, "I'm coming, Mama," and went inside.

Thank you, Lord. Maybe He hears my prayers—sometimes.

She retrieved the mail from the box, turned the key, and stepped into the stillness of the dark, empty house.

So depressing.

Trudy tugged at chains to open the massive drapes. Sunlight flowed across the room, lighting dust bunnies floating in the air.

Better.

She repeated the move throughout the house, pushing aside curtains, pulling back heavy drapes. She drifted into the den and eyed the stereo. She didn't dare change the radio station. No USB plugs. That eliminated using her phone for music. She glanced over the CD cases lining the shelf.

Hmmm. Possibilities.

Gertrude liked old jazz music.

Maybe. I can live with some jazz.

She chose a greatest hits with multiple discs that looked upbeat.

Hoping for music to inspire some cleaning, she turned the volume up and went in search of the vacuum cleaner. Pulling it out, she switched direction and reached up for a duster. Might be a better option to start.

As music filled the home, Trudy worked from room to room. By the end of the first CD, she banished most of the dust. Pulling the heavy Kirby into the den, she started there and vacuumed. By the end of the second CD, the house looked cleaner.

Windows? Not that inspired.

She put Mr. Kirby back into the kitchen pantry, retrieved the bathroom cleaners, and changed the CD again. By the end of the third and final CD, Trudy felt good about her progress. Before heading upstairs, she rummaged through the refrigerator, tossing out expired items.

Lots of expired items.

Shaking her head, she retrieved a cardboard dinner from the freezer and popped it in the microwave. As she half-chewed, half-swallowed the food—if she could call it that—she considered the locked box in Gertrude's closet.

Next on her list.

Food finished and fork washed and put away, she ventured to the bedroom, determined to pick the lock.

How hard could it be?

Old and not heavy duty. Fireproof maybe, but not a top security lock. Besides, Gertrude might have the key "hidden" in an obvious place.

In the bedroom, she paused beside the jewelry box.

Too obvious.

She searched through drawers and a trinket box. No luck.

The jewelry box beckoned. With an easy click, it opened. Beneath a string of pearls, a small silver key peeked out.

Could it be that easy?

Clutching the key, she opened the closet door, flipped on the light, and kneeled on the floor. The key slid easily into the lock—and turned.

Unbelievable.

Trudy carried the box to the writing desk and opened it up.

She sifted through items. Typical stuff. Insurance papers,

Gertrude's birth certificate, her social security card. At the very bottom, she pulled out an envelope, yellowed with age. Carefully opening it, she looked at the papers inside. Marriage certificate.

*Ha! So, she **did** get married.*

There in black and white, she saw Gertrude Ryan and William Dade. The other paper in the envelope stole her breath.

Annulment?

Dated three months after the marriage license.

Why would Gertrude get an annulment? Especially if she suspected a pregnancy.

Trudy looked at the bottom of the document.

Not Gertrude Ryan or Gertrude Dade. Euleseus Ryan.

Euleseus? Who the heck was Euleseus?

She peeked at Gertrude's birth certificate.

Father: Euleseus.

The man everyone described as mean.

Pieces gravitated in Trudy's mind. The pictures she first found—not a traditional wedding. They eloped. Trudy felt certain. Made sense. The father didn't like the boy, so when he learned of the marriage, of course he got mad.

But why did he sign the annulment and not Gertrude?

She looked back through papers and noted dates.

Doing the math in her head, she snapped her fingers.

"Why that sneaky little Gertrude. She lied about her age to get the marriage certificate. That's why her father could get it annulled. He might or might not have known about the baby— assuming a baby existed. Maybe he suspected it?"

Somewhere above her, a creak suspended Trudy's words.

With her heart picking up pace, she looked up, listening intently.

Someone in the house?

"Stop it, Trudy. Old houses creak." She chuckled.

THUD.

What was that?

Something knocked over?

Impossible.

I'm the only one here.

CREAK.

I'm not alone.

Hide.

A gun. In the desk.

She stuffed the certificates back in the envelope, thrust it back into the bottom of the box, and replaced the other documents.

Listening, she locked the box, placed it in the closet, and closed the door softly. Moving back to the dresser, she replaced the key exactly as she found it, peeping from beneath the pearls.

CREAK.

Trudy tiptoed into the office and opened the top drawer. No gun.

Crap.

She peered up the stairs.

Nothing.

THUD.

Heart pounding, mind racing.

She stopped. Listened.

"Get a grip, Trudy. You're imagining things." The words spoken to the empty room didn't convince her.

She filled her lungs. Released the air. Slowing her responses, she relaxed.

"Guess my snooping in this old house has my brain tricking me. How silly."

CREAK.

Or not.

Someone's there.

She cowered at the bottom landing.

Grabbing an umbrella from the entryway, she ascended the stairs, staying close to the wall.

Three steps up.

She inhaled and held her breath.

CREAK.

Several more steps, always looking up.

THUD.

Only a few more steps to the landing.

Girl, you're insane. Go back down and call the cops.

She took the last steps, gripping the umbrella, ready to clobber the intruder.

CREAK. THUD.

CREAK. THUD.

BOOM!

Trudy jumped backward into the wall.

She screamed.

Lightning flashed outside the half-moon window in a small sitting area across from her.

Ragged breaths tumbled over each other.

Another CREAK and THUD hit as a shutter banged against the house, opening and closing.

Her knees buckled and Trudy slid to the floor, her back still against the wall. She didn't know whether to cry or laugh.

"Some intruder." She shook her head. "I need to get that fixed—pronto."

As her heart slowed, Trudy used the umbrella and stair railing to get up. Crossing to the window, she looked outside. Trees almost even with the window swirled and whipped against the house. Dark clouds rolled in, thunder and lightning accompanying them. She opened the window, trying to secure the shutter. She caught it on the next swing, but the wind tore it from her grip. No way to keep it from banging.

"Not like I'm staying in this house alone tonight anyway,"

she said to the wind. "Blow all you want." She let go.

CREAK. THUD.

Laughter burst from her. She slammed the window and locked it.

Turning around, she took in her surroundings, peeking into the two bedrooms. She sneezed. Needed cleaning.

Dust lined the furniture. She wrinkled her nose at the stale air. With the coming storm, she should hurry home. Upstairs could wait.

Then, the door into the forbidden attic room. She hesitated. Ignoring misgivings, she crept up the stairs. Her hand on the knob tingled.

She turned.

It opened.

Hidden

Half expecting a rank odor, Trudy sniffed.

Pleasant. Not rank at all.

Around the room, exquisite furniture poised, ready to receive guests who never entered. Trudy paused and then crossed the threshold, drawn by the beauty. An elegant quilt covered the antique bed, care taken to place coordinating pillows against the intricately carved headboard. The matching dresser and vanity sat against another wall. Beside the window, a well-worn rocker looked out over the lawn as if waiting for the owner to return and spend the afternoon rocking while reading or perhaps sewing.

Mom was right. Gorgeous pieces. I can't imagine how much Gertrude could get if she sold them. Not something I want to suggest.

Ever.

She fumbled her way to the dresser, running a finger over the surface.

Not a speck of dust.

Unused, from what Mom said, yet pristine. Photos lined the top—pictures of two women who both looked like younger versions of Gertrude. The sisters? Her great aunt never talked about her sister. They almost looked like twins. Several frames held the image of an adorable little boy who reminded Trudy of her childhood photos. Tears pooled as she recognized one from the pictures they used at her dad's funeral.

Did Gertrude keep them in the room for her mother?

In the forgotten room, sorrow ran up Trudy's back, sending tremors down it. A mixture of emotions inundated her being, filling her from the atmosphere. Trudy shivered despite the warmth.

What spirits lingered? What secrets might the walls yell if given voice?

She turned to another wall where an ancient trunk beckoned her, begged her to explore its contents. Behind it, a tattered quilt hung, providing a backdrop that differed from the rest of the room.

Kneeling beside the trunk, she tried the latch. Locked, of course.

Crossing to the vanity, she found several hat pins.

That'll work.

With two in hand, she crouched beside the trunk again, looking furtively at the doorway. The wind, creaks and thuds continued, but all else remained quiet. Downstairs, music continued filtering up the steps from the stereo. Her hand shook as she played with the lock, doing her best not to scratch anything as she maneuvered the makeshift picks.

CLICK.

Nice.

Trudy opened the lid and peered inside while her cheeks burned. If Gertrude ever found out…

Too late. She couldn't turn back. Instead, she brushed away the shame and dug into the trove of hidden treasure.

In the top tray, several trinkets and jewelry pieces lay in a single layer, including a simple gold wedding band. She dismissed it and lifted out the trays. Eyes widening, a breath caught in her throat. On one side, dozens of dingy envelopes dared her to open them. She studied the return address and exhaled.

For a moment, she considered it.

Maybe after exploring everything else.

Reading Gertrude's letters from William… That breached a place she didn't want to go—yet. She hoisted out a quilt filled with wedding circles. She knew the pattern from the one her mom inherited from her grandmother. Tradition.

In the trunk, a lacy white dress sucked the air from Trudy's lungs. The same one from the picture in Gertrude's closet.

Without warning, tears trickled, and then poured like a flood.

Not a woman who wanted a marriage annulled.

Trudy clenched her teeth, thinking about a harsh man she never knew—and thanked God she didn't.

What father did such a cruel thing to his daughter?

Impatient with herself, Trudy brushed away the tears. Like a fragile dish, she lifted the dress. Beneath it, several small boxes created a uniform line.

More jewelry?

Maybe, but they didn't look much like jeweler's boxes. She opened one, surprised by a medal of honor. Each contained other medals she assumed belong to William.

She slumped to the floor, unwilling to continue looking at the precious objects. She hoped she could reverse pick the lock.

Although she considered keeping out the letters, she couldn't betray that sacred trust. Her heart burned to read the words, but it felt too invasive. With the care of a new mother, she replaced each item, shut the lid, and used the hairpins to lock the trunk again.

Maybe one day she'd visit this treasure trove again.

Standing up, she lost her balance, and to keep from falling, she grabbed the hanging quilt. It gave way and fell on top of her when she landed hard.

"Stupid quilt." She chuckled, eying the corners with a realization that thumbtacks didn't hold a person's body weight. Pushing herself off the floor, she looked up, straight at a closet door.

"Why would Gertrude hide a closet door?" She glanced around the room, feeling as if someone watched her. "Get a grip. No one's here but you."

She twisted the knob, the door swinging open.

Dank, mustiness and old moth balls gagged her. She backed up and started to close the door—until a monstrous object stopped her.

A massive, old-style safe stood against the back wall, its combination dial and cast-iron handle staring at her, taunting.

Just try to break into me, girlie.

She stared back, knowing it could have thousands of numeric combinations. And somehow, she knew—it contained everything she needed to understand Aunt Gertrude's anguished heart. For a long time, she stood there, afraid to move toward the safe, yet not wanting to leave it.

Hidden.

Inaccessible.

Unbreakable.

As her phone played a familiar ring tone, she jumped and looked at the display.

Dr. Thompson. She didn't expect that.

"Hello?"

"Hi Trudy. I'm sorry to call so late. It's been a busy day."

"No problem. Is Gertrude OK? What happened?" Her heart thundered.

"Yes. Everything's fine. That's why I called. I went by to check on her today—had issues getting another patient admitted and settled. Gertrude is an incredible woman."

"Well, I guess that's one way to describe her." She chuckled.

"I'm amazed at her physical progress. She far exceeded my expectations."

"Yep. That's my auntie. She's an overachiever."

"I have no reason to keep her in rehab, although..." He hesitated.

"Although what?"

"The nurses confirmed the dementia, Trudy. I'm sorry. I hoped I got it wrong, but we can't deny it now. I even experienced a touch of it myself tonight. Without more tests, I can't confirm the level, but I suspect she's reached the moderate phase."

"What does that mean?"

"We'll try some various meds, try to slow it down, but her memory could go fast or linger off and on for years. Every person progresses differently." He sighed. "I wish it was better news. She really wants to go home."

"Ha. She wanted to go home before she ever went to rehab." They both laughed.

"How soon will you release her?"

"I can give you another day or two, but after that, insurance gets testy. They don't like paying that bill."

"I understand. Can she stay alone?"

"For short periods, but I don't recommend all day. Physically, she still needs help. I'll arrange for home health care and at-home physical therapy. That should help for a while, but you need to make some permanent decisions."

"I've been looking at options, but I thought I had a little more time."

"Since it's so late in the day and a weekend, I won't do anything until Monday, and it can take at least 24 to 48 hours to set everything up. You probably have until Tuesday or maybe Wednesday. Will that help?"

"Yes. I'll make it work. Thank you, Dr. Thompson."

"You're welcome. I still want to see Gertrude in my office—monitor how she's doing."

"Of course. You've been fantastic—even if she does try to play matchmaker with us."

They laughed again and wished each other a pleasant evening.

Trudy looked back at the forbidding monster of a safe. She swore it laughed at her. Shaking her head, she closed the door and tacked the quilt back to the wall.

I must get that combination from Gertrude before she can't remember it any more. But how?

Ready for Home

Gertrude fidgeted beside the front door, watching for Trudy.
She said today. I know she said today.

The aide approached. "Ms. Ryan? Are you OK?

"I'm just waiting for my ride. She will be here soon."

Laughing, the aide shook her head. "Ms. Ryan, it's only 6:00 a.m. I don't think she's coming this early. You haven't had breakfast, and the administrator won't be here until at least 8:00 to sign you out." She gently took her arm. "I can help you back to your room, or you can wait in the dining hall. They at least have coffee brewed—even if you still have at least 30 minutes before they serve breakfast."

Gertrude jerked her arm away. "I do not need help back to my room." She huffed at the aide and ambled toward the window. "She said today."

"Yes ma'am. I believe you are going home today. But not yet. Why don't we get some coffee? I can sure use a cup. I still have an hour before I go home, and I could use a little pick-me-up." She smiled. "What do you say? Coffee?"

"Oh, alright. But just one cup, and then I am coming back here to wait for T…" She hesitated. "Trudy."

"Yes ma'am." The aide walked beside her, but Gertrude inched just out of her reach. No touching before the sun rose.

The two women shuffled across the lobby into the dining room.

Dining hall. What are we? At summer camp. Ha.

Sitting down, Gertrude opted for the aide to bring her coffee.

Might as well let them wait on me for one more morning. After all, I am paying for the service. Once I get home, who will I order around? Trudy? Too much like me—independent.

A smile played at her lips as she pictured her namesake. They shared more than looks and a name. Maybe that explained why she liked Trudy better than any other relatives. Plus, she had Ben's heart. Ben. Oh, how she missed that man.

A tear slid down her cheek as the aide returned with two steaming cups of coffee. She flicked it away.

"Here you go, Ms. Ryan." The aide set down the cup and took a chair next to Gertrude. "What are you thinking?"

Pursing her lips, Gertrude shook her head.

None of your business.

The aide touched her hand.

Again with the touching. Good grief. I just wanna go home!

"It's OK. You'll be fine at home."

"I miss my son."

"Oh. Does he live far away?"

"Well, I guess if you call Heaven far away, yes."

Red covered the aide's youthful face. "I'm so sorry. I didn't know." She scratched her nose. "I should've figured as much. I mean, I never saw any men—other than Dr. Thompson—come to visit. Is Trudy your only relative?"

A chuckle rose and escaped before Gertrude could stop it. "Ha, the only one I want to visit. I have another great-niece and their mother. No use for either of those all-about-me women."

"Oooh. I have some of those relatives myself. Always about them."

"Trudy, though—not like that. Like her daddy—my Ben—she always puts others first. Sometimes to her de…" She sighed. "What's that word?"

"Detriment?"

"Yes. Why can't I remember the simplest things?"

The aide shifted in her chair and sipped the coffee. "We all do that at times."

"Yes, but I am no fool. They say I have dema."

"I know."

"Well, you see me almost every day. What do you think?"

She sat back, fidgeting with her fingers. "Ms. Ryan, I'd be lying if I said I don't see potential signs. But I'm not a doctor. Heck, I'm not even a nurse—yet. Just an aide."

Gertrude sipped coffee and leaned back. "In my heart, I know that nice young doctor probably got it right. I forget far too many things, and sometimes, I feel so confused."

"I'm sorry, Ms. Ryan. Deep inside, you're a sweet lady—although you try to hide that part of you."

They both laughed. Tension eased from Gertrude's shoulders. *Laughter—marvelous medicine.*

"I can be harsh, but I do not know why." Tears fought her eyelids, but she refused to let them flow. "So many days, I try to focus, but everything around me swirls in chaos. No voices. Nothing like that. Yet, while I fight to think, everything blurs, like everyone and everything around me keeps screaming and I can't hear my thoughts." She bit her bottom lip. "Does that sound crazy?"

"Not at all. I can't imagine what dementia feels like, but I had a few others tell me something similar." Tears filled the young woman's eyes. "I hate that for you, Ms. Ryan. I want you to be OK when you go home."

Gertrude patted her hand. "Oh, I will be fine, my dear. I may not have full faculties all the time, but I am not worried. Once I get home, where I know my surroundings and have my normal routine, I will be just fine."

I dare not let her see the fear gripping me even in this moment.

The charge nurse came through for a cup of coffee and addressed the aide. "Oh, there you are."

"I was just getting Ms. Ryan some coffee and chatting for a moment. She's going home today."

The nurse put on a plastic smile. "Yes, I know."

Gertrude tilted her head and stared down the nurse. "Don't be mad at her. She needed to straighten out my wayward mind, and she did a fine job of it."

The smile relaxed as the nurse shook her head. "Misty is a good aide. But I need her to help me now. We have to get **everyone** ready for breakfast."

"Of course. I left Ethel snoring like a warthog. You probably have to wake her, and she will not have a clue who you are or where she is."

All three women chuckled.

Misty stood. "Do you want more coffee, Ms. Ryan?"

"No. I am fine. Go work before I get you in more trouble."

Misty smiled and left Gertrude to her thoughts.

Even before the accident, Gertrude felt her brain slipping away.

Did not like it.

Sure did not want to admit it.

But she knew the truth, and it was not setting her free.

Leaving Rehab

The sun peaked through the window, rousing Trudy from a restless night with little sleep. She blinked against the morning light, pretending her mood matched the sunrise—a promise of a bright day filled with hope and happiness.

It didn't work.

Ugh. Today's the day. Gertrude comes home. Then what?

No clue. In her vast experiences with various jobs, caregiver never came close. At least Dr. Thompson arranged for home health and PT for a while. But that might not happen until tomorrow or the next day.

Her mother's words trickled through her mind, that insistent warning she couldn't handle Gertrude.

Maybe Mom...

Trudy stopped herself. "Oh, no you don't," she declared to the empty room. "I made peace with never being enough for you, Mom. I can do this—for Daddy and for Aunt Gertrude." She pushed back the covers, got up, and immediately made the bed. "I refuse to leave my house in a mess today." After deciding to stay with Gertrude, at least until she could get around better, Trudy might not see her cottage for a while.

With fresh resolve, she opted to grab breakfast and coffee on the go rather than make a mess to clean. After a quick shower and dressing, she packed essentials, grabbed her laptop, and headed out the door to the office. Although Peter told her to take the day off, Trudy had a few things she wanted to wrap up and files to retrieve before making the move to working from home most of the time. Besides, during her visit the previous afternoon, the rehab administrator admitted they needed until noon to complete all the paperwork and make sure Trudy had help once she took her great-aunt home. She had time and didn't want to start her morning potentially dodging word bullets from Gertrude.

The real trick—figuring out how to work and watch her aunt at the same time.

C'mon. How hard could it be? Not like having a toddler who streaks across the room naked.

She and all her coworkers cringed for a young mom on maternity leave who had that happen during a video conference call. At least Trudy didn't have to worry about something like that.

Still, she knew they might have a few challenges. But she'd make Gertrude understand the need for quiet and privacy during calls.

No worries.

Right?

At 11:47, Trudy entered the rehab doors, praying silently for a peaceful aunt.

Nurse Taylor greeted her. "Hey, Trudy."

"Hi, Nurse Taylor. How's Gertrude today?"

"She's… Gertrude."

Trudy winced. "Not a good day?"

The nurse waved her off. "Not a bad day. Well… Down here in her pajamas and ready to go before I came on at seven. Then she decided to change into clothes. She still isn't dressed, fussing over what I took out of the closet for her to wear. She can be sooooo picky."

Laughing, Trudy shook her head. "That's a good sign. She always fussed over her clothes, wanting them perfect. That sounds more like the old Gertrude." She sighed. "You know, several times I noticed her hair disarrayed. Caught her in pajamas late in the afternoon. That should've told me something wasn't right with her."

"Well, if that's the old Gertrude, you may want some bad days. Most of the time she didn't argue and let me help her dress in whatever."

"I suspect she wants lunch out, so she needs to look nice." Trudy smiled. "She adores eating out as a special treat."

"Why not? She deserves a celebration." Nurse Taylor grinned. "She's been a star physically."

"Mentally?"

"Oh, we saw moments. More confusion than anything, though. Just remember, don't argue or try to correct something she gets wrong. Life will be much easier that way."

"I'll try to remember. Thank you."

Trudy strolled down the hallway, hoping Gertrude picked her clothes so they wouldn't have *that* to deal with on a day that looked more promising than she expected. Yep. Gertrude fussing over clothes—good day.

She reached the door and knocked gently.

"Come in."

Pleasant voice. Good sign.

She pushed open the door, stopped, and threw a hand over her mouth.

"Trudy, I'm so glad you're here. Those aides can't get a thing right."

Gertrude stood before the closet wearing a slip, hiked up in the back and caught in her underwear. Trudy closed the door and crossed the room, not sure whether to laugh, cry, or simply fix the messed-up undergarments.

"What are you looking for, Auntie?"

"I can't find my navy-blue slacks and jacket anywhere."

"I don't think I brought those. Remember? We stuck with comfortable clothes to make rehab easier."

"But I'm going out today. I can't wear some old jogging suit. What if one of my friends sees me?"

Trudy looked down and shook her head. "Well, I expected you'd enjoy lunch out, but I doubt we'll see any of your friends." She looked back at her aunt.

"Lunch out?" Gertrude brightened. "I love lunch out."

"I know you do. And with you going home, we have every reason to celebrate. But we gotta get you dressed first. You certainly can't go out in that slip."

Gertrude looked down. "Oh, my goodness no. Is this even my slip? I seldom wear a slip. Especially with pants. What was I thinking?"

Trudy chuckled. "I wondered that same thing." She shuffled through the closet. "How about these new leggings I bought you with a long-tailed shirt? You'll be comfortable and cuter than a bug's ear."

"Ha. I always told you that."

"Yes, ma'am." She laughed. "I always wondered if you meant it as a compliment or an insult."

"Definitely a compliment. I thought you looked adorable as a little girl. I still think you are a lovely woman, Trudy." She sighed. "I suppose cute will have to do for today."

"Do you want some help getting that slip off?"

"No. I have it." She took the clothes from Trudy, flung them over the walker, and trudged to the bathroom. "I shall take this old body in here to keep from scarring you for life." She wiggled eyebrows on her way past.

"OK. I'll just pack up the rest of your things so we can blow this joint."

"Sounds like a plan to me."

The suitcase packed within minutes, Trudy sat on the bed waiting for Gertrude to finish dressing. The nurse and admin knocked and entered without waiting for an answer.

"Where's Gertrude?" the admin asked.

"She's dressing."

"Good. We brought the paperwork. I'm sure she's ready to go home."

"Yes, very ready."

The admin smiled. "The nurse tells me the two of you had many conversations and that you are in touch with Dr. Thompson's office."

"Yes, sir. I tried to learn as much as possible while my great-aunt was here."

"That'll help."

The nurse almost whispered. "We also included information about Alzheimer's organizations in the area. We saw too many signs to ignore them."

Trudy shook her head. "I know. At least today seems like a good one."

The admin handed a form to Trudy. "We need you to sign a few places."

Sign here tabs denoted where they needed her signature. She glanced over the paragraphs and signed.

Putting everything in a folder, they handed it to Trudy, who quickly slipped it into her bag as Gertrude exited the bathroom.

"Oh hello, Nurse..." She crinkled her nose. "I am going home."

"Yes, you are," the nurse replied. "And your great-niece will take such good care of you. But listen to her, because we don't want to see you have to come back."

"I will not be back. I can assure you."

Gertrude rounded the bed and looked in the suitcase. "Trudy, please get my brush and things from the bathroom. Looks like you already got the clothes."

"Yes, ma'am."

With everything in her bag, Trudy offered a hand to Gertrude.

"I am fine, thank you. I have this fun little friend to help me walk." She patted the walker. "But do not worry. It is a short-term friendship." She smiled and turned toward the door.

Yanking a long piece of tissue paper from the back of Gertrude's pants Trudy shook her head at the nurse and followed her aunt through the door.

Home Again

Following an uneventful lunch, Trudy drove Gertrude home. She dreaded the front steps and getting her great aunt up them without a quick solution. Before leaving rehab, the physical therapist assured them Gertrude could take the few steps onto the porch. He warned Trudy to keep a close eye on her, though.

The words replayed in her mind as they turned onto the last street.

She gets a little too ambitious and doesn't want help. What an understatement. *Just make sure she doesn't take the steps alone. I can imagine her rushing up them, losing her balance, and falling backward.*

Well, that couldn't happen. Another fall might devastate her.

As they pulled into the driveway, Gertrude cursed under her breath.

"Auntie. Did you just say sh…"

"Language young lady."

They both laughed.

"I'm sorry." Gertrude sighed. "Did you tell Kit to expect me today?"

"No ma'am. She'll bake that chocolate cake and stay all night to help eat it—if we let her."

"Exactly. But she's sitting on her porch, like a cat waiting for a rat."

Trudy looked at the neighbor's house. Indeed, Kit sat in the porch swing, a book held in front of her face.

"She's reading, Gertrude."

"So?"

"Maybe we can sneak in without her seeing us." Trudy shrugged. "One can hope."

Gertrude shook her head. "Not with Kit. She knows every

coming and going in the neighborhood. She…"

Trudy tuned out the rest of what her aunt said, trying to figure out a scenario where they could get past the nosy neighbor. She wished her aunt had an attached garage. Without one, she considered pulling the car farther up, getting as close to the back as possible. But she rejected the idea, remembering the front had only three steps. The back? Six.

Trudy shut off the engine and opened her door.

Every hope for a peaceful homecoming crashed to the ground with Kit's holler.

"Trudy! It's so good to see you."

From her peripheral vision, Trudy couldn't ignore the overly bright flowers on Kit's dress speeding toward them. "Crap." She forced a smile as Kit reached the driveway. "Hi, Kit."

"I kept an eye on the place. Saw your car the other night, but that storm. Oh, my goodness, I figured if I stepped outside, the wind would blow me down the street." She craned her neck to see around Trudy. "Oh my. Is that Gertrude in the car? She's home?"

Trudy nodded. "Yes, they released her today." Her mind raced, searching for a way to send Kit home without offending her. She had it. "We stopped for lunch, and I'm afraid I let her overdo it. You can say hello, but I really want to get her inside to rest."

"Oh, I understand. Completely." She stepped around Trudy and ducked to see Gertrude. "Hi neighbor. I'm so glad to see you looking wonderful."

"Thanks." With Gertrude, you never got pretenses. Civil, but no warm fuzzies. At least that didn't change—yet.

"I know you're tired, hon, so I won't bother you now. How about I make a meal, complete with chocolate cake? I'll bring it over around 6:00 tonight. Does that sound good?"

Gertrude's eyes rolled. "Whatever."

Kit smiled, stood and turned to Trudy. "She's not too friendly today, is she?"

"She's tired, and I think maybe hurting a little. Even though she's home, Gertrude still needs rest and therapy to be 100% again. It may take months to fully recover."

"I can imagine. When Mama broke her hip…"

The droning continued for several minutes before Trudy broke in. "I don't mean to be rude, but it's rather warm out here. I must get my aunt inside now."

"Of course. I'll see you later."

Great.

Trudy watched as Kit crossed the yard, went inside, and yelled through the house loud enough for every neighbor to hear. "Mama! Guess who's home?"

Trudy gathered her things while Gertrude opened her door. "Auntie, wait for me. I'll come around and get your walker."

Storm clouds brewed in the older woman's eyes. "I don't need that contraptable."

"Yes, you do. The therapist said be sure you use it, especially outside."

"I don't care. I'm not an invalid."

"I know, but it keeps you steady. You don't want to fall again."

"I'm not gonna fall." Gertrude moved, trying to hoist herself up from the car. "Your car sits way to low, dad blab it."

Trudy shut her door and rushed to the passenger side. Fortunately, Gertrude couldn't get out alone. She grabbed the walker and opened it before gently taking her aunt's arm.

"Don't tug on me." Gertrude tried to stand, failed, and tried again. "Dang it. Just let me pull myself up using your arm. And next time, we take my car."

"Yes, ma'am." Trudy stood still as Gertrude held tight.

Reluctantly, she snatched the walker and rushed down the

sidewalk.

Trudy slammed the door and clicked to lock it. She'd retrieve the bags and her laptop later. Running to catch her aunt, she passed her and reached the steps first. "We gotta be careful here."

Gertrude sneered at her. "For what? You think I can't climb three little steps?"

"I'm sure you can, Auntie. But how do I explain it to Dr. Thompson if I let you fall again?"

Rolling her eyes, Gertrude huffed. "You and that stupid doctor. I am fine."

She maneuvered the walker onto the first step, pulled herself up, tottering. She paused. Moved the walker up, took the second step, tottering again. Trudy reached out but didn't touch the older woman. Gertrude steadied herself, moved the walker up to the porch and stepped up again, pushing the walker forward. Her hands shook as she moved toward the door.

As Trudy walked around her aunt, Gertrude pushed against the screen door, wrinkles creasing her forehead and nose.

"Allow me, Auntie." Trudy pulled the screen open, inserted the key, and unlocked the door.

Gertrude grabbed the knob, turned it and went inside. She looked around as if she never saw the place before. "Why are all the drapes open?"

"I did that. It felt so dark and gloomy in here."

"The drapes keep out the hot sun."

"I thought you liked the heat, Gertrude. You always complain about being cold."

"Maybe. But you will want to make it cooler in here, and then I get to pay the elelity bill." She moved to the wall, yanking the cord until the drapes closed completely. "Besides, I like it dark. It fits my mood."

"Very well. I'll close the rest of them. Let's get you settled. Do you want to sit in the den or perhaps have a rest in your bedroom?"

"A rest? You mean a nap? You think I need a nap, like a toddler? I'm not tired. I don't care what you told K... That woman from down the street."

"Auntie, I think you are tired. And yes, maybe you need a nap. It's been a rough morning with more movement than usual."

"How do you know what exercise I get? You are not my nurse."

"I'm your great niece, and I want to help you if you let me."

The volume increased as Gertrude grew more agitated. "I suppose you'll put me to bed and kill me in my sleep. Then you can have all my money. Well, I won't go to sleep. You hear me? And if you come in my room, I have a gun under my pillow."

The senselessness of Gertrude's words made Trudy cringe. She didn't remember seeing a gun, but then she didn't look under any of the pillows.

Warnings bounced around her brain.

Don't argue with the dementia patient.

How could she not argue with these unreal accusations?

Taking a deep breath, she stepped back. "Auntie, I promise I do not want to kill you."

Gertrude licked her lips. "I don't believe you." She turned, wincing, and shuffled toward the bedroom.

Compassion flooded over Trudy. "Auntie, is your hip hurting."

"Of course not."

"Do you want some tea?"

"No."

"It's time for your medicine."

Gertrude whirled, agony covering her face. "Is that how you plan to kill me? Fill me with too many painkillers?"

Trudy shook her head, counting to ten. "No ma'am. I just want you to be comfortable. Just one pill."

"Whatever."

By the time Trudy got a pill from the prescription bottle, a glass of water, and straw, then went to Gertrude's room, her aunt had removed most of her clothes and stretched out on the bed. She entered quietly, cautiously.

Gertrude turned her head toward the door. "Hi Trudy, dear. What do you need?"

"I… I… I brought your medicine and some water."

"Oh, thank you. My hip is aching something awful."

She allowed Trudy to help her sit up slightly and swallowed the pill.

"I think I'll take a little nap. Just a short one."

Trudy sighed. "Good idea. Sleep as long as you want. I'll wake you before dinner."

Discreetly feeling beneath the pillows, she retreated from the room and softly closed the door behind her. Leaning back against the wall, she fought back tears.

Could she really do this? And for how long?

A Quiet Evening

As Trudy finished work, shut down her laptop, and considered what to make for dinner, despite Kit's offer, Gertrude's door popped open. Trudy's breath caught as she whispered a prayer for grace.

Entering the dining room, Gertrude smiled. "Oh, hello, Trudy. Are you still here? I thought you surely went home by now."

Trudy relaxed. "No, Auntie. I don't think you should be alone—at least not until you're more stable on your feet."

"I am fine, dear. This walker helps me get around without any problems."

"Still, I promised if they released you, I would make sure not to leave you alone for more than an hour. I came prepared to stay for as long as you need me."

Gertrude shook her head. "You should be out enjoying life, not sitting with a grumpy old woman. Besides, I feel much better."

The grimace on her face said otherwise.

"Maybe. But a few days with you won't hurt me. They arranged for an in-home physical therapist, and a home health nurse will come by each day, too. I can sneak out to work while they are here and come back later with my laptop. That way, I can go to the office for meetings and do the rest of my work here." She grinned. "I kinda like working from home most of the time, anyway."

"Well, I suppose it will be all right for a while. But I really am fine." Gertrude hobbled toward the kitchen.

Trudy jumped up from her chair. "I was just wondering what to make for dinner. What sounds good?"

"I seldom eat much for dinner. A bowl of oatmeal or something like that. Sometimes I just have popcorn."

"Auntie. That's not a balanced diet."

Gertrude shrugged. "An apple with peanut butter. Definite favorite." She wiggled her eyebrows as a smile crept slowly across her lips. "Right now, I want to go sit outside for a spell. Breathe fresh air and visit my flowers."

"That sounds nice."

"Maybe you can bring some iced tea and join me."

"Ooh. Good idea. I made a fresh pitcher while you napped. Right behind you."

Trudy watched, her heart thumping, while Gertrude headed out the back door. "Just sit down, and don't try going down those steps."

Gertrude turned her head, rolled her eyes, turned back toward the door, and let out a tremendous sigh.

Quickly grabbing two glasses from the cabinet, Trudy filled them with ice, poured the tea, and followed her great aunt.

Opening the door, she half expected to see the old woman trying to maneuver the steps. To her surprise, Gertrude sat at the bistro table, moving nothing but her eyes. A cool breeze brushed wisps of hair around the older woman's face. She brushed them back and smiled up at Trudy. "This is so much nicer than that pitiful garden at the center."

"You have a gorgeous yard, Auntie. I don't know how you keep it so amazing." Trudy sat down the glasses and took the second chair.

"Ha. Lots of hard work. How do you think I stay in such good shape?"

"So, that's your secret. Now I know."

"No secret. The sprinklers take care of watering, but the weeds do not pull themselves."

"It'd be nice if they did, wouldn't it?"

"Then what would I do for exercise?" A smile glowed across Gertrude's face, matching the sun's reflection. She gazed out across the yard and then turned to her roses. "Oh, no."

"What is it?" Trudy's eyes flashed wide.

"That pesky weed. It must be a foot tall."

Trudy saw it between the roses. "I'm sorry, Aunt Gertrude. I cleaned inside, but I didn't think to check the yard."

"I think that caused me to fall."

"The weed?"

"Yes. I wanted to get my hoe and dig it up." Gertrude leaned back her head, scrunching her forehead. "I headed down the steps... I remember that. And then..." She closed her eyes, shaking her head. "I just cannot figure out why I fell. These steps never gave me any problems before."

"The paramedics told the doctors you kept saying something about a rat. Did you see one that day?"

"No! I do not allow rats in my yard. Ever. The ext... pest guy comes every month to make sure of it." Gertrude rubbed her arms. "No rats."

"Hmmm. I don't know then. Sometimes, our feet just don't move the way we expect."

"Well, I must take care of that weed. Right now."

"No you don't." Trudy moved to the steps. "I got this. Is the shed locked?"

"Always." Gertrude's eyes darted around the yard and at Trudy. "I have a secret." She looked around again, especially toward Kit's house. Standing, she moved a couple steps to a decorative house plaque and stood in front of it. After a moment, she turned around and held out a key. "Here you go. Now you can get the hoe."

"A hidden key holder? That's genius." Trudy took the key. "It looks like an ordinary plaque hanging there."

"Yes, and if you tell a soul, I'll haunt you when I die. No

one—and I mean no one—knows this secret."

Trudy reached up, locking her lips with an imaginary key. "Your secret is safe with me."

What other keys lived in that little house?

After retrieving the hoe and work gloves, Trudy returned the key and went to work while watching how Gertrude opened the plaque. She dug up the offender from among the roses. Gertrude directed her to multiple other weeds, and she worked until the sun dropped behind the trees.

"Much better." Gertrude relaxed in her chair. "We should get some supper now. It is almost bedtime."

"Yes ma'am. Let me just put these tools back in the shed."

As Trudy returned and picked up the weeds to put in the trash, a bushy-tailed squirrel scampered across the fence and jumped onto the porch railing. "How cute."

"Not cute. Thieving, destructive rat."

"C'mon, Auntie. He's a friendly squirrel, not a rat."

"Same difference." Storminess covered Gertrude's face and her eyes flew wide. She grabbed her walker. "Get inside, quick. And tomorrow, make sure the extrimnator comes."

Gertrude slammed the door behind her.

Reality Hits

Gertrude sat beside the table, grateful for the solitude of her backyard. Despite a few weeds here and there, the brightness cheered her—except for those occasional mornings when it looked… off. She never quite put her finger on why it seemed strange at times. She still loved her yard, the flowers. The squirrel kept his distance most days, and for that she thanked God.

The PT guy and nursing aides? THEY still showed up daily. For that, she did not feel grateful. Although she should. After all, she got to come home from that nasty place where they monitored everything. At least Trudy allowed some moments of privacy. Not so much with the home health people. And they changed too often. How could she remember a name when the same one seldom returned?

She disliked all of them, always trying to make her change clothes in front of them. Even the man who came, claiming to be a nurse. He just wanted to see her naked. Maybe catch her in the buff so she couldn't chase him when he stole money or jewelry. She did not trust a single "aide" or "nurse."

At least the PT guy—oh, what was his name—kept coming back. He tortured her, though, and no one seemed to care a bit. Her hip always hurt more when he finished the exorcism.

She settled back into the deep cushions, thankful she didn't have to see anyone today. She reached for her Bible and opened it to a bookmarked page. The words blurred, making no sense. Blinking, Gertrude took a sip of coffee.

Umm. Delightful.

She might forget some things, but never coffee.

She picked up her Bible again and focused. "You are fearfully and wonderfully made."

Am I? My mind no longer works right. I knew it for a long time, but every day, it slips more. Even if I wanted to deny it, now I have no choice. With Trudy here all the time, I see the concern on her face, and if honest, sometimes she feels like a stranger.

Impatient with her emotional weakness, she flicked a wayward tear from her cheek.

I will not give in to this disease—battle it, fight against the memory loss. I can do this.

Who am I kidding? Nothing will change the future.

A cheery twittering grasped her attention. She let her gaze follow the sound until it lit on a bright red spot in a nearby tree. The bird looked back, daring her to say something.

"Well, you are a beautiful one! Thank you for that lovely song. I need encor… help today."

The bird chirped one more time before flying to another tree beside the fence.

"Ah. I bet you have a nest out there. Well hidden. Watch out for that pesky rodent." She shook her head. "Trudy thinks he looks so cute. Ha. He is nothing but a glorified rat."

The squirrel dared not made an appearance while she rested in the comfy chair. She liked it much better than the hard ones at the center, thankful to sit on her back porch and enjoy the day. Her mind flitted around the yard, like the bird who slipped up, grabbed a seed and took off again, uninhibited by her presence.

She searched her brain, trying to recapture the proper name for the bird.

Red… No. Not red. Canary? How silly. Not right. Car… Ha. Cardinal. I remember.

The act of searching for the word made her head ache. How long before she failed to remember the simplest things?

Something so simple, and I lose that. I have secrets. Lots of them. Like the safe upstairs. It contains… I should tell Trudy, before I forget.

A chill ran over Gertrude despite the morning warmth.

No. I won't burden her with all the junk of my life. I can't. I won't. Some things need to stay secret, hidden in the past where they belong. Why bring up all that old nonsense? I refuse to think about the past, let alone speak of it.

But if I die, she will never know the truth.

Better that way. I do not want her looks of pity because of ANYTHING in the past.

Still…

Gertrude looked up at clouds. For a while, she searched for shapes, pushing other thoughts from her mind. Most days, she had no problem brushing off the niggling thoughts that tried to consume her. As the temperature rose, she decided to go inside. Maybe take a nap.

Grasping her walker, she placed the Bible and coffee cup in the attached basket and headed to the door. Inside, she proceeded to the study with a plan in mind.

"Hey, Aunt Gertrude. Are you OK?" Trudy looked up from her typewriter.

"Yes, dear. I'm fine. Warm from being outside."

"Do you want some water? Tea maybe?"

"No. I might like a cup of coffee. Perhaps one of those delectious muffins. Would you be a dear and bring it to my study? I want to sit in there a spell."

"Of course." Trudy rose and stretched. "I need a break, anyway. Mind if I join you?"

"I want to be alone."

"No worries. I still have work to do. I'll just bring your coffee and muffin." She stopped and retrieved the cup and saucer from Gertrude's basket.

"How did that get there?" Gertrude frowned. "Oh, of course. I had it out on the porch with me. I thought I put it on the counter."

"I'm sure you meant to. I distracted you." Trudy turned to the kitchen. "I need to make fresh coffee and heat the muffin for you. Do you need help getting to the study?"

Always treating me like a child. She and those blasted people who come by all the time.

"I'm not a child. I can make it to the study by myself."

"I know." Trudy sighed. "I get overprotective. One of my weaknesses."

"Well, stop it, then."

Gertrude trudged out of the room, weariness wrapping its arms around her body. Tears played at her eyelids, but she shoved them down, refusing to let them spill.

In the study, she sat in the over-sized office chair. Pulling out her best stationery and a pen, she began a letter.

Dear Trudy,

If you read this, it means I am gone from this world, learning my way around Heaven with Ben and Jesus as my guides. I have things to tell you. Things I could never speak in life, but you must know.

When Trudy walked into the room, Gertrude covered the letter with a clean sheet of paper and stared into space.

She did not want her great niece to see the letter—yet.

Pretend. Use the disease to hide what I do not want her to know.

"What are you doing, Auntie?"

"Oh, just thinking. Did I pay my electric bill before the fall? All that time away from here, I must owe hundreds of dollars."

"I took care of all that, Auntie. Remember? You called the bank so I could pay your bills."

"Oh. Good. I sure do not want the electricity turned off during the summer heat."

"Absolutely not. I got it. You don't need to worry about any of that."

"I know. I can count on you to keep things going." She looked down at the paper. "You can go now. I have everything I need."

Trudy hesitated. "Are you sure? I can hang out in here for a while."

"No. Go back to your work. I am fine."

"Very well. But I'm just in the next room, so holler if you need me." She moved toward the door. "I'll check on you in a while."

Gertrude shook her head and sighed. "I am fine." She forced a smile.

Trudy brushed her shoulder gently as she turned to leave.

Picking up the pen, Gertrude closed her eyes and considered what to include and how to get the finished letter to her attorney.

Introducing Bessie

Waking early, Gertrude dressed herself, selecting a pullover dress without buttons.

No one seeing this naked body today.

She padded through the house and slipped through the back door. Scrunching into the chair cushions, she peered at the sky. Dark clouds rolled, matching her mood after a sleepless night of strange dreams and a hip that kept aching.

She opened her Bible to a familiar passage, hoping it made sense.

Suddenly, a touch to her arm spiked her heart rate.

"What the…?" Gertrude looked up into a smiling brown face. "Who are you? And what are you doing on my back porch? You scared me."

"Hello, Ms. Ryan. My name is Bessie. They sent me over to check on you today. I'm your new nurse and certain we will become best friends."

"I doubt that." Gertrude blew out a puff of air. "It's Saturday. Why are you here today? None of you work on weekends."

"I'm afraid it's Monday, not Saturday. Your great niece, Trudy, needed to go into the office for a few hours, so I'm here to keep you out of trouble until she returns. Besides, I often stop by on a Saturday or Sunday to check on my favorites, so get used to seeing me—even on weekends." She laid a hand on the Bible. "Oh, that's one of my favorite passages. 'You are fearfully and wonderfully made.' I still find myself amazed by the way our bodies work."

"Bodies, yes. Not so sure about my brain. It don't feel so wonderful these days."

"I know, Ms. Ryan. But I'm here to help with that as much as

I can. Now, I'm gonna take your vitals and jot that information down. They make me do that."

"And I can tell you hate it."

"Actually, it's the least favorite part of my job. Necessary, though, so let's get it out of the way, and then you and I can have a pleasant visit."

"Visit?" Gertrude rolled her eyes and shook her head. "I suppose you can call it that. I call it an intrusion on my morning."

Bessie laughed. "All about perspective." She busied herself with various tools.

If Gertrude ever knew the names of all the gadgets, the terms bounced off her mind as the woman prepared to do whatever she planned to do. Not that any of it mattered. She looked across the yard, hearing the woman's voice yet not registering anything she said.

Looking up, Gertrude squinted at the woman. "Who are you?"

"Bessie. Your new nurse."

"Oh, yes. My mind tilted for a moment.

"Understandable."

As the nurse asked pointless questions, Gertrude tried to remain focused. Instead, her mind wandered.

I know my mind quit working right, but I never seem to get it back on track. I hear this woman talking, but I don't have a clue who she is. Should I know her?

Time passed, the woman leaving only for a minute, returning with coffee.

She left again and returned with eggs, bacon, and toast.

More questions. Senseless muttering. Questions that meant nothing.

Just go away. Leave me alone. I want to sleep.

Blinking, Gertrude looked around the yard, filled with pretty flowers. Home.

A woman sat beside her, writing things in a notebook.

Gertrude rubbed her temples. "Do I know you?"

"I'm Bessie, your nurse. I think you dozed off for a quick nap."

"I never doze off." Straightening her back, she sniffed. "I take naps on purpose, when necessary."

"Naps—always necessary."

A younger woman walked onto the porch carrying two glasses filled with something. Familiar.

"I brought out some iced tea. Thought you could both use some."

"Thank you, Trudy." The nurse accepted the glasses from her and set them on the table. "We're almost finished out here, now that our sleeping beauty woke up."

"She seems lost today."

Are they talking about me? As if I don't exist. I'm right here.

"I'm not lost, and I can hear you talking about me." Gertrude stood, placing a hand on her hip.

The older woman patted her shoulder.

"Don't touch me." She swatted the woman's hand. "I don't know you."

The hand moved, and the woman breathed deeply. "OK, Ms. Ryan. I'm not here to hurt you. Sit down and have some tea."

"I don't want tea."

The young woman stepped forward. "It's your favorite—raspberry hibiscus, with fresh mint from your garden."

Gertrude crossed her arms and clenched her fists. "Do I know you?"

"I'm Trudy, Aunt Gertrude. Of course, you know me."

"No. You are **not** my Trudy. She has lovely, long blond locks."

"I cut it years ago and quit putting hair color on it. But I assure you, I am Trudy."

"Don't lie to me. Who are you really?"

"I'm your great-niece."

"No."

"I…"

The older of the two touched the younger one's arm. "Let it go."

Those crazy old biddies. I gotta get help. Call Ben. He'll come save me.

She considered running to the shed, but she dared not leave them alone. They might go into the house and steal everything. Standing, Gertrude pushed past them, holding to the chair and door frame to steady herself. Inside, she turned, closed the door, and turned the lock. Her legs shook as throbs moved down one.

God help me!

Feeling her way through the house, she looked at the stairs. Shook her head. Searching, her heart pounded against her ribcage. She moved across the room, bracing herself against a wall. Past an open door, she saw a bed, a familiar book on the table beside it. Safe inside, she closed the door. No lock. Her gaze shifted, looking for a hiding place. A door near the corner. Closet. She tottered to it. Inside, she buried herself behind a row of clothing and held her breath.

For moments, she stood there, frozen.

A male voice came softly. "You're safe."

Closing her eyes, she breathed in and out several times, listening.

Nothing.

She quietly opened the door, moving to the bed. Falling across it, exhausted, she wept and fell asleep.

Wisdom

"Crap." Trudy shook her head. "She does this all the time—locks me out of the house."

"Please tell me you have an extra key to get in."

Trudy smiled. "Of course. Right where she won't look—in her hidden key holder."

Bessie chuckled while Trudy retrieved the house key. "I had to crawl through an unlocked window the first time. Not my finest hour. Fortunately, no one saw me and called the cops. The next day, I made several copies and hid them in various places around the house."

"Smart woman. She won't go out the front, will she?"

"No. At least, she hasn't so far. I lock the deadbolt, and when she goes haywire, it seems to throw her."

"Good. Let's talk out here then. Give her a chance to calm down."

Trudy paced while Bessie took a chair beside the table.

"It keeps getting worse. Sometimes, she wants to argue for hours. Back and forth. I get so frustrated."

"Don't argue with her then."

"What?"

"Are you a mom?"

"Yes. My son's a Marine, and my daughter's in college."

"Do you remember her at around four?"

"How could I forget? We fought every morning over what she could and couldn't wear."

"Every morning?"

"Well, most mornings. At least until I learned to give up and let her dress crazy. I got so tired of fighting, I quit caring if she looked weird. I let her go to school in a sun-dress one day with snow predicted. Of course, I made her wear a coat, and when she complained about being cold all day, I smiled. At least she didn't do *that* again." Trudy chuckled. "Eventually, her taste improved, and she listened if I reminded her to dress for weather."

"Then you understand."

"Understand what?"

"Sometimes, you let an argument go. Your great aunt lost reasoning abilities. Trying to reason with her won't work anymore than it does with a four-year-old child. Especially on bad days."

Rubbing her temples and plopping into the other chair, Trudy blinked. "I can see that. But how do I keep from arguing about the important things? Taking medicine or a bath? Brushing her teeth or hair? Simple, everyday things. Gertrude used to be the most fastidious person I knew for looking good. Now, she walks around in pajamas half the day. She comes out here in underwear. Shouts that she already took a bath or brushed her teeth when she didn't go anywhere near the bathroom. She accuses me of outrageous plots—stealing her money and jewelry, trying to lock her up. I can let go of some arguments, but not those things. How do I deal with that?"

"Grace, my dear. Grace."

Trudy scrunched her nose. "Grace?"

Bessie nodded.

"As in God's grace? That doesn't mesh for me."

"Maybe you don't fully understand grace then."

Trudy leaned forward, heat rushing across her face. "I grew up in church. I know about grace. And this situation has no grace in it."

"Are you sure?"

"Show me where there's an ounce of grace in any of this. For me or Gertrude."

Bessie sunk into the cushions and sipped her tea. "Define

grace, Trudy."

"What?"

"Define grace."

"Unmerited favor. Everyone knows that."

"Good, churchy definition. What does that even mean? Unmerited favor."

"It means God showing you favor you don't deserve. The ultimate favor, of course, being Jesus forgiving our sins, dying for us, all that."

A smile crossed the seasoned face, light shining from amber irises. "Good. I'm glad you know that part. But there's more."

"More?"

Bessie rubbed her hands together, like someone itching to give away a secret. "See, favor is only part of grace. And honey, in your situation, you need to understand the rest of grace."

Relaxing, Trudy leaned back. "I'm not convinced you have a clue what you're talking about, but I can listen."

"Like you, I questioned the whole grace thing when I faced a tremendous trial in my life. Someone dared throw second Corinthians 2:9 at me. I wanted to slap that friend when she said, 'You know what Paul said. God's grace is sufficient for you, just like it was for Paul.' I refrained from hitting her, but I sure huffed out of that room before I lost control and changed my mind."

Bessie stopped for a sip of tea.

Trudy tried to imagine this strong woman facing down someone and managing not to slap her. Bessie best not throw that verse her way. She didn't have the same restraint.

"You know, when I got home, I looked up that verse, and the use of grace stumped me. Like you, I believed grace meant unmerited favor, and that definition didn't fit Paul's situation any more than it fit mine. Or yours."

"So, what happened?"

"I studied the word grace. I mean deep studied. After weeks of digging into dozens of verses and looking at the Greek word *charis*, I came up with a better definition."

Trudy waited, leaning forward again, intrigued by the wisdom pouring from this woman of deep faith. "And?"

"That's when my definition changed, and I walked away with fresh understanding. Now I believe it means divine intervention that changes you." Bessie let that settle over Trudy.

"Divine…"

"Divine intervention that changes you. In my experience, God's "favor" means He works to make us more like Jesus. And that doesn't always look the way we expect."

Trudy swallowed hard. "So, you're saying God wants to use this situation to change me?"

"Well, I'm not God, but when I surrendered my emotions and frustrations to Him during that trial, and every tough time since, He usually showed me something I needed to change. My revised definition of grace makes a lot more sense than 'unmerited favor.'"

"Hmmm."

"Trudy, you have a rough road ahead. I won't lie to you about it. Gertrude will get worse over time. You may have moments filled with goodness. Fantastic days when she seems almost normal. But many days will be like this one or somewhere between the two."

"How do I do this, then? I won't put her in a home and ignore her. My mom and sister don't understand, but I promised my dad to look after Gertrude."

"Your dad's gone?"

"Yeah. A few years now. He loved Aunt Gertrude. She raised him after his parents died in a car crash. He was only five, so he viewed her more as a mom than his aunt. I can't dishonor his memory by turning away. No matter how hard it gets for me."

"That's a tough choice. I pray you can honor him until she passes. But I know you can't if you don't find a way to let God help you. If you have anything between you and Him, you may want to put that to rest sooner than later. I don't know anyone who deals with Alzheimer's well unless they have a true devotion to the person or God. Preferably both."

"I'll certainly keep that in mind." Trudy looked at the back door. "Please tell me you're coming back, Bessie? She's run off so many aides, and even the seasoned nurses cringe when she goes off on them. I could use your wisdom."

A laugh rose from Bessie's belly and worked its way past her throat, bouncing off the house and filling the yard. "I'm not scared of no little thing like your great aunt. She can be a tough one, I'm sure. But she's scared, and I get that. I come in with the Holy Spirit, filling me up to deal with anything she tosses against me. I don't wear Velcro, so nothin' gonna stick." She patted Trudy's hand. "I won't abandon you, hon. Just know, we may get to know each other well. So be sure you really want me around."

They both laughed, and the tension knotting Trudy's shoulders fell away.

Bessie stood. "Guess we better go check on Gertrude now."

"Yeah. Lord, give us your grace."

Bright Morning—Maybe

Gertrude hobbled into the kitchen, eyes bright.

Trudy looked up from her laptop. "Good morning, Auntie. How are you this morning?"

"Ready for coffee."

"Sit down. I'll get a cup for you."

"You are working. I will get it." Gertrude motioned with her hand. "I am not an invalid."

Stretching, Trudy rose. "I could use a break, anyway. Are you hungry?"

Her aunt took a seat, positioned to look out the window. "A little. You know, I woke up thinking about Granny's special biscuits. I loved the smell as they baked. Then she cut them open and slathered butter and fresh honey over them. And then that first bite. Like manna from Heaven." Her mouth spread into a wide smile. "Let's make some."

Sitting a mug on the table, Trudy hesitated. "Do you have the recipe?"

Tapping her temple, Gertrude nodded. "Right here."

"OK." Trudy paused. What did she have to lose? Lucid moments grew rarer. She dared not waste this one. "Let's do it. Do you mind if I write the recipe down? I always wanted to know how you made such terrific biscuits, but I'll forget."

"Suit yourself." With that, the old woman rose, rubbing her hip. "I need to move a bit myself—work out this stiffness."

Gertrude moved to the kitchen and retrieved a bowl from the cabinet. She poured herself a mug of coffee and tapped her lips. "We need flour, baking powder, salt, milk… And lard. Granny used that nasty Crisco."

"I don't think we have any lard, Auntie."

"Check the pantry. If not, we can substitute butter. It will work fine."

"OK. I'll get the ingredients."

Gertrude busied herself turning on the stove and taking two round cake pans from the cabinet while Trudy rushed around, pulling ingredients from the pantry and fridge. She shook the milk carton, hoping it had enough left.

"I'm not sure we have enough milk, Aunt Gertrude."

"Get a can from the pantry. I always keep several in there. Mama always kept canned milk in case we ran low. She watered it down sometimes, so Irene and I could have a glass with breakfast. Besides, it makes anything that needs creaminess taste better."

Putting the carton back in the refrigerator, Trudy grabbed a can of evaporated milk from the pantry, thanking God for the normal version of Gertrude.

The two women worked side-by-side, mixing ingredients.

"Get me that rolling pin," Gertrude directed. "And spread out the waxed paper. It makes a fine covering for easier cleanup. I figured that one out. Granny always made a gigantic mess on the counter. Mama too, and they rushed to wipe it up before the menfolk saw it. But flour still showed up in cracks and on the floor."

Trudy followed her aunt's instructions, jotting notes as they worked. "How do you remember the amounts?"

"Years of practice, child. Your daddy loved Granny's biscuits. Well, he loved my version of Granny's biscuits. He used to tell me I made them better than anyone."

"I remember him saying that. Mom attempted them one time I think, but she used a recipe she found in a cookbook. They didn't taste like yours. Now I know why. Pretty sure she used Crisco too."

"That messes them up for sure." Gertrude rolled and cut the dough. "Now the ultimate trick. Place them in these cake pans and make sure the sides touch. That way, they rise **up**, not out."

Less than a half hour later, the two women sat across from each other, savoring every bite and sipping coffee.

After consuming her third biscuit, Trudy pushed the plate back. "I'm stuffed. Exquisite, Auntie."

"Yes. Granny outdid herself this time." Gertrude dabbed her lips with a napkin. "I think I'll go take a nap now."

She laid the napkin on the table, stood and looked at Trudy, her eyes narrowing. "Leave the dishes. I'll clean them later. Have a good day, dear. It was very nice meeting you. Please lock the door on your way out and come again soon."

Gertrude rubbed her hip as she limped away.

Trudy stared at the empty chair.

What just happened? How could she remember the recipe, the sweet memories, and then, in minutes, forget me?

She dropped her face into her hands, sitting alone at the table. Which Gertrude would come back after the nap?

Trudy picked up the scribbled recipe. A droplet slid down her cheek and splashed on the paper. Better rewrite it while she remembered the steps. Aunt Gertrude might not remember the next time she hungered for the delectable taste of childhood.

A Sweet Reprieve

The TV droned in the background.

Incessant. Mindless.

All day. Every day.

Gertrude seldom watched TV in the past, and then only educational programs or a mind-challenging game show. Since coming home from rehab—she did nothing but watch it. Not even good movies or anything thought-provoking.

Senseless junk that did nothing to stimulate a decaying brain.

Trudy pressed her lips together, squashing the scream demanding to escape. She rolled her head, begging the neck muscles to release. Tension clenched her head while she peeked around the corner. Gertrude needed to interact, use her brain for something while she still could. The sitting, doing nothing didn't help.

Maybe a walk around the garden. She loved the garden.

Too late.

With dusk settling, the anticipated mosquitoes promised to drive them back indoors almost immediately.

She made a mental note to encourage her charge to go out early in the morning before the heat intensified for the day. Maybe they should make that part of her daily morning routine. She jotted a note for Bessie.

Worth a shot.

In the meantime, Trudy needed something encouraging her aunt to engage with life—move around, talk. Something. Anything.

She stepped to the doorway. "Aunt Gertrude, would you like to do something other than watch TV?"

A grunt came from the other room. Trudy drifted through the

doorway. "Aunt Gertrude?"

"I said NO." The snap caught Trudy by surprise—why, she didn't know. Irritation hung thick in the air most days like a thick smoke that fought to suffocate both of them.

She sucked air, not trusting her voice enough to speak.

Her thoughts drifted back to childhood, sitting in front of her great aunt.

A checkerboard on the table with sodas and popcorn between them promised an afternoon of fun. Back then, Trudy counted on the popcorn bowl never running dry. A second soda—probably not. An added glass of Kool-Aid? For sure. Gertrude never let her win, but sometimes Trudy beat her aunt.

Sometimes.

A scream on the TV brought her back to the nastiness of reality, whacking Trudy with the harshness of an assault. She refused to cry. Tears did no good.

Grace. Give me grace, Lord. I can't do this anymore today.

Suddenly, an idea popped.

Why not?

Trudy started to pose the question, but decided against it. Why bother? Everything she asked brought a searing "no."

Instead, she retreated into the kitchen.

Fifteen minutes later, Gertrude shuffled in. "Is that popcorn I smell?"

Success!

"Yes ma'am."

Gertrude smiled. An actual, genuine smile. "I love popcorn." She picked a piece from the massive bowl and popped it into her mouth.

"I know. Me too. It reminds me of being a little girl and spending the afternoon playing checkers with you."

"Oh my. I'm not sure I remember how. It has been so long."

Were those tears slipping between the old woman's wrinkles?

"I remember, Aunt Gertrude." Trudy gently took her great aunt's arm and led her to the table. "We don't have sodas, but I made sweet tea."

Two glasses, perched on coasters, flanked a checkerboard, red and black pieces facing off.

Gertrude slipped onto one of the chairs. "I used to like checkers."

"Maybe you still do." Trudy placed the bowl, overflowing with popcorn, between them. "Wanna try it?"

Gertrude nodded. "You go first."

The next couple of hours passed quietly, the click of checkers bouncing against the board mixed with the occasional "crown me."

Gertrude won more than she lost.

The stiffness in Trudy's neck eased its hold.

Without warning, the grandfather clock chimed nine. "Time for bed," Gertrude announced.

As she limped past, a soft touch brushed against Trudy's shoulder. For the first time in weeks, the television rested.

Oh, the beautiful sound of silence.

After assisting Gertrude with dressing and crawling into bed, Trudy returned to the breakfast nook. Picking up the checkers and board, she packed them into their wooden box and closed the lid.

When she opened the cabinet to replace them in their rightful place, she stopped.

Dare she?

Yes. She dared.

Trudy carried the box into the den. Between the sofa and a straight-back chair, a round table waited. It held nothing but a box of tissues, which she moved to the coffee table. Opening the box, she tested her theory.

"Ooh. Perfect fit." She stepped back, admiring the placement of the checkerboard in the table's center. Room for drinks on either side, she'd figure something out for a bowl of popcorn. Arranging the red and black pieces, the last traces of stress retreated.

"There. Maybe I can entice more interaction. It worked tonight." She shrugged. "Maybe not. At least I tried."

If every evening went like this one, she might survive this messed-up season of life with Gertrude. If not...

She refused to think about that option.

Trudy turned off the lights and headed to her room, praying for the peacefulness to continue and hoping they both slept without interruptions.

Job Disturbance

Over the next couple weeks, Trudy settled into a daily routine—a strange somewhat routine. She never knew which flavor of Gertrude to expect each morning.

Some days, she emerged, wearing a robe or fully dressed, puttered through the house, and retreated to her favorite spot on the porch. Sweet as honey, she sat beside the table sipping coffee and enjoying the yard. Occasionally, she tried reading her Bible. At Trudy's suggestion, she more often listened to a recorded voice reading it.

Then, the other days.

Oh, the bitter, burned coffee flavor. On those days, Gertrude stayed in her room until Trudy or Bessie forced her to dress and come out for breakfast. Tempers flared on both sides, and at Bessie's insistence, Trudy tried not to argue with her great aunt.

She tried.

Often failing.

Preparing for a video conference call, Trudy hoped for a honey day. At least Bessie kept Gertrude occupied while she worked. The queen of distraction, Bessie taught her new ways to deal with the disease every day.

With her laptop and coffee, Trudy peeked in at Gertrude, curled into a teeny ball, fast asleep. Her great aunt, once extraordinary, looked as fragile as a china doll. A soft snore eased from the sleeping ball, ending with an almost snort, then resuming.

Smiling, Trudy turned and tiptoed to the study. Since coming home, Gertrude avoided the room most days. She complained about her glasses not being the right prescription, so she couldn't see the words well to read.

But at the suggestion of a trip to the optometrist, she bristled. "Why? So he can charge me a bunch of money to get it wrong again?"

Instead, Trudy introduced audiobooks. At first, Gertrude whined over everything about the recorded reading of a book. After a few days, though, Trudy caught her listening more than watching TV. A small success. How much her aunt remembered or understood... That didn't matter. It kept her from utter boredom and mindless programs.

Gently closing the French doors, Trudy sat at the desk with her laptop opened. At precisely 8:25, she launched a link for the meeting and checked a few more emails while waiting for Peter and her co-workers.

A ping on her phone announced a text.

Bessie.

"Flat tire. I'll be a bit late, but on my way. Nice man stopped to help."

"No worries. Gertrude still sleeping. I'm getting on a video call. Let yourself in."

The meeting started with the house quiet.

As Peter launched into the third item on the agenda, Gertrude burst through the door.

"Where is it? What did you do with my journal? And my purse?"

Trudy stared at her monitor in horror. Gertrude—dressed in nothing but a slip—flitted behind her.

She searched bookshelves.

Flung magazines off the side table.

Pushed Trudy away from the desk.

Peter's voice stopped. Trudy looked back at the screen. She clicked the video icon.

"Well? Where did you put it? You hid it. I know you did!"

Horrified, Trudy clicked the microphone.

"Aunt Gertrude! What the heck? I'm on a call in here." Her

temper flared, heat rising from her belly to her hairline. "What are you doing?"

"I need my journal and my purse. Where are they?"

Breathe. Calm. Stay calm.

"Gertrude, I don't know where you left them."

"I had them in my room. You took them."

"No, I didn't." Trudy's volume rose.

Gertrude pushed her farther aside, crawling under the desk, opening and slamming drawers.

Glaring, she clenched her fist as if ready to hit Trudy.

Suddenly, she stormed from the room, screaming through the house.

Trudy clicked on the video and mic icons, furtively watching behind her.

Peter stopped again. "Are you OK, Trudy?"

She couldn't help but notice the deep red of her reflection. "Yes. I... I... My aunt's a bit agitated. I'll be back in a few minutes."

Clicking on the video and mic again, she rushed to Gertrude's bedroom. Purse. Bottom of bedside table. The journal waited on the rocking chair. "Oh, Gertrude." She looked around. "Where are you, Auntie?"

Venturing into the living room, Trudy froze. The front door gaped.

"Oh crap! God, help me. Give me grace!"

Pulse accelerating, she raced outside just in time to see Kit cowering in front of Gertrude, her hands raised against the flailing fists of the old woman.

"GERTRUDE!"

Jumping from the top step to the grass, Trudy ran across the lawn. "Gertrude. Stop! What are you doing to Kit?"

The neighbor's eyes flared wide, her mouth hanging open.

"Gertrude. Stop. It's Kit. She didn't do anything to you."

The old woman cocked her head, looked at Trudy then back at Kit. "I'm sorry."

She turned to Trudy. "You didn't take it. He did."

"Who did?"

Gertrude's face twisted. "Father."

"Father?"

"Yes. He doesn't want anyone to know." She crumpled against Trudy. "I won't tell. I promise. I won't tell any of it. The truth'd kill Mama. I won't tell."

Compassion washed over Trudy, replacing the anger and embarrassment. "It's OK, Auntie. It's OK. He's gone."

"I need my journal. Gotta write. Find Will. Save me. Will. Find my journal. Run away! Gotta…"

"Gertrude. I found your journal. I know where it is."

Gertrude's eyes widened.

Trudy took her arm gently. "It's in your rocking chair. Let's go get it."

She glanced over her shoulder at Kit. "Sorry," she mouthed. "Later."

Great. Now the whole neighborhood will know Gertrude's lost it.

"OK." Gertrude tottered, grabbing Trudy's arm to steady herself.

The two women reached the driveway as Bessie pulled off the street.

Bessie bolted from the car, leaving the door open. "What happened, Trudy? Why is Ms. Ryan out here in the street practically naked?"

Trudy's hands shook as Bessie slipped an arm around Gertrude. Her smooth voice calming. "It's all right, Ms. Ryan. Bessie's here. Everything's gonna be OK."

The call!

"I gotta get back inside, Bessie. You good?"

Bessie nodded.

Trudy tore across the grass and bounded up the steps, hoping she didn't miss the entire meeting.

Settling, though out of breath, she clicked the video and mic. Peter finished the last item and wrapped up the meeting.

Trudy shook her head, blinking, refusing to release the flood of tears.

When Peter paused, Trudy swallowed hard. "I'm so sorry everyone. The nurse had a flat this morning, and when we started, Gertrude was still asleep."

One lady smiled. "It's no problem, Trudy." With misty eyes, she continued. "None of us knew you were going through something so terrible. My grandma had Alzheimer's. It's rough."

She couldn't respond. Not without a deluge escaping from her eyes."

One of the younger guys cleared his throat. "At least she had everything covered. Man, if she'd been naked…" He overemphasized a shuddering shrug. "That's not an image I could unsee. Nor do I want to try."

Laughter broke the tension, even for Trudy.

"Trust me. I have seen her without the slip. You're right. You don't want that in your brain." Trudy laughed. "Thank you all for understanding."

Peter released those in the room and others on the call. "Trudy, stay on, and I'll recap the meeting for you. If you're OK."

She nodded, still quivering from the morning.

"I'm OK. Mortified, but OK. Her nurse is with her now." She blew out a sigh. "She went outside, Peter. She never unlocks the deadbolt to go out front, but she did today. I better do damage control with the neighbor, too. Probably all the neighbors. They're a nosy bunch."

Peter chuckled. "I'm sorry. I shouldn't laugh."

"What else you gonna do?" Trudy took a sip of coffee. Bad decision. "Oooh. Cold coffee. Yuck."

"What set her off this morning?"

"I don't know. One minute, she's sleeping. The next... Well, you saw the next. I didn't even know she woke up."

"Remember when we talked about FMLA?"

Trudy nodded.

"You might want to take a leave."

"Peter, she could go on like this for months, years. I need this job. I LOVE this job."

"I know. I'm not trying to kick you to the curb. Trust me. I don't want you to leave permanently." He sighed. "I'm concerned about you trying to keep up with everything here while you bear the load of caring for your aunt."

"When Bessie's here, it's good. She's a saint. Maybe an angel. So patient with Aunt Gertrude. Please, Peter. Don't make me go on leave. Work keeps me from joining Aunt Gertrude on the journey to senility."

"I'll give it some thought. See if I can come up with special projects for you. But think about it. The time may come when you don't have a choice. About FMLA—or what to do with your aunt."

Thank God for Bessie

Emerging from the study, Trudy peered around the corner. Too quiet.

"Bessie? Aunt Gertrude?"

No answer.

Trudy took deep breaths. Front door closed. No screaming.

She rushed to the kitchen. Through the window, she found the two ladies putting seed in the bird feeder. Gertrude fully clothed, of course.

Dear Bessie. You sweet angel.

One more deep breath, fresh coffee, and Trudy pushed open the back screen. "Good morning."

Bessie smiled. "Good morning, Trudy. Did your meeting end well?"

"Yes, Bessie. Yes, it did. Thank you."

Gertrude turned. "Good morning, dear. We needed to feed the birds. Poor little things. I thought you fed them, but not a seed one in this feeder."

"I'm sorry, Gertrude. I intended to first thing this morning, but I had that early meeting, and it slipped my mind."

A hearty laugh broke from her aunt. "And you think I have demeninga."

Trudy and Bessie joined the laughter.

"You got me, Auntie. Maybe it's contagious."

"Oh, Lord, I hope not." Gertrude shook her head and dusted her hands. "There. Now, the birds will come and... ser... sing for us." She turned toward the house. "I might need a nap."

Bessie crinkled her forehead. "This early?"

Sighing, Gertrude nodded. "I fell asleep early but had the strangest dreams. Kept me awake until dawn! And then..." She straightened, glancing around the yard. Looking, listening. "I'm tired."

Bessie offered an arm. "Well, let's get you settled for a nap, and I'll have lunch ready when you wake up."

Trudy stayed on the porch, watching dark clouds gather. No rain in the forecast, but a storm brewed. A nasty one. Nothing could make this day worse than it started.

Heading back indoors, she found Bessie in the kitchen, doing what she did best—cooking something delicious and comforting.

"How do you do it, Bessie? Except for the wayward words, Gertrude acted almost normal just now."

"The disease, hon. It comes and goes. You learn to roll with it."

"I try, but I fail more than succeed. Like this morning."

"You did all right."

"No. If you hadn't showed up at that moment... I calmed her some, but she stayed agitated. One wrong word and..." Trudy shivered. "I should probably go over and talk to Kit."

"What exactly happened?"

"I have no clue. I peeped in around 8:00—still sound asleep, even snoring. I got online, checked a few emails, and logged on for a video conference. I never heard a sound from Gertrude until she burst through the door, wearing nothing but a slip, shrieking about her journal."

"Wait. She burst into the study where you were on a video call?"

Trudy rubbed her forehead. "Yes."

"They could see her?"

"Ummhmm."

"Any fuddy-duddies on the call?"

"Possibly. A couple of them almost never smile."

Laughter poured from Bessie like a broken dam.

"It isn't funny."

Bessie tried to gain control of herself but couldn't. Tears trickled down her cheeks. She brushed them away. "Oh, Lordy. I can't help but imagine those faces."

A chuckled worked its way up and out of Trudy. "Well... Yeah. They looked quite shocked." The laughter bubbled up and out. For a full minute both ladies enjoyed the freedom of humor in an otherwise devastating moment.

The nurse cleared her throat. "OK. What happened after that? How on earth did Gertrude end up next door?"

"After I excused myself and muted the mic—of course, I already shut down the camera—I went to find her. The journal was right there on her rocking chair. No sign of Gertrude. I rounded the corner and saw the front door open. My heart never raced like it did in those seconds."

"I can imagine."

"When I stepped onto the porch, Gertrude stood in front of Kit, trying to slap at her with both hands. Poor Kit. I took hold of my aunt, somehow stayed calm, and led her back toward the house. That's when you pulled up."

"Wow. What did Gertrude yell when she busted in?"

"Gibberish mostly. She thought I hid her journal. But outside, she mentioned Will, Father, the journal again, running away. Most of it didn't make sense."

"Who's Will?"

"From documents I found, William Dade. Gertrude married him. Her father had it annulled, but it didn't matter. Will went off to the military and died from some stupid infection."

Bessie's eyes shot wide. "Did Gertrude tell you this?"

"No. I accidentally came across some photos and the telegram about his death." She hung her head. "I broke into a lock-box and found the other documents. I don't have the guts to ask Aunt Gertrude." Trudy brightened. "But now that she mentioned him..."

"It might open a door."

"Bessie, do you think her father could be part of why Gertrude acts so angry? That and Will dying?"

"Hon, anything we refuse to forgive and let go of creates bitterness in us. Do you think when Jesus said forgive, he meant it for the good of scoundrels who do us wrong? We forgive so the anger doesn't fester and grow into bitterness. Maybe Gertrude doesn't talk about her father or Will because she doesn't want to think about them. Thinking opens the door to forced dealing with the past."

"You are a wise woman, Ms. Bessie."

"Ha. Years and years of experience."

Gertrude's words drifted across Trudy's consciousness. "You know, she said some things outside that have me wondering more about her father, too."

"Like what, hon?"

"That he didn't want anyone to know. But she wouldn't tell. Didn't want to hurt her mom. I'm not sure." She shrugged. "Maybe she just meant the way he treated Will and her. I think they eloped, so maybe he didn't want the neighbors to know that."

"Could be."

"I found a card that said Baby Dade."

"You think Gertrude had a baby?"

"If she did, she never told anyone. And I haven't found anything to suggest she did—other than that card."

"Hmmm. You know, it could be something from this Will character. Maybe an old keepsake from his birth."

"I never thought of that. It's possible. No, the date's wrong."

Trudy refilled her mug while Bessie worked on lunch.

"You know far more about Alzheimer's than I do, Bessie. If I ask her about these things, will it trigger an episode?"

"Oh, don't get me to lying, girl. I have no way of telling how she'll respond. It could be fine, or it could throw her into a tizzy. She mentioned a dream. I doubt she remembers it now, but that probably set her off this morning. Maybe she had a nightmare about her father."

"Makes sense I guess."

"Keep a record of her outbursts. Sometimes, that helps identify triggers. We can't control dreams, but if memories of her father throw her into agitation, avoid bringing them up—no matter how badly you want to know the truth."

"So I shouldn't ask?"

"Didn't say that. Just tread lightly. And prepare for anything."

"Thanks, Bessie. I don't know how I'd make it without you."

"That's why I'm here, my dear. Now skedaddle outa my kitchen and get back to that high-falutin' job of yours." She smiled.

"Not so high-falutin'. And after this morning, only God's grace will keep Peter from demanding that I take FMLA."

Trudy returned to the study, her mind full of questions without answers.

Did she dare ask?

If she didn't, how would she ever know the truth of Gertrude's life?

One thing she knew for certain. She had to work up the courage to ask soon. If she waited too long, not even Gertrude would know.

Confronting Gertrude

At supper that evening, Gertrude said little.

"Auntie, are you alright?"

"Just tired, dear. Too little sleep last night, restless nap, this bothersome hip." Gertrude picked up the chicken breast and took a bite.

Trudy pressed her lips together. Gertrude didn't eat with her fingers—maybe fried chicken, but certainly not a baked breast smothered in a mushroom wine sauce. Bessie put the dish together before leaving. Trudy just popped it in the oven for an hour, filled with gratitude for the nurse extraordinaire.

She cleared her throat. "You had a bad dream last night, huh?"

Gertrude huffed. "Like I remember any dream."

"Outside this morning, you said some things."

"I didn't go outside this morning—at least not until Bessie came and took me out back."

"You don't remember going to Kit's house?"

"Why would I go over there?"

Trudy sighed. "You got confused, couldn't find your journal."

"I certainly do not remember any such nonsense."

Biting her bottom lip, Trudy pressed. "Who's Will?"

Gertrude froze. Her bottom teeth scraped her upper lip. "Who told you about Will?"

"You did, Auntie. At Kit's house. You wanted to find Will. Have him rescue you." She paused. "You wanted to run away."

Glaring, the old woman pushed away from the table. "I am finished eating now."

"C'mon, Auntie. You don't have to tell me about Will. Just finish eating."

"There is no Will." Gertrude grabbed the table, pulled herself up, and tottered to the den.

Sighing, Trudy pushed her half-eaten dinner away and leaned her forehead against her palm.

Why won't she talk about Will? I want to know about this love of hers.

She cleared off the table, put away leftovers, and washed the dishes, vaguely aware of Gertrude's pacing. Down the hall, in-and-out of the kitchen, around the dining room. Pacing. Bessie warned her about the possibility of agitation if triggered.

With the last dish put away, Trudy approached Gertrude, guilt riding her like a monkey. "Auntie, do you want to go for a walk in the garden? We can cut some roses."

Gertrude stopped pacing for a moment. "The steps."

"Oh, yeah. I forgot. How about a nice cup of herbal tea and take it out on the porch?" Then it hit Trudy. "Wait a minute. You took the front steps fine this morning."

"I think not. But if I did, that explains why this stupid hip aches so much tonight."

"Well, maybe the walking around the house aggravates it. With the sun going down, the back porch might be pleasant."

Sighing, Gertrude tilted her head toward the door. "I like the rose hip tea. Make that one for me. I shall go sit outside."

"Fantastic idea. I'll be out in a few minutes. Do you want your walker?"

"Heavens no. I hate that thing."

"Please be careful going out the door."

"Quit treating me like an infant. I know how to walk." She brushed past Trudy, but at the door, she reached over and held the trim as she stepped across the threshold.

With a slight hum, Trudy heated water and measured the tea into a pot, placing it and two china cups on a tray. When the kettle boiled, she poured it over the tea, snapped on the lid and headed outside.

A gasp escaped when she opened the storm door. Gertrude, wearing a broad smile, bent slightly at the bushes, inhaling the scent of roses. Pushing down a scream, Trudy set down the tray and flew down the steps.

"These flowers smell delightful. We should cut a few and take them inside."

Trudy clenched her teeth before blowing out a breath. "Yes, Auntie. That'd be wonderful."

Gertrude wrinkled her nose. "What? You don't like them?"

"They're beautiful. I… I just expected to find you sitting on the porch, not down here with your roses."

"Oh, I always enjoy a stroll around the yard after dinner, dear. Ben used to play while I pulled a few weeds or cut a few stems. Ben's my son you know."

A thick knot climbed into Trudy's throat and stuck there. "Yes, I know."

She gently placed Gertrude's hand on her right arm and covered it with the left hand. The two wandered through the yard, admiring flowers. Several times, they stopped while Gertrude closed her eyes and breathed, threw her head back and murmured, "Hmm."

At the shed, Gertrude froze. Trudy looked at her aunt's face. Smoldering flames covered her eyes, her forehead wrinkling. She stared at the door, jaw tightening, letting go of Trudy's arm. "He deserved it."

"Who deserved what, Gertrude?"

"Euleseus. Ignorant, controlling, perverted man."

"Your father?"

"I didn't call him Father. No father does the things he did."

Trudy swallowed a lump, hesitating, wondering. If she asked, would it trigger an episode? Finally, she whispered. "What did he do to you?"

"I tried locking my bedroom door, but he had a key. He

walloped me for locking it, but I didn't want him to touch me. Not the way he did. It didn't matter. After beating the tar outta me, he 'loved' on me. I puked afterward."

Gertrude's gaze locked on something unseen while Trudy held her breath, not wanting to break the story. "Then, I met Will. I loved him, and that old man chased him away. Didn't matter. Will saved me, but he didn't come back. He left and didn't come back. And Mama… she never hurt anyone. And he…" Daggers filled the stormy eyes. "He tied her up. Left her to rot in poop and pee. I locked him in the shed, and I don't regret it at all. He got what he deserved in there." She sniffed. "I hope he felt the rats nibbling before he died."

As realization hit, Trudy's heart pounded.

Did Gertrude purposely kill her father?

Her mind raced back to the documents she found. Death certificates. Heart attack.

Not on purpose, but she might have caused the heart attack by accident.

Anger washed over Gertrude's face, a glow of wrath and justice mixing on her features as the sun dipped beneath the horizon.

A sudden breeze chilled Trudy. She trembled and slipped her arm around Gertrude. "It's getting dark and chilly. We should get you inside."

Gertrude's head snapped in Trudy's direction. Blank eyes stared at her. "You… who?"

"It's me, Auntie. Trudy." She kept her voice even, calm. "We're in your yard, but we need to go inside now."

Suddenly, her aunt blinked. "Trudy? Why are we outside in this chilly evening air? Are you trying to make me catch pneumonia?"

"Not at all. We got caught up in the fragrance of the flowers. Dusk slipped up on us."

Her aunt rubbed her hip. "I know you want me to do the PT,

but those steps. Hard on an old woman."

"I know. Here—lean on me for support. I got you."

They limped across the yard, painfully climbing the steps, tea forgotten.

Inside, Gertrude patted Trudy's arm. "Thank you, dear. I am exhausted. Could you bring one of those pain… pills?"

"Of course. I'll be in to help you into bed in a minute."

"Good. Good." Gertrude limped across the kitchen, grasped her walker, and headed to the bedroom.

Puzzle pieces slipped into place, filling details of an abused daughter who grew into a bitter old woman.

Lunch with Irma

Trudy dreaded meeting Irma, although she welcomed a break from caring for Gertrude. With Bessie there, she had nothing to worry about and the afternoon free—all of it to herself. At least after she endured lunch with her sister.

Endured? I used to treasure meeting Irma for lunch.

Lately, Irma felt like a stranger. Wrapped up in herself, in Zane and those demanding kids of theirs. Trudy longed for the relationship they had through high school and into college years.

Thrust deep in the reality of life, they played their parts, and Trudy wondered if either of them liked their roles much.

She shrugged off the negative thoughts and entered the bistro one minute late—good for her—but of course, Irma sat there, not a hair out of place and looking as if she stepped from the pages of a magazine. Even in jeans, she wore a sophisticated air.

How does she do that?

For a split second, Trudy stood, marveling at the gracefulness of her sister.

She looked down at her leggings and over-sized shirt.

Frump. I've become a frump.

Face it. At her best, she never compared to her sister's flair.

Irma spotted her and rushed over. "Trudy! You look so cute and comfortable today. C'mon. I got a perfect table overlooking the lake."

Of course, she did. She always made everything perfect. Was Irma's comment serious—or facetious? Trudy couldn't read her sister any longer.

Cute and comfortable? Really?

No.

Frump—pure frumpiness.

Lunch arrived, and between bites Irma droned about her kids and husband.

"I swear, Trudy. I can't keep up with it all. The kids both have sports and several school clubs. I love that they enjoy all the church activities, but sometimes, I wish one of them could drive. I play chauffeur all the time."

"Why don't you have Zane help with getting the kids where they need to go?"

"Zane? Are you kidding? He works 80 hours a week. We barely see him. I try not to complain. I mean, he pays for anything the kids and I want or need, and I get to enjoy lunches like this without having to worry about the cost. I'd like to have him home more, but he loves his job. I can't deny him the chance for a promotion—maybe reaching the top of the company someday. All he asks is that I have dinner ready when he comes home. Although, he usually takes it to his study and works there—when he doesn't stay at the office. That's become more frequent lately."

Trudy raised her eyebrows. "That's interesting."

"Oh, c'mon. I trust him. Nothing's going on. They've been in the middle of a huge audit lately. That's all." Irma sighed. "Of course, I still volunteer with several organizations while the kids are in school. Did I tell you they elected me to the board of the Ladies Society Club? Second vice-president. I plan all the programs. It's a good thing we have someone clean the house every week."

Busy. Consumed with everything but helping with our great aunt.

Trudy squashed the rising irritation. Why couldn't Irma give up a half day to let her take a break?

Finally, after an hour that felt like a day, the waitress brought the check. Irma snatched it and pulled out her wallet. "So, how is Gertrude doing?"

"Good days, bad days." Trudy swallowed a lump. "I have so many messed-up emotions, Irma. I get angry at her, trying not to lash back when she's irritable or downright mean. Then other times, it's almost like the aunt I remember from childhood and before Dad died. One morning, we made Granny's famous biscuits. She knew every amount and all the ingredients. Oh, my goodness, they tasted amazing. But then a minute later, she treated me like a stranger, as if I came to visit for the first time."

"No way."

"Yes. She does that—lucid one day or part of the day, and then seeing things, confused, depressed. Dealing with dementia is enough to make a caregiver lose her mind right along with the one affected. Craziness."

"At least you have work. That has to bring you back to reality and a sense of purpose."

Trudy stirred her coffee. "I took a leave. At least a partial one."

"No. You didn't. Please tell me you didn't."

"I worked from home for a while, as much as I could. But you know our aunt. She demands attention when she wants it. After a few weeks, it just didn't work any longer. I never knew when she might rush into the room during a call and start shouting. She did one morning—in nothing but her slip."

Irma threw her hands over her mouth. "That's so wrong, Trudy. You can't let her make you lose your job!"

"I don't want FMLA, but at least Peter supported me in the decision. We tried some off-the-wall work for a while, and he still gives me minor project work I can do without joining calls or going in for meetings. Fewer hard deadlines. It seemed the best thing for now."

Dropping her hands, Irma's jaw tightened. "But Trudy, what about your promotion? And who knows how long the old woman might hang on before giving up to the Grim Reaper?"

"Irma. That's not nice."

"I can't help it. She never treated me all that well. You were always her favorite. But this? Trudy, it could end your career."

"I don't think so. I can always work on a promotion later. My career will wait. Aunt Gertrude can't live alone now."

"What about the home health care aides? Don't they come?"

Trudy chuckled. "Yeah, right. She ran them off faster than she chased off the kids down the street. Only one can handle her BS, and that's Bessie. She comes every morning and leaves at lunchtime, which allows me to work for a while or kick back if I need to. Lot of wisdom in that woman. Bessie gives the BS right back and doesn't take much off Auntie. At the same time, she treats her with respect and gentleness."

"Well, good for Saint Bessie. But you should put Gertrude in a home and forget about the old bat."

The words hit like a whip, pushing months of suppressed anger to the surface. The strength to press it back down drained as heat rushed through Trudy's body and into her face.

"How dare you?"

Irma froze, her eyes widening. "Now, Trudy…"

"Don't 'now Trudy' me." She drew in a breath, held it for 30 seconds, and released it in a huff. Didn't help. "You never understood our aunt. Yes, she can be harsh, and at times, I detest that woman. But you don't know everything, little sister. You're so self-absorbed with your life, you never once offered to help. Then, you sit there telling me what I ought to do?"

"I have my husband and the kids…"

"Your husband's an a-hole. And the kids? They're old enough to help around the house, but you do everything for them. And I mean EVERYTHING."

"Calm down, honey. Let's not make a scene."

"What? One of your friends might see you fight with family?"

"Trudy, no. I just don't want to see you lose everything over an old woman who's filled with bitterness. She's not worth it."

"Maybe not. But Daddy thought she was, and I promised him

I'd look after her. I will NOT break that promise by throwing away our great aunt."

Irma looked out at the lake, her eyes growing red and watery. "I know. I was there." She looked back. "I'm not like you, Trudy. I can't handle Gertrude, her biting remarks. I never could. I don't see what you see—what Daddy saw. I just can't."

"Not if you don't try."

Irma stood, tossed two 20's on the table. "Lunch is on me. I gotta go." She turned, took a deep breath and walked away.

Trudy glared at her sister's back, then slumped in the chair.

Great. I alienated my sister.

Left alone at the table, Trudy stared at the lake. So unlike her to talk to Irma that way. What happened? Had she lost herself in the middle of life and all this mess of dealing with a demented— and yes, bitter—old woman?

Her teeth clenched, her head throbbed, and she fought tears yet again. She hated crying, and lately, the river of droplets flowed nonstop. As acid filled her esophagus and unsavory thoughts trampled her mind, a cardinal flew to the rail and looked straight at her.

Frozen, she looked into the bird's eyes. He didn't move other than cocking his head a few times, eyes locked on hers.

The bitterness haunting Aunt Gertrude in her demented state—not so different than what flowed through Trudy's subconsciousness. With a couple of decades… Trudy grabbed her glass of water, sudden dryness filling her mouth.

I do not want to end up like my aunt. I refuse to die a bitter old woman, alone and unloved.

All the more reason she couldn't leave Gertrude.

"I can't," she whispered. "No one deserves to die alone, abandoned by everyone. I won't let that happen."

The bird chirped and darted away.

In Irma's Self Defense

Irma rushed from the restaurant, vacillating between anger, frustration and concern. She huffed and mumbled all the way to her car, a flood of emotions fighting to take top place.

Her phone rang.

"Mom. She'll take my side on this."

She slipped into her car and answered the phone, starting the engine so the call would shift to the speakers.

"Hi, Mom."

"Hi, honey. How was lunch with your sister?"

"It went well—at least until I finally asked about Gertrude. I tried not to bring her up, but I was afraid Trudy might think I didn't care."

"Well, you really don't, do you?"

"Of course, I do. Maybe not so much about Gertrude, but I worry about Trudy."

"Why? What did she say?"

"It isn't so much what she said. More the way she looked."

Concern filled the space as Irma waited for her mother to respond.

Finally, she asked, "How did she look?"

"Haggard. Trudy never had a flair for fashion, but..." Irma paused. She didn't want to sound overly critical. "She looked a little frumpy, Mom. Barely put together. We used to meet for lunch, and she at least looked professional."

"Oh, Irma. You and your always perfect style. If that's all you're worried about, I'm sure she's fine."

"Maybe." Irma sighed. "Mom, did you know Trudy took a leave of absence from work?"

"She mentioned considering FMLA, but no, I didn't know

she moved forward with it. That's insane. Why doesn't she just put Gertrude in a facility?"

"I think she should. But don't say that to her. She'll chew your head off."

"Taking care of anyone takes a toll on a person. Maybe she needs some help."

"I'm sure she does, but I can't do it."

"You could give her a break once in a while."

Irma couldn't believe she heard right. "Me? The way Gertrude feels about me?"

"She's nicer to you than she ever was to me. I swear she never thought I deserved your father. She tolerated me, but we never had a genuine friendship. Honestly, I didn't care, except it hurt your dad." A sadness filtered through the speakers. "I think you should offer to go over. Who knows? Maybe you can develop a semblance of a relationship with your great aunt. If I didn't have a bad back, I'd offer. But if she falls or needs help, I can't do anything."

"And I can?"

"Physically, yes, Irma. If Trudy needs help, you owe her to at least offer it."

"Thanks, Mom. I'll think about it." Irma suppressed rising anger. "I gotta run."

"OK. Consider it, baby. Besides, the old woman has a little money stashed away, and that house's value could be worth the pain of temporary groveling. If nothing else, you might work your way into her will."

Good ol' Mom. Always looking for easy money.

"Sure. I'll call you later. Bye, Mom."

Irma disconnected the call.

Not on her life. No amount of potential inheritance covered the added stress of sitting with Gertrude for one hour.

Besides, she couldn't take care of Gertrude. Mom and Trudy

didn't understand.

Irma sighed, talking to herself. "I have a husband and teenagers who need me. All the school functions and volunteering at the school and church. I barely make it home in time to get Zane's dinner. He'd throw a fit if I had to stop off and check in on Gertrude, making his dinner late. No, that won't do."

So what if he got home later every day? As sure as she made even a quick stop, he'd come home right on time to a cold stove. Sure way to get the silent treatment for the remainder of the evening. A lot of times he fell asleep in his office, but on that rare occasion when they went to sleep at the same time... She didn't dare do something to mess *that* up.

But Trudy? All alone in the evenings with nothing to do. No one else in that cute little cottage of hers.

"She can take care of Gertrude. Besides, they get along. Trudy gets along with everyone, even that crotchety old biddy." Her voice reverberated through the car.

She wished for half the patience of her sister. Somehow, Trudy knew the best way to respond to Gertrude. Like velvet gloves, the right words poured from her sister's lips. Truth with gentleness—such a gift.

"I'm doing her a favor. Taking care of Gertrude gives Trudy something to fill those lonely evenings. A win-win for both women."

Was she trying to justify herself?

No way. She had responsibilities. Trudy...

Maybe Trudy worked on her paintings some nights. A true artist. Her sister should pursue a different career. Still, she took pride in Trudy's accomplishments—raising two kids alone and working her way up the corporate ladder. Never make upper management—not cutthroat enough for that. Still, she did well in building a career, even if it didn't use her artistic abilities much. Maybe someday.

In all honesty, Irma hoped she looked as good when she made it to Trudy's age. Had to admit, she stayed fit over the years. For a while, Irma worried as her sister melted to almost nothing after Mitchell left. She kept most the weight off, still trim. They often passed for twins. Sometimes they mistook Irma for the older of the two. That chapped her every time.

Ohhh. A reminder. She picked up her phone. "Hey Google, create a task. Hit the gym first thing in the morning, or I won't get there at all. And I can't miss a day. I need those two hours for my sanity."

Irma sighed. So much to do.

Nope. She could never take care of Gertrude—not even if she wanted to.

Which she didn't.

Insight to Gertrude

Trudy stood in the doorway of the sunken den. Shutters closed, the dreary dimness darkened her mood more than usual. Some days, she wondered how much more she could stand before breaking.

Gertrude sat in the dimness, staring at nothing.

"Auntie, shall we turn on the light?"

"No. I like the dark."

I don't, Trudy thought, gingerly stepping down into the gloom. Early, cloudy—one of those days certain to leave her aunt muddled, depressed and belligerent.

"I brought your breakfast." Trudy placed the tray on a table next to her aunt. Peeping slits between window blinds filtered the gray morning. Why did this have to be a gloomy day? She hoped from the beginning that bringing Gertrude home from the rehab center helped with memory and mood.

How could a such a dreary day help with anything?

Maybe later when the sun broke through, at least both their moods might improve

"Gertrude cradled her coffee, holding it like precious treasure. She sipped. "Nice. Now this is coffee." She looked up. "Thank you for bringing me home."

"You're welcome, Auntie. I know how much you love this house."

"It has been in my family for decades." She gazed at the window as if seeing through the blinds. Do you think I will forget that?"

"I hope not."

"My mind feels like the sky today. Stormy and gloomy. I am missing a few cogs, Trudy. I know it, but I cannot stop it." A mistiness dusted her eyes.

Trudy kneeled beside her aunt's knee. "I know." She touched the old woman's hand. "I just don't know how to help you."

"You are the only one who ever tried to understand me, child. After your father passed, anyway. Thank you for that."

"Daddy loved you so much. How could I not?"

Trudy wanted this moment to last. She dared not move and break the clarity. It might not come again.

Suddenly, Gertrude leaned forward.

"Child, what are you waiting for? Eat your breakfast so you aren't late for school. Hurry now."

"What?"

"The bus will be along any minute. Hurry! I promised your father you wouldn't miss any more days, and they don't tolerate tardiness. Hurry now."

And in a flash, the sweet moment passed as Gertrude ventured back into an altered place. A moment from the past perhaps, but more likely, a place found only in the darkness of her mind.

Picking up a fork, Trudy said, "OK, Auntie. You eat too."

Gertrude reached over, opened the blinds, and didn't respond.

Finally, she sat her coffee cup on the side table, blinking as she looked around the room.

"Are you ready to eat now?" Trudy moved to hand her aunt the tray.

"I already ate."

"No, you didn't. See? Here's your food. I can warm it up if you want."

"That's not my food. Why do you want me to eat it so bad? You put poison in it, didn't you?"

"Auntie, don't be ridiculous. You just finished thanking me for taking care of you. It's me. Trudy. You know I'd never hurt you."

Gertrude squinted and turned her head slightly, cutting her eyes back toward Trudy. "You aren't Trudy. I don't know who you are."

She looked around, eyes growing wild. "HELP! Trudy, come quick! Help me!"

Trudy backed up. "Gertrude. It's me. I swear."

"Get out. You get out of my house. I'll call the police. I will. You can't rob me. Please, don't hurt me." Sobs broke from the old woman as her gaze darted around the room.

"I'm leaving. I won't hurt you." Keeping her eyes on Gertrude, Trudy backed toward the door. "Just calm down."

"Trudy. Where are you? HELP!"

Trudy reached the doorway, turned and slipped out the door. She ran to the kitchen and made it through the back door before a tsunami of sorrow overwhelmed her.

Now what? She doesn't know me. I can't leave her alone, but I can't go back. Lord, help me. Grace? There's no grace in this.

The door creaked behind her. Trudy whirled, wondering what she might find.

Gertrude stood there, a cup of steaming coffee in her hand. "What on earth are you doing out here on such a nasty day, Trudy? Come inside and get some coffee."

Trudy wiped her face with her fists.

"Child, what is the matter? Why are you crying?"

The sobs came then, wrenching her body. Gertrude sat her coffee on the bistro table and wrapped her arms around Trudy. "There, there. It will be all right." She patted her back. "Come inside and tell me what happened. No one can get away with hurting my girl."

A quivering breath caught Trudy off guard as the tears ended.

Gertrude grabbed her coffee and gently led Trudy inside.

A roller coaster. I'm riding a fracklesnacking roller coaster.

Back in the kitchen, Gertrude pulled a cup from the cabinet and poured coffee into it, carrying it to the table where Trudy sprawled on a chair. "Here. This will make it all better."

Trudy laughed. "Coffee? Make it all better?"

"Of course. Coffee is the nectar of gods, you know. My personal favorite vegetable."

"Coffee isn't a veggie."

"Seriously? Did your mother tell you that? I happen to know, coffee is the best bean God ever created. Since when is a bean not a vegetable?"

Trudy burst out laughing. "Oh, Gertrude. Only you could convince someone that coffee is indeed a vegetable."

A smile played across the old woman's face as she eased into the chair next to Trudy.

"Now. Tell me why you were bawling?"

Do I tell her the truth?

No. Definitely not. Make something up. Fast.

"It's nothing really."

Think. Think.

"I… I had a fight with Irma."

"What about?"

"She made fun of my outfit the other day at lunch."

Gertrude cocked her head. "So what? Irma always had that thing about the newest styles. Although, I admit, she has good taste in clothes." She stopped for a sip of coffee. "Look, Trudy. What you wear matters at the appropriate times. But if you want to go comfortable… Well, that is just how you dress. It fits you."

Smiling, Trudy nodded. "I know. It normally doesn't get to me. But all this stuff… I'm tired."

"What stuff, dear?"

"Life, work, being away from home… It gets to me sometimes. And then, I get so mad at Irma. We barely talk anymore."

"Well, that is not a huge loss. All she talks about is that no-good husband and those lazy kids."

"True. But she's my sister."

Gertrude patted her hand. "I am sure the two of you will patch things up in no time. My sister and I argued—a lot. But we looked out for each other, and in the darkest times, she stood up for me, and I did for her."

Opening. Do I dare?

This moment may not last long.

Dare.

"Auntie, I never knew your sister—my grandmother. Tell me about her. What was she like?"

With closed eyes, Gertrude smiled. "Sweeter than you can imagine. I have no idea what would have happened to me if not for her."

"There's a story in that statement."

"Yes, but I think you have work to do, and I am missing my morning talk show. Besides, my breakfast went cold on me. Would you be a dear and reheat it for me? My hip is aching a bit. Rain on the way."

"You think?"

"Ha. The hip does not lie."

Gertrude limped toward the den. Trudy followed, picked up the breakfast and headed back to the kitchen. When she returned, Gertrude had the TV blaring, but she looked up and smiled when Trudy sat down the tray.

"Thank you, dear. Now go get your work done. We can talk later."

"Yes, ma'am. Maybe over lunch."

Accusations

Eyes fluttering, Trudy peeked at the clock. 4:41. On a Saturday.

No! Go back to sleep.

She closed her eyes, breathed deeply, and snuggled down beneath the warmth of an old quilt.

Drifting…

BANG!

Eyes wide opened, Trudy shot up in bed.

THUNK.

BANG.

"What on earth?"

Grabbing a robe, she rushed down the stairs. Lights everywhere.

"Gertrude?"

No answer.

More banging. A clank—from the kitchen.

She rushed around the corner. Gertrude, fully dressed with an apron covering her clothes, pulled a large pot from the butler's pantry.

"Gertrude. What are you doing?"

The old woman looked at her as if Trudy was the crazy one. "I'm getting ready for canning. Don't worry. I'll make breakfast first, but we must get these peaches put up."

"Peaches? What peaches, Auntie?"

Gertrude glanced in the sink. She scratched her head. "They were there last night." She snapped her fingers. "I know. That Best woman. Probably put them in the fridge. They do better when they aren't cold. It'll take longer to blatch them." She opened the refrigerator, moved a few things around, pulled open the fruit drawer. "That's odd. They aren't here either."

Whirling back to the butler's pantry, she shuffled to the open door. "Maybe she just put them in here to get them out of the sink."

Gertrude rummaged through boxes, moved cans and appliances. She glared at Trudy. "Did she steal them? Don't we pay her enough? I woulda given her some blasted peaches if she asked. I can't stand thievery. Fire her when she comes this morning."

Trudy sucked in air and blinked. "Gertrude, we don't have peaches. I wanted to buy some a few days ago, but it's way past peach season. You must've been dreaming about peaches." She crossed the room and put an arm around her aunt. "It's the middle of the night, Auntie. Let's go back to bed and try to get some sleep. Yeah?"

"It is not the middle of the night. It's practically morning. Lazy bones. No wonder you don't have a job anymore."

Oh. Wrong thing to say.

Breathe. Don't argue.

Breathe. Let it go.

Not Gertrude. Not rational. Can't reason.

Breathe!

"Gertrude, I still have a job. I took time off to try to keep you out of trouble. I am anything but lazy. Who do you think cleans this house while you recover?"

Gertrude blinked. "Lucia does, of course."

"Lucia. Who is Lucia?"

"She's the housekeeper. Comes every week."

Deep breath in. Deep breath out.

In. Out.

In. Out.

"Auntie, I don't know about any housekeeper, but I haven't seen one."

Gertrude smacked her forehead. "What's gotten into me. Of course, not. She took some time to stay with her mama. Something about old and sick. I forgot. How silly."

Placing a hand aside her cheek, Gertrude sighed. She shuffled around and pulled out a frying pan. Trudy watched in horror as she went back to the fridge and retrieved eggs, bacon and bread.

"I can make breakfast for you, Gertrude. Why don't you go out on the back porch and have your coffee? I see you made some already. Should I get your Bible and journal for you?"

"Maybe. I'm suddenly quite tired. Maybe I should rest for a minute." Painfully, slowly Gertrude headed to the back door.

Trudy grabbed a mug and filled it with coffee. Looked strong enough to crawl after her great aunt. She winced and wrinkled her nose, vowing to throw it out and make a fresh pot—a less thick pot.

Sitting beside the table, Gertrude stared out over the dark yard. "Why is it so dark out here?"

"The sun is still sleeping, Auntie. Here's your coffee. Shall I turn on the porch light?"

"Yes, please."

"Take a minute. I'll go make breakfast."

"Lovely. Do we still have some of those bran muffins? I need one today."

"Gotcha. I'll check. I think we might have one left."

Trudy went back inside, not looking forward to the long day ahead.

With fresh coffee brewing, she got to work frying bacon and eggs. Locating one last muffin, she made a mental note to pick up more from the store. Thank God the bakery kept them in stock. She hated the idea of making, much less eating the things. But Gertrude liked her bran.

Just as she was about to plate the food, Gertrude came back in and slammed the door behind her. She went to the front door.

Trudy watched, making sure she didn't open it. Even with an alarm on it, she constantly worried about her aunt leaving and getting lost—or worse, going to Kit's house again.

As she turned in full circles, Gertrude scrunched her forehead. "Where are my car keys?"

Think. Quick.

"I put them away. You can't drive."

"Nonsense. Of course, I can drive."

"Noooooo. You can't."

"Don't be ridiculous. I have a car and a license. I can drive."

"Auntie, you can't." Trudy racked her brain. Not herself, how could she convince her aunt?

Painkillers. That's it!

"The painkillers. They can make you drowsy, so it isn't safe for you to drive. I put the keys away so we could find them later. When you can drive again."

"But I am not taking them this morning. I do not need them today." The calmness in Gertrude's voice shook Trudy. Her aunt threw daggers from her eyes then. "You want to sell it, don't you? You probably already did. Well, I won't let you."

Trudy took an extra deep breath, willing herself to stay calm. "I didn't sell it, Gertrude. It's in the garage like always. But I won't let you drive it. Besides, it's barely 5 a.m. Nothing is open for you to drive to."

A growl came from Gertrude's throat. "First the car. Then you'll go after my money. Well, it's hidden. Safe from prying eyes. You'll never find it." The volume grew. "I won't let you take my money like you did my son. Do you hear me? You can't have it!"

With a turn, Gertrude stormed from the room. The bedroom door slammed, followed by the sound of something being dragged across the floor.

Great.

With a shake of her head, Trudy loaded two plates with

breakfast. She covered one with a cloth, picked up the other, and poured herself a cup of coffee. Not really hungry, she had to eat—do something to strengthen her body. She didn't dare go back to sleep until she knew Gertrude had settled.

The words drifted across Trudy's head.

Like you did my son? Does she think I'm Mom?

More than ever, Trudy wanted to break into that safe upstairs, but she knew if Gertrude caught her in the room, she'd go berserk. More than usual.

Still, she wondered about the secrets. If she didn't figure them out soon, they'd be lost in Gertrude's mind, locked away tighter than any safe.

Unraveling the Puzzle

Trudy stared across the yard as she finished the last few dishes, taking a moment to assess the past weeks. Months? The days all ran together, some good and others bad. She smiled at some of the sweet times with Gertrude, walking through the yard, cutting flowers and displaying them in the large vase on the dining table or in smaller vases throughout the house. Although her aunt insisted on leaving drapes drawn most days, the splashes of color made the drabness bearable.

Shudders shook her body as she thought of other memories—accusations, senseless arguing, confusion. And the nighttime wanderings. More than once, Trudy woke to loud noises only to find Gertrude pacing or pulling pots and pans from cabinets.

Several times, she panicked when discovering Gertrude's empty bed. She raced through the house, calling her aunt to no avail. Then, she always found her in the most unlikely places— the closet curled up on the floor with contents from the hidden box, snoring. Another time, she looked for a full hour before rechecking the den, where Gertrude slept peacefully on the divan.

Trudy sighed deeply. At least life on Gertrude's journey to senility never proved boring.

The kettle's whistle snapped her back to reality. She finished preparing two cups of tea and headed to the den, oddly quiet for a change.

At the door, she stopped. In the recliner, Gertrude held a massive photo album Trudy didn't remember seeing. The older woman gazed into the book—no lines across her forehead and the hint of a smile playing at her lips.

Contentment.

Hesitant to break the mood, Trudy watched from the doorway.

Gertrude finally looked up and smiled. "Why are you standing there letting my tea form icicles, child?"

"I didn't want to interrupt. You looked deep in pleasant memories."

"Come over here. I want to show you these photos."

Crossing the room, Trudy sat the teacups on the side table and pulled up a footstool. Sitting beside her great aunt, she peered at the album. One picture of two astonishing young women caught her eye and tugged at her heart.

She pointed. "Who's that?" She looked again. "If I didn't know better, I'd almost think it was a picture of me."

"I can see that. Although you are prettier than I ever looked. As a teenager, you had that smile that lit the entire room."

"Wait. That's you?"

"Yes, with my sister, Irene."

A lump formed in Trudy's throat. "Irene. My grandmother."

Tears glistened as Gertrude nodded. "People always said we looked alike."

"Almost like twins. Way more alike than Irma and me. But I look like both of you, don't I?"

"I always thought so. Your mother denied it, but your daddy agreed."

"Oh, Auntie. Both of you looked so beautiful, although I see sadness in your eyes."

"We took this picture not long after Irene got married. Our father signed for her just before her 17th birthday. I didn't blame her. I wanted to leave with her. And she wanted to take me, but the old man said no." A visible quake shook her.

Laying a hand on her arm, Trudy leaned in. "How old were you?"

"Hmmm…16, I think. Mama had me less than a year after

Irene. Maybe that is why people thought we were twins—so close to the same size most of our lives, and my sister was the tiny one."

"What was she like? I don't think Daddy remembered much about her except the scent of musk. He always bought Mom musk oil, and she hated it. I loved it, so I used to sneak into her room and put it on—as if they couldn't all smell me." Both women laughed.

"Irene loved anything that reminded her of the woods. Her favorite place. I always preferred gardens and the scent of roses. We were some pair. When she and Fred died, I had to put musk oil on Ben's pillow to get him to fall asleep. He used to beg me to put it on his stuffed animals too, and he took one almost everywhere we went." Sadness washed across her face, so Gertrude turned the page.

The next several pages held candid shots of an adorable baby and toddler. "Daddy?" Trudy blinked, not willing to let the flood building behind her eyelids rush down her face.

Gertrude nodded and cleared her throat. "Such a beautiful boy. He hated me calling him beautiful. He used to say, 'I not butiful. I hansum.' But he had such a beautiful spirit, like Irene. She made a great mother for him."

"Isn't that you in a lot of the photos?"

A smile danced across the wrinkles. "Yes. Irene and Fred let me come to live with them months before Ben arrived. We were both…" She froze, her eyes twitching. "We were both convinced I needed to be away from my father."

Trudy hesitated. "Why? Because of the way he treated you and your Mama?"

"It was just time."

Smoldering in the green eyes told Trudy to change the subject. "So, Irene married young. Why didn't you ever marry? You were certainly stunning. I can't imagine you not having a hundred suitors."

The eyes cleared for a moment, then clouded again, an explosive storm building in them.

Crap. Shouldn't have asked that.

"Father. The boys all heard about him. A few dared to risk it, and I learned to sneak out the window and down the tree beside my bedroom. What he didn't know… Let's just say, the only way I had a chance at marriage—not let him know about the young man and elope. He wanted me for himself."

"Gertrude, are you saying your father…"

"He called it loving me. But I knew other girls did not have daddies loving them the way he did me." The brooding in her eyes thickened.

"I'm so sorry, Auntie. He should never have done those things to you."

"Will. He wanted to save me, but he insisted on getting a blessing. Did not happen. Ever." Her bottom lip quivered. "He went and joined the military 'to make a better life for us' and died instead."

"Is that when you went to live with Irene and Fred?"

She nodded. "I couldn't stay in that house any longer. I hated my father for keeping me from Will. Oh, we still saw each other, but I missed Mama. I came over during the day, and she started fading fast. Her memory—like she checked out, unable to deal with reality. But she told me to stay with Irene. So I did."

"That's so sad. With all Mom's faults, I still love her, too. Not like I did Daddy. I can't imagine having a father like yours."

"He got what he deserved—dying alone. He killed Mama slowly. He destroyed my life and tried to do the same with Irene and Ben. We kept Ben away. The old man didn't deserve to know such a sweet little boy." Gertrude's face grew red, her hands shaking, bottom lip quivering. She stood, pacing. "He messed up my life. And Will… He supposedly loved me, but not enough to come back. A stupid infection. Why didn't he get it treated? Why did he ignore it? I hate them. Both of them." The pacing halted. "You know, I served God throughout the years, despite the evil I lived under. Where was He? I am cursed, not blessed. What a fool I played. And now? Now, the 'good' Lord wants to erase my mind. I wish He would erase these bitter memories. If I have to forget anything, why do I have to remember this... this... garbage?"

Gertrude stormed from the room, the tea and photos dismissed.

As she watched her great aunt stomp toward her bedroom, the dam crashed. Through a wave of sorrow, Trudy grieved.

Oh, the sweet aunt she wished for and the grandmother she never knew.

A Look at Inner Bitterness

Trudy wept after Gertrude left the room. Not for what she became, but for the woman buried all those years—a broken soul who couldn't forgive. She moved to a chair and let the tears roll.

When did this bitter diatribe start?

Gertrude's life seemed good. A big house—inherited. No mortgage. Closets full of expensive clothes—brands Trudy dared not dream of owning. Two cars in the garage. Trips. Not one, but several rooms with full bookcases, including multiple first-edition copies. Everything a woman could want.

Maybe not everything, but close.

Why then did Gertrude ooze bitter gall? Her words, though sarcastic, dripped anger. Her eyes flashed like lightning. Through a stiff demeanor, she held people at bay. If she had a dog, he'd probably cower before her. But this wasn't the woman Trudy remembered from childhood.

Or was it?

As the dementia took hold, meanness leaked from her. Was that the true Gertrude? Irma and Mom insisted she always acted like that toward them.

Looking back, Trudy had to admit the truth. She saw it often. Never directed at her and usually not toward Irma. Mom received well-placed verbal blows as often as the wind blew. Perhaps Irma got into trouble because she practiced her brand of rebellion. Passive-aggressive. She always played that game well.

Herself? She never uttered a peep, hating confrontation.

The kid down the street? Poor little guy. Gertrude always flung threats in his direction. Over the years, he crossed to the opposite side of the street to make sure he didn't step on the grass, still followed by ranting from the elderly woman.

Embarrassing.

Most of the time, he stayed in the middle of the sidewalk, but that never mattered. Her aunt waited for him to mess up.

All this hidden under a flourish of "God's just blessed me so much." On the surface, always a good Christian woman. Generous in appearance, writing checks for the church and charities. That surface concealed a bubbling interior of toxic gunk, and Trudy just received a massive dose of it aimed mostly at Gertrude's father, but also at Will and even God.

In the past, the slime stayed under control most of the time. As the disease stripped away filters, the blackness flowing in Gertrude's veins spilled, spurting yuckiness on anyone who dared come near.

What deep secret drove her to such a bitter epitaph? Was it just the father's abuse and losing her husband? Was that enough for such a well of anger? What other secrets lay hidden in the closet, locked safely from all eyes?

With the passing of each day, Trudy feared she might never find the truth. Without it, she could not help her aunt find peace in her final years.

Then, a worse thought snaked its ugly way to the surface.

Could she harbor bitterness that ate away her gentle spirit and compassion too?

No. Not possible.

At least not to the extent of Gertrude's inner raging.

Words from her psychologist floated through her brain.

Forgiveness sets you free. Forgive for yourself, not for those who wronged you.

She worked through so many issues, forgiving her ex for cheating on her, for the verbal abuse, for all the pain he caused. Still, as she watched Gertrude, memories mounted from the recesses of her mind. She didn't want to remember all the bad times, but every time Gertrude yelled at her, accused or berated her, long-forgotten events spilled over from those buried memories.

Forgive all over again.

And again.

And again.

Seventy times seven, right? Ironically, Gertrude quoted those verses still, but she never forgave her father. Maybe the truth of his evil character explained it. Hard thing to forgive. But it went deeper. He might have built the base, but Trudy sensed more—things she didn't know but despaired over learning.

She searched for hints from vague conversations she shared with her dad. Oh, how she missed him. Did he know about Will? She didn't remember him mentioning anyone in Gertrude's life. Then again, it all happened before his birth.

The tiny footprints on that birth announcement tiptoed across her frontal lobe. Maybe that contributed to Gertrude's anger. No clue about the baby—boy, girl, survived, died in infancy? Obviously, her great aunt didn't keep the baby. No one knew anything about her having a child.

Trudy ran her fingers across her forehead. Her head ached from trying to solve the mystery. Without answers from Gertrude, she feared the secrets might all die with her aunt.

She closed her eyes, leaning her head back against the chair. Did any of it matter? After all, Gertrude chose clinging to the events of her past, refusing to forgive her father and God only knew who else. Who was she to break through to the bitter old woman? She had no license or education to help anyone.

She couldn't even help herself.

Overwhelmed with weariness, a fresh wave of sorrow flooded Trudy. Tears continued cascading, creating endless rivulets of emotion. She brushed them away impatiently, but they didn't stop.

Don't cry. Don't let the weakness show.

Alone in the silence of Gertrude's den, she wondered where that came from. Who told her not to cry? Mom? Dad?

No.

No one told her. She cultivated that belief during her marriage, refusing to let her ex-husband see tears even when she had no power to stop them.

A surge of anger exploded, pouring heat through her body. He stole her best years. He taught her bitterness, and she hated how he did that to her.

He didn't do it.

What?

He didn't. You created that belief in response to how he treated you.

She detested hearing those words in her head—especially because she knew where it originated. She recognized the voice. She didn't always hear Holy Spirit speak as if he sat in the room with her, but when she did, he always spoke truth.

"You're right."

Forgive him.

"Again?"

Forgive him. And then forgive yourself.

"I can't, Lord. I want to, but I'm not sure I can. Not him or myself. Why was I such a weakling? Why didn't I see the real him before we married?"

The room responded with silence.

Figured. Even God didn't have answers for her.

She turned out the light, went upstairs to her room, crawled into bed, and cried herself to sleep.

Sweaters, Skirts, and Secrets

"I'm ready to go." Gertrude's bright voice surprised Trudy.

"Go where?" She looked up from her laptop.

Standing inside the French doors leading to the study, Gertrude did a twirl—a slow twirl, for sure, but a twirl nonetheless.

"Do you like my outfit?"

Trudy gawked.

What on earth?

Gertrude sashayed into the room, two empty, fuchsia arms flouncing around her hips. A sweater collar squeezed around her midsection, the zipper slightly off-center, with about an inch revealing black underwear. A powder-blue silk shirt hung whompy-jawed with half the buttons hanging below the left bottom, and a gap revealing a missing bra. A navy blazer turned wrong side out and a bright orange paisley scarf completed the outfit.

Biting her bottom lip, Trudy let her gaze drift to the floor. Knee-high white trouser socks topped a pristine, white sneaker on the left foot and a red ballet-style flat on the right.

"Well?" Gertrude flung out her hands, palm up. "Whadaya think? Pretty, huh?"

Trudy covered her mouth, determined not to let the laugh building in her gut erupt.

"Interesting color combinations. I think... the white tennis shoe... looks... far more comfortable."

Looking down, Gertrude gasped. "Oh my. I... Well... I wanted your opint on that."

"Definitely, the tennis shoe. And where are we supposed to be going?" She looked up at the corner of the room, the chuckles begging for release.

"To see Dr. Tomassina. Did you forget?"

Checking the calendar, Trudy shook her head. "No. No, Gertrude. That appointment—last week. We saw Dr. **Thompson** last week."

"No, we did not. You better not make me miss seeing that handsome young man. I plan to dazzle him with my lovely attire. If you don't want him, I might as well pursue him. Always wanted a doctor in the family."

Unable to contain herself any longer, Trudy lost it.

"I'm sorry, Auntie. Really, I am." The laughter bubbled and spilled over.

Gertrude crossed her arms over her chest. "What's so funny?"

Trudy blew out a quick breath. "I have no idea. I guess the picture in my head with you and Dr. Thompson..." Gales of laughter ripped free. After a minute, Trudy gained control. "Auntie, I don't think Dr. Thompson is man enough to handle you."

At that, Gertrude chuckled. "You might have that right. He is young and inexperienced. I could teach him a thing or too on how to please a woman."

"Ew. Please tell me you aren't talking about... you know... that."

"What? Sex? It isn't like you never did it. I mean you have kids and all."

"Yeah, but I do NOT want that picture in my head, Gertrude. I... NO!"

Bessie poked her head around the corner. "What's so funny in here?" She froze, her gaze lingering on Gertrude. "Hon, did you need help getting dressed this morning?"

Gertrude flung her hand. "No. You two have no sense of style. None." She swayed her hips, walking to the straight-backed chair. "And Trudy thinks I wasted it because she believes we already saw Dr. Tomlin."

Bessie pinched her lips between her index finger and thumb. "You saw him last week. He praised your progress with that hip. He should see you this morning with that little swing going on." The nurse wiggled her hips until all three women let their laughter run amuck.

The longer they laughed, the harder and louder it grew.

Finally, Bessie wiped her eyes. "Oh. That felt fabulous."

Trudy brushed away a sprinkling from her cheek. "I don't remember the last time I laughed until I cried."

Gertrude nodded. "Glad I could be your source of… hummus."

"Seriously, Auntie. Don't you want to change?"

"No! I like this outfit. It's what I wanna wear today."

Bessie weighed in. "You might get warm in that. How about we pull out your khaki Capri's and a comfortable shirt and go cut a few fresh flowers? Those on the table look a bit wilted."

Rubbing a hand across her mouth and lower jaw, Gertrude narrowed her eyes. "Are you trying to steal my outfit for your honey?"

A smile played at Bessie's mouth, but she raised her eyebrows and donned a perfect poker face. "No, Ma'am. I could never pull that off like you, Ms. Ryan. Where did you ever come up with that idea?"

Pursing her lips, Gertrude rose. "Oh, Irene and I spent hours as young women trying different styles. I almost stole her Fred. Such a boring man, though, I let her have him."

"You what? Aunt Gertrude. You didn't?"

"Nah. But I had you going for a second there, didn't I?"

Bessie chuckled. "Don't you get us going again. If I start laughing, I might not ever stop."

Gertrude wiggled her eyebrows. "You know, I don't want to cut flowers. I need to go see Irene—check on her and the baby."

Bessie started to answer, but Trudy gave her a quick head-shake. "Is the baby OK?"

"So far. But Irene finds it hard to stay in bed, and the baby isn't big enough to survive birth now. You know that, Mama."

"I forgot. But you should change first."

"Nonsense. Irene will get a kick out of this outfit. Of course, it doesn't hide much, does it?"

"Modest enough."

"Yeah, but it is snug around the waist. Maybe I should wear something a tad looser. Don't want the old man to see my secret."

"Your secret? Gertrude, are you pregnant?"

Bessie's mouth parted, a hand flying to hide her surprise.

"Mama, I don't tell my secrets. I love you, but you can't keep things hidden like you used to. If the old man knew…"

Trudy swallowed. "I promise. I won't tell."

"You can't tell what you don't know."

"But if you are…"

"I'm a big girl now, Mama. You don't need to worry about me. I have everything under control."

With that, Gertrude turned and swayed from the room, sweater arms waving goodbye.

Irma Scorned

Bleary-eyed, Trudy stumbled into the kitchen, breathing in the aroma of… something baking, bacon, coffee.

COFFEE.

She rubbed her eyes and retrieved a mug from the cabinet. Turning, she blinked at Bessie, who faced her instead of the stove.

"Well, good morning, Sleeping Beauty."

Trudy ran a hand over her hair. "Mornin'. Not sure about the good part."

"Rough night?"

"What was your first clue?"

"Hmmm. Perhaps the dark circles beneath those baby greens. Or maybe the hair that looks like a rat ran through it and tried nesting. It might be the size of that mug you filled with coffee."

"Long night. I made the mistake of staying up drawing, headed to bed around midnight, and woke abruptly to a screaming alarm before 2:00."

"Oh, no."

"Oh, yes. Gertrude. Standing on the front porch, looking up at the stars, oblivious to the screech behind her."

Bessie tried to suppress her laugh to no avail, turning back to the bacon. "I'm sorry, Trudy. It isn't funny."

Trudy chuckled. "Kinda was for a second. I mean, Aunt Gertrude stood there, totally innocent in her silk pajamas. Doing nothing but looking up. When she finally turned around and caught sight of me, do you know what she said?"

"I can't imagine."

"She covered her ears and said, 'I hate the sound of sirens. Hope it wasn't someone we know. Come back inside, so we can pray for the poor person in the ambulance.'"

"No idea, huh?"

"None." Trudy took a sip. "Of course, I already disengaged the alarm before we had first responders show up here."

"So, what happened after that?"

"She paced. Sat. Paced some more. Turned on the TV and flipped through a few channels before turning it off. Then she went back to pacing, saying, 'I gotta go. Gotta check on Mama. Gotta see if Irene's OK. Gotta call Ben. For hours. The same thing.'"

"I'm sorry. Did you try to calm her, distract her?"

"I tried everything you told me to do. Even took her out to the garden, made some herbal tea and had her drink it. Almost gave her a painkiller, but thought better of it."

"Probably a wise decision. You don't want to depend on those things to make her sleep. In my experience, they don't put the patient out. Then you have an adult child who becomes disoriented, dizzy, and finally collapsing after she wears herself out."

"This isn't her first pace-through-the-night episode."

"I know. Probably won't be her last either. It's common."

"It's exhausting. I didn't want to go back upstairs only to have her breach the front door again. But I couldn't get her back in bed no matter what I tried. We even played checkers for an hour."

"Who won?"

"She did. Even in her demented state, she still whips my butt at any game."

"I wish I could say it'll get better, but you know it won't. More than likely, it'll get worse."

At the gentle chime of the doorbell, Trudy jumped. "Who on earth? We expecting someone?"

"Not that I know of. Want me to answer it?"

Trudy looked down at rumpled pajamas. "Please. I'll go change and run a brush through my hair."

After changing into jeans and a t-shirt, Trudy gathered her hair, secured it with a clip, and raced back down the stairs to greet the rare visitor.

At the entry to the formal living room, she pulled up, tingles racing through her body.

"Irma?"

Her sister sprang from the sofa, crossing the room in two long strides, and wrapped her arms around Trudy.

"What is it? What's the matter?"

"Nothing." Red-rimmed eyes didn't lie.

"You're lying. What happened? Is something wrong with Mom?"

"Can't a girl come see her sister without something being wrong? Besides, you said I should come see Aunt Gertrude."

"Weeks ago. I'm not an idiot, Irma. Something's going on with you."

"I…"

A loud gasp drew their attention to the doorway. Gertrude eyed Irma and then took a few steps backward, ramming her arm into the frame.

Irma stepped toward her. "Hello, Aunt Gertrude. You look wonderful."

Gertrude's gaze darted around the room. She stared at Irma. Trudy. Back at Irma.

"Not good." Trudy softened her voice. "Auntie, you remember Irma? She came to visit us. Why don't you come sit down, and I'll get us all some coffee."

Gertrude shook her head. "I don't like coffee."

"Maybe some tea. A nice herbal blend."

The older woman rubbed her arm and turned toward Trudy. "You… Do I know you?"

"Of course, Auntie. I'm Trudy. Your great niece. Ben's daughter."

"Ben? I have a son named Ben, but you aren't his daughter." Irma eased backward.

Trudy sighed and moved to her aunt's side. "Not surprising. After last night's wandering, I'm sure you are tired. Come sit in this comfy chair." She gently took Gertrude's arm, trying to lead her.

Gertrude jerked the arm back, accidentally hitting Trudy. "No. You two must leave. NOW. I'm calling the police."

Bessie approached with a cup of coffee and moved in front of Gertrude. "Good morning, Ms. Ryan. I'm glad you're awake. I have a nice breakfast for you, complete with your bran muffin. I know you like those."

Wild eyes searched Bessie's face. "I know you. You're my nurse."

"Yes, ma'am."

"These two women—they got in somehow. Trying to rob me. We need help. Call the police."

Gently placing her arm around the thin waist, Bessie spoke in calm, even tones. "Ms. Ryan, I know you haven't seen Irma in a while, but I promise she won't hurt you. I won't let her. And Trudy never hurts you. She's your friend. Trudy keeps you outta trouble."

Gertrude patted her lips with fingertips and cut her eyes toward Bessie. "I don't know."

"I know. Let's get some food for you. See if that helps." She held the coffee toward Irma. "Her you go, dear. I hope it has enough cream and sugar."

Irma nodded as she accepted the mug. An almost silent, "Thank you," squeaked from her lips.

With their aunt gone, Trudy collapsed on a chair and giggled. "Irma, if you could see your face."

Irma straightened her shoulders and closed her mouth. She swallowed hard before taking a seat on the sofa again. "I don't see anything funny. That freaked me out."

Trudy broke into a chuckle. "I could tell by your gaping mouth and inaudible, 'thank you.'"

"I repeat. NOT funny."

"Lighten up, sis. I get this at least once a week, where she looks at me stunned. And I'm here most days and every night."

"Are you serious? She forgets you?"

"Uh… It's called dementia. Common sign—forgetting people you know well."

"But why did she know the nurse?"

"Who knows? Maybe because Bessie always comes in a uniform, Gertrude feels she can trust her. Believe me, we went through a lot of aides and nurses before her. I told you, she has a way with our aunt."

"Great aunt. I had no idea she'd gotten so awful."

"Not all the time. She has moments of lucidity. A few days, she almost seems normal, except for failing words. We get some interesting renditions of object names."

"What was that about wandering last night?"

Trudy tilted her head back. "Ah, the nightly treks through the house. I don't know what she looks for, but she gets antsy and paces. She tries to cook sometimes. That's scary. Lot of muttering, most of it senseless. I learned a few things from her, though."

"Like what?"

"Her father—horrible. She never used the word, but I think he molested her."

Irma's eyes flew wide. "What?"

"Yeah. Makes sense why she detested him and never wanted to talk about her younger years. It came out during one of her less than memorable moments when she thought I was her mama."

"No way."

"Yep. Way. And get this. Aunt Gertrude married someone."

"No, she didn't."

"Yes. Looks like she lied about her age, and her father had it annulled."

"So what happened to this husband? He just abandoned her?"

"Military. Between Korea and Vietnam. He died of some infection. I found a telegram."

"Did Gertrude admit that?"

"Bits and pieces. She won't say much about Will."

"That is the wildest thing ever. Who knew?"

"I know." Trudy lowered her voice. "Irma, I think all this stuff explains the bitterness, and I want to help her let go of it all. But if she won't talk about it when her mind works, I don't know how."

"I don't think you can, Trudy. She thrives from pushing people away with her caustic ways."

"Maybe. But it's like the deep wounds infected her soul, and she can't treat them any more than the doctors could save her husband. I don't want her life to end with all that gunk inside."

"You can't work miracles, girl."

"No. But God can, and I'm praying for one."

"Ha. I thought you didn't believe in God answering prayers."

"It feels that way for me most of the time. But Bessie said something one day that got me thinking."

"Bessie must be something else."

"She's a woman of deep faith, despite troublesome times in her life. When she's here, it's like God's presence fills this house. I wish she could be a live-in instead of here a few hours every morning."

"So what did she say that got you thinking? Mom and I have tried for years—without success, I might add."

"Grace means divine intervention that changes us. God's favor doesn't always appear favorable."

"I never heard such a thing."

"Me either. I can't explain it like she does, but I keep contemplating that conversation. Maybe God will use all this with Gertrude to do something in me."

"Whatever. You are one of the best people I know, Trudy. What could God want to change in you?"

"Plenty."

Irma waved her off. "Maybe your sense of style in clothes. That part of Gertrude should rub off on you."

They both laughed.

Trudy tilted her head. "So, why did you really come by today? And why were you crying on the way?"

"It isn't important. My troubles seem small after what I saw today." Irma blinked rapidly, fighting fresh tears. "You truly are special. The way you stepped in and tried to calm Gertrude."

"I failed. As usual. But I keep learning from Bessie. I'm telling you, she must be an angel."

"I believe that."

"You are my sister, and I care about you, too. What's going on?"

Irma chewed at a corner of her upper lip. "I think Zane's having an affair."

Stiffening, Trudy swallowed a lump. "I'm so sorry, Irma. Are you sure?"

A slow nod. Tears pooling. "I saw a text. Pretty damming."

Her teeth gritted, Trudy shook her head. "That bas…"

"I don't know what to do. How can I survive without him?"

"You're stronger than you know, little sister. He doesn't deserve you."

"But I never had a genuine job. I can't earn a living. I need him."

"Do NOT let him destroy you." Trudy stood, crossed her arms, and tromped to the window. "We can figure this out."

Irma eased beside her. "It'll be OK. I'm sure when I confront him, he'll end it. We have the kids to think about. Yours were older when…"

"It doesn't matter. Betrayal is betrayal. If you can forgive him for sleeping with another woman, you're better than I ever thought about being. I sure couldn't. I didn't. The kids survived, and yours will too."

"We'll see."

"Don't fall for his crap. Lose the asshole."

Irma smiled. "I told Mom. She said I should work things out. Forgive him."

"Of course, she did. I went through it, Irma. Remember? Forgiveness or not, he doesn't deserve a second chance. No cheater does."

"Are we talking about Zane or Mitchell?"

"Both. They always were good buddies."

"Zane messed up, but I have to try. I can't give up."

"Like I did? The disappointment and embarrassment of our mother?"

"She's not embarrassed by you."

Trudy breathed deeply. "Look. You do what you must, but when you figure out that Zane won't end his little tryst, I'll be here for you."

"I'll remember that. Thank you." Irma headed to the door. "I meant what I said. You are a special woman. I wish I had your strength. I don't."

Trudy faced the door, blood boiling through her veins.

If I could get my hands on Zane, I'd hurt him right now. How can he do this to my sweet sister?

She turned and peered out the window, forcing back the bile in her throat as her sister's slumped shoulders disappeared inside the Lexus.

No money in the world excused staying with a wayward man.

Trudy's Anger

The morning with Irma somersaulted in Trudy's mind throughout the day. She tried working.

No use.

Leaning back, she cracked her neck, willing the stress to leave. It disobeyed.

Mid-afternoon, dark skies and a low, distant rumble matched her grumpiness. Too much grumpiness—for too many days. In Gertrude and in herself. The house groaned with sorrow. Bitterness spilling over into the dreary mood.

So not me. This house. This old woman. Rubbing off on me. Corrupting my mind.

She slumped.

Who was she kidding? The years of subdued anger tugged at her heart and mind.

As the first drops of rain pelted the roof, Trudy lost control—again. Tears cascaded, unbidden, and for once, she didn't attempt stopping them. Years wasted in bitterness flooded her with regret.

Why did she hold all the bad stuff inside?

"I don't want to end up like Aunt Gertrude," she whispered to the swaying trees. "I can't be so angry anymore."

"Why are you angry, dear?" The softness of Aunt Gertrude's voice surprised her. "What's wrong?"

Trudy flicked away the tears and turned to her aunt.

How much did she hear?

Questions colored Gertrude's eyes as she tilted her head.

"Auntie. You're up from your nap. Shall I make tea?"

The old woman shook her head. "Not now. Tell me what's wrong. Did I do something to upset you?"

Trudy crumbled. "Oh, Aunt Gertrude." Sobs broke. "I

wasted all these years working, trying. Never enough. I made so many stupid decisions, letting people hurt and disappoint me far too many times. I thought I forgave everyone. I tried. But I keep seeing all this junk from my past, and anger bubbles up all over again." She took a deep breath. "What's the matter with me?"

Gnarled hands reached out and grasped Trudy's. "Oh, honey. I fear I taught you too well the wrong lessons. I never forgave my father, and it permeated all my world. Somehow, let it all go." Tears pooled in Gertrude's cloudy eyes, but dared not escape. "Then forgive yourself, and put down that big stick."

"Big stick?"

"Yes. The one you use to beat yourself." She released Trudy.

"But how? How do I let go?"

"Forget. You can't be angry about what you don't remember."

Trudy doubted that. Her aunt remained in bitterness despite the dementia. Perhaps her mind held fast to the deepest wounds and couldn't hide those memories. Maybe if she forgot the bad stuff before the dementia stole everything from her...

Gertrude broke her thoughts. "What does an old woman have to do for a cup of tea?" The harshness returned.

Trudy knew her aunt was right. She must find a way to let go of the past—forever. Before it was too late, and the regrets that lay buried deep made their way to the surface if she, too, became demented.

An inner murmur calmed Trudy.

Give it to the Lord, child. That's how.

As Trudy prepared tea and a snack, she prayed, "Lord, take this bitterness and all the terrible memories. Take them as far as the east is from the west. I don't want them to haunt me years from now."

Knowing the anger still seethed, she forced a smile and carried the tray to her aunt,.

Gertrude's Repentance

Fierce drops pelted the window as Gertrude sipped her tea. A cardinal swept from below and dropped into a nest, high above the window.

Such a beautiful bird.

Carefree.

Independent.

The rain bounced against the tree, dripping, running a race to see which drops hit the ground first. The poor bird, hidden in the nest puffed itself against the chill. Not much shelter from the horrid thunderstorm.

Maybe not all carefree.

Branches swayed, whirling as the tree fought to stand upright. She hoped the storm didn't dislodge the nest.

Some carefree life. A lot like me. I always claimed how God blessed me. And He did. My sweet Ben, and his beautiful Trudy. When he named her after me, I cried. Did not let anyone see those tears. A proud, sophisticated woman hides her emotions. But hiding them only made the bad ones stronger.

Now what? Is this despair all that's left for me?

Gertrude stared across the yard, her bottom lip quivering. She never wanted to be so angry. The shed loomed against the dark sky. Scenes from her life poked her brain, pinpricks of moments, feelings, pain, memories.

Anguish.

So tired. I'm ready, Lord. I can't bear this sorrow any longer.

A soft yet firm voice spoke. "Gertrude."

She jerked her head up, scanning the room.

No one.

Great. Now I hear voices, too?

"Gertrude. You know My voice. You know who I am."

Silence roared at her.

"Lord?"

"I see you. I know your pain, your sorrow."

"It's too much. I can't bear it."

"I never meant for you to carry it. Let go, my beloved. Forgive and let go, so you can come Home in peace."

Gertrude ran fingers across her cheek, wiping away the wetness. She whispered, "How? I want to, but I don't know how."

"Forgive your earthly father, as I always forgave you for any sin."

Forgive that you may be forgiven. Not exactly right, but somewhere in the Bible. She remembered that much.

"I tried to forgive him. But I couldn't. He hurt me. Deeply. In more ways than I can count."

"I know, and because you never forgave him, he wields that power against you—all these years later, daughter. Don't you think it's time to take care of this?"

"Oh, Lord. Help me. Show me how to forgive that man."

"Just speak it."

"I… I for…"

She clenched her fist. "I can't. I don't forgive him!"

"Gertrude. What he did doesn't deserve forgiveness, and whether he repented doesn't matter. No sin reaches beyond my mercy. You know that. If anyone seeks My forgiveness, you know Jesus paid the price, and I forgive—no matter how heinous the crime. As my beloved daughter, you can too. Don't let another man's sin continue destroying the joy and peace in your soul."

"Lord, I want to be able to forgive—to release all this pain." Quiet sobs shook her body.

After several minutes, the voice returned. "Speak it again. And mean it."

Gertrude peered around the room. Should she get on her

knees? Like that could happen. She clasped her hands together. "Oh, Lord. I don't know if I can forgive him, but I sure want to try. Forgive me for clinging to it all this time."

Sudden peace flooded her mind. She closed her eyes and drew in the deepest breath she'd taken in years. Releasing it slowly, she looked through the window. In the setting sun, a rainbow appeared over the shed. "OH. Thank you, Lord."

Her wrinkled hand swiped the wetness from her cheeks again. As she leaned back, Gertrude calmed. The pinpricks continued, and one-by-one, she prayed over each bit of pain.

So many wounds. Why did I wait until my final days before letting God heal me? I wasted my life with bitterness eating away inside.

For a long time, Gertrude sat in the stillness, bitterness trickling from her soul through her eyes. Finally, exhausted, she took another deep breath, rubbed the wetness from her face and closed her eyes again. Like a soft blanket on a chilly night, warmth covered her, replacing the remaining sorrow with comfort. A slow smile grew.

She opened her eyes and yawned.

I should find Trudy, say goodnight, and get to bed. I do not trust myself to speak right now. Drained. How do I explain this evening? It makes little sense to me—this sudden peace. Perhaps forgiveness did its work.

Pushing up from the chair, she steadied herself before crossing the den and ventured toward her bedroom. At the French doors, she peered into the study. Trudy, at the desk, her head buried in her hands.

Poor girl. She looks tired too. In a minute.

Gertrude eased past and found a gown on the end of her bed. For a change, she slipped out of clothes and into the softness of flannel without help.

"Nice. I think tonight will be my best sleep ever. No nightmares. No sorrow."

She smiled.

The sound of sobs tiptoed through the hallway.

"Trudy?"

No idea what happened, but the precious child needed her, and for once, she had enough peace to offer comfort.

Trudy's Healing

After leaving Gertrude with her tea, Trudy retreated to the study. She wanted to shake all the negative emotions, but Irma kept popping into her thoughts. She opened her computer.

Work. Focus on anything but Irma and her mess.

It worked for a while, but the thoughts continued pounding her, making her head throb until she finally gave up trying to ignore them.

How could Irma stay with a cheater? She didn't. She kicked her ex out with the trash. Maybe she should have given Mitchell another chance—stuck it out a little longer. Would he have changed? Quit cheating?

Her phone chirped.

She glanced at it. A text from her daughter.

"heard from dad. got caught again. she left."

Trudy shook her head, the answer to her question clear.

He didn't change. Still his old cheating self.

She typed a reply. *"Sorry to hear that. Don't know why he doesn't learn."*

"I know. he's torn up this time."

Trudy's jaw tightened. She didn't want any part of this. Been there too many times.

"I can't help him, baby girl. And you can't either. He has to change his ways."

"But mom he needs you, needs someone who cares"

"That isn't me. He burned that bridge. I know he's your father, but I can't help him. Not anymore. I'm sorry."

"You gotta forgive him please just call him"

Trudy laughed. Call him? Comfort him when he sinned—again? Not on her life.

Memories rushed from every direction, pummeling her with

pain and sorrow.

How can I let go of the past when it keeps coming back to bite me?

As emotions bubbled deep, they clawed their way to the surface. She tried pushing them back down, but they battled for release. Despite her best efforts, they escaped, leaving her in a pool of despair, harsh sobs shaking her body.

Sitting at the desk, she rested her head in her hands and let the sobs escape.

A bony hand rested on Trudy's shoulder.

Great! Gertrude. Just what I don't need.

"What's the matter child? Why are you so sad?"

Did her aunt even know her?

She didn't want Gertrude to see her crying. She didn't like anyone to catch her crying.

"Nothing. I'm fine." She wiped away the tears, demanding the sobs cease.

"You don't sound fine, dear. Tell me what's troubling you."

Trudy stared at her aunt.

She's not my aunt. She has no idea what's happening.

The young woman sighed. Gertrude couldn't help having Alzheimer's. None of this mess was her fault.

"Auntie, sometimes life seems too hard. It gets to me."

"I'm sorry, dear. Life isn't easy, is it?"

Trudy half-listened as the old woman spoke in a comforting tone, words that could bring relief if not coming from the one who caused a good deal of her sorrow lately. What happened to the aunt who truly comforted her in the past? A disease stole her, just like a drunk driver stole her dad. Neither situation fair, but life didn't always play fair, did it? How much longer could she hold on without letting bitter bile fill her heart? Maybe it already did.

Gertrude stopped talking, placed a finger on Trudy's chin and lifted it, the same way she did a lifetime ago. Trudy forced a smile, knowing her aunt wanted to capture her attention.

"Trudy, do not end up like me. Do not cling to the bitter sorrow of life. Release it, and allow Father God to heal it. I have. Finally."

The younger woman gasped.

Did she just call me Trudy? She recognizes me?

She looked up, catching the stream that followed the path of a wrinkle. The two women embraced, a gentle yet firm hug. Trudy melted into her great aunt's arms, fresh sobs breaking through her resolve not to cry.

Gertrude pulled back a little. "Promise me you will deal with this. Let it go, baby, and let God pour his oil on your head. Figuratively, of course. I do not want oil all over my desk." She grinned.

"Thank you, Auntie. I'll try."

Stepping away, Gertrude said, "Do more than try. You'll feel better. I love you, sweet Trudy."

"OK."

"I'm tired, need to sleep now. Goodnight, dear." And with that, the demented woman returned, shuffling toward her bedroom.

"I'll be there in a minute, Auntie."

She should follow, make sure Gertrude got into bed without any problems. But she already had on a nightgown. She'd be fine for a minute. Besides, Gertrude nailed it. She had to rid herself of the bitterness.

Immediately.

Trudy slipped into the quiet darkness of the foyer and kneeled beside the table holding the ancient family Bible. For a moment, she waited there, wondering if she still knew how to pray in earnest. Taking a deep breath, she poured out her heart.

Father, God, I haven't talked to You in so very long. I blamed You when Daddy died, and then Gertrude getting sick… All too much. I can't do this anymore.

She paused. Didn't feel right. The anger pulsating in her heart popped up long before that.

OK, let's get real. I'm mad—have been for a long time. Maybe it started before the cheating SOB You let me marry. OK—the one I chose to marry.

Trudy softened.

You tried to warn me didn't You? I knew in my heart he cheated with Sally days before he asked me to marry him. I think he asked, so I didn't dump him. He hated being alone. I knew, but I didn't want to be alone either. Still, I didn't deserve him abandoning us—his son, daughter and me. She doesn't remember the way he treated us, even before he left. Ignoring our needs, not caring about anyone but himself. And yes, I blamed You **and** *him for so long. I don't think I ever forgave him.*

Realization hit with a gut-punch that bent her in half.

Oh, Lord. I never forgave him. I didn't. I held this junk for almost 20 years. How do I let it go? How do I let any of this go? I don't want the bitterness, Father. Even a demented old woman has more sense than I do. I still don't know what made her so bitter, but she said she released it finally. I can't be 80 and still holding on to this garbage.

Sobs racked her body as Trudy continued.

Show me how to forgive. Teach me to release all this bitterness.

In the quietness, serenity flowed over Trudy. Warmth surrounded her, holding her like a mother embracing a small child. She had no explanation, no words to adequately describe the emotions tearing through her soul, unraveling and repairing rips in her heart.

Peace. Pure, simple peace.

Father, I want to forgive. Help me forgive—the husband who left me, the man who took my father, the HR manager who wouldn't give me more time, Aunt Gertrude for keeping secrets and growing old and senile. Most of all, forgive me for holding these terrible wounds for so long, for blaming You. Forgive me and help me move forward.

She continued pouring out her heart, at moments almost

shouting again, but pulling back so she didn't disturb her great aunt. She wept, prayed, reflected. Wept more. Things she buried climbed to the surface. As each wound blipped on her mind's radar, she prayed about it, forgiving and asking for forgiveness. Finally, she slumped.

Father, most of all, I need Your forgiveness for letting all these wounds separate me from You. I know none of it came from You, but You can still use it. Even with Mitchell—maybe. He needs You, too. More than ever. I'm a mess, but he has a history too. I don't want to be with him again, but my daughter needs me to care about him. I can do that for her—with Your help of course. Thank you.

In the afterglow, she sat back, closed her eyes and breathed deeply before rising. No longer smelling a musty house, Trudy inhaled a scent of freshness she couldn't explain.

She smiled, almost dancing to the kitchen. Couldn't forget Gertrude's nightly cup of herbal tea. Glancing at the clock, her mouth flew open. Wow. More time with God than she realized. Gertrude might already be asleep, and she might not understand. But Trudy couldn't wait to tell her aunt that she, too, released her bitterness.

At the bedroom door, Trudy knocked softly. "Auntie? Are you asleep?" She pushed the door open.

In the rocker beside the bed, Gertrude slumped to the side, her hand resting on the open Bible. That didn't look comfortable.

Trudy touched her great aunt's shoulder. "Aunt Gertrude?"

No response. No movement.

"Gertrude." Trudy touched the hand. Slightly cool, but warm. She waited in horror, searching the chest. No rise or fall.

"Gertrude?"

She shook the old woman. "Aunt Gertrude. Wake up. Please."

Still nothing. She watched, expecting eyes to open, or a sudden expansion of the chest.

Nothing.

"NO!"

Tears burst from Trudy's eyes, relentlessly echoing her soul.

Gone without warning, Gertrude managed to give her one final gift. The insistence to forgive.

Trudy kneeled beside her great aunt. "I released my bitterness too, Auntie. I let it go. Thank you for wanting to fix me at the end." Trudy wiped away her tears. "I guess no one will ever know the secrets that left you so broken. They don't matter now, do they? Rest in peace, dearest one. I still love you."

Trudy turned from her aunt and picked up the phone to call Bessie.

"Hello? Trudy?"

"She's gone, Bessie."

"Oh dear. Let me throw on clothes, and I'll be right there to help you find her and…"

"No, Bessie. She's gone."

"Ohhh. Are you sure?"

"Yeah. I think."

"I'll get there as fast as I can."

As they disconnected the call, Trudy peered at Gertrude's NIV Bible, Luke 6:37 highlighted in yellow.

"Forgive and you will be forgiven. Yes, Gertrude. No matter how difficult, we must forgive."

She kissed her aunt's forehead and silently went to wait for Bessie.

Friends and Allies

The word of Gertrude's demise spread like butter on a hot biscuit. After the best night's sleep Trudy had in years, she awoke to a doorbell ring. She threw on a robe and hurried down the stairs while Bessie ushered Kit through the living room toward the kitchen.

Screeching to a halt, Trudy blinked. "Hello, Kit."

The neighbor handed Bessie two dishes and turned to Trudy. "Oh, Trudy. I'm so sorry to hear about Gertrude. After that one day... Well, she scared me, so I stayed away. Maybe I shouldn't have. I had no idea..." Her voice faltered, red rimming her eyes. "If I knew..."

"Don't worry, Kit. Gertrude surprised us all. We knew she had dementia, but I sure didn't expect her to just go without warning. Trust me, she scared me that day with you and several times after." Trudy chuckled. "Good days and not-so-good. I can at least say the last months were anything but boring."

Kit nodded. "I can't imagine. Mama doesn't walk well anymore, but she's sharper than a straight pin. How awful for you to experience all that with Gertrude. I loved the woman, but she..." Kit sniffed. "I don't want to speak ill of her."

"I know. She had a mean streak. Years of pent-up anger, I think. Before the end, she made peace with her past."

"Did you... Were you...? I'm just gonna ask. Did you watch her take the last breath?"

"No. I found her, still warm, but very much gone."

"I don't know what I'll do when Mama goes." She placed a hand over her chest. "I don't know if I can stand it."

"Hopefully, that won't be soon. But when it happens, you'll get through it."

"I suppose. Well, I'm sure you'll have visitors soon. I hope you don't mind, but I told a few neighbors, and I called the pastor."

"Thanks for the heads up. I should probably get dressed."

"Yes, of course. If you need anything, let me know. In a strange way, I loved her. Alongside that meanness, she hid a soft heart."

"That she did." Trudy walked Kit to the door, then headed to the kitchen.

"Bessie, what are you doing here?"

"I figured you might need help getting through this morning. Didn't know whether to expect your sister or maybe your mom."

Trudy's eyes widened as she gasped. "I haven't told them. Oh my goodness. I need to call them."

Bessie placed a steaming mug in Trudy's hand. "Go put some clothes on, hon. I suspect the next-door neighbor has the entire street lined up for comfort food."

"You're right. I'll call Irma and Mom, too. Not sure either one cares much. I'm so glad you came over, even if you didn't have to."

With a snort, Bessie turned away. "The old woman kinda grew on me. And if I'm honest, so did you." She turned back. "You look different this morning."

"Grace, Bessie. God's grace."

Pushing back tears, Trudy strolled from the kitchen and climbed the stairs slowly, realizing she had a rough day ahead—full of decisions.

At the landing, she climbed the steps and glanced into the forbidden bedroom. The quilt hung crooked, no doubt her rushed attempt at pinning it back in place. Unable to maneuver the stairs, Gertrude didn't know what she discovered. It seemed senseless now, that idea of trying to recover the past. Still, she wondered about the contents of the safe. Did it hold anything of value or simply a void as vast as the hole in her heart?

She started to go in, but the chime of the doorbell stopped her. More guests. Dress. Go make arrangements. Deal with the safe later. If she could figure out the combination.

In her bedroom, Trudy called her sister, who picked up after only one ring. "Hey, Irma."

"Hey, Trudy. How's it going?"

"Gertrude…" She swallowed a knot. "I found her around midnight last night in her rocking chair. She's gone, Irma."

For a few seconds, Irma didn't answer. She finally responded. "Are you OK?"

"Yeah. I didn't expect it so soon."

"Well, it's gotta be a relief. I mean with her not recognizing you sometimes, and that meanness coming out."

"It's weird though. Last night, I almost felt like the old Gertrude came back. Caring, comforting me. The last conversation you and I had… Let's just say it raised some anger I left boiling in my gut. She caught me crying and urged me to forgive and let it go."

"Gertrude did that?"

Trudy laughed. "I know. The epitome of bitterness wanted me not to keep mine."

Irma chuckled. "Maybe she had a moment of repentance."

"I think she did. I seriously think something happened in her before that. She had a softness to her that I never saw—except with Daddy. She loved him with everything she had."

"Yes, she did. I am sorry. Shall I call Mom for you?"

"If you don't mind. I slept late, and the neighbors keep popping in with food and words of sympathy. I need to put on some clothes and go finalize all the details with the funeral home, too."

"I'll take care of making calls to family—although we don't have all that many relatives to notify. Then I'll meet you at the funeral home. No one should have to go through that alone."

"Thank you. See you later."

Trudy disconnected, blinking and shaking her head. She fully expected some snide remark, not an ally.

Glad she didn't. I don't want to be angry with my sister. Mom probably won't show the same restraint. Not sure I need that right now.

She showered and dressed, then headed downstairs.

More strangers sat in the living room, Bessie serving them coffee and plates filled with goodies.

"Hi, I'm Trudy."

One woman wiped her mouth before replying. "We know. Gertrude talked about you all the time, showing us your picture. She was so proud of you and your sister. Is she here too?"

"Irma? No. I just talked to her though. I didn't call last night."

"Understandable, dear. The nurse insisted we help eat this cake. I hope that's alright."

"Oh, yes. Please. People in the neighborhood brought food over early this morning."

"Well, we ladies from the church will bring some, too. And the pastor should come by later today."

Trudy didn't know what to make of the sudden show of affection. For a moment, anger tickled her throat, wondering why none of them visited earlier, but she pushed it aside.

The other woman said, "Several of us talked to Gertrude over the last few months, but she insisted you didn't need anything. Proud woman, but we all loved her dearly. She had those moments when her words came across harsh, but inside, she was a softy. Just don't repeat that, cos she'll come haunt me for saying it." She smiled.

Trudy nodded, not sure how to react. The clock chimed. "I hate to leave, but I really need to go take care of arrangements. Please stay for as long as you like. If Bessie needs to go, just lock up when you leave."

"We plan to stay for a while, if you don't mind," the first woman said. The second nodded. "That way, you can tend to business, and we'll serve guests for you and leave the kitchen clean. You don't need all that to worry with."

Not trusting her voice, Trudy nodded. She sniffled. "Thank you. I'll be back as soon as I can."

Bessie came around the corner as Trudy grabbed her purse. "You OK?"

"Yes. I just want to get this stuff taken care of. These church ladies say they plan to stick around, so if you need to go…"

"I do have a patient or two I need to visit. I'll drop back by later to check on you."

"I'm fine—or will be after I take care of the arrangements. Irma's meeting me there."

"Good. She should. You know where I am if you need me."

"Thanks, Bessie. Last night—strange. I'd like your take on it. But for now, I really gotta go."

"I look forward to hearing the details. Go, hon. And be safe."

"Always."

The Will

Trudy pulled into a parking space near the attorney's office, relishing the chance to walk. She missed the long walks that so often cleared her head and helped with controlling weight. Gertrude didn't care for walks other than puttering in her backyard garden.

But Gertrude no longer ruled her days—or nights.

Instead of energizing her, every step grew heavier. As she looked around, familiar sights stared back, covered in a subtle grayness. Stepping through the door, she peered around the cozy waiting room.

No one.

I spent all these months alone—except for Bessie. Why should today be any different?

She sniffled, approaching the receptionist. "I'm Trudy Ryan, here to see Mr. Bastian."

"We all hated to hear about your grandmother's passing."

"My great aunt."

"Right. I always forget she never adopted Ben. She couldn't have treated him more like a son than if she gave birth to him."

"I know. She loved him so much, and he loved her."

Don't cry. Don't you dare let this flow start. It will never stop if you do.

"Mr. Bastian said people filled the chapel at her funeral. Quite the character, that Ms. Ryan. But she had a golden heart."

"Yes. She hid it well most of the time, but I saw the genuine Gertrude, and I loved her."

"I'm sure." The receptionist glanced over Trudy's shoulder. "Isn't your sister coming?"

Trudy shrugged.

"Have a seat. I'll let Mr. Bastian know you arrived."

"Thank you."

She moved to an over-sized chair and slumped into it, trying to push thoughts down. She didn't want to think. To remember the good or bad from the past months. She searched for a tissue. Maybe holding one could stem the tears before they dribbled beyond control.

As the door opened, she looked up. Her heart jumped, a lump forming in her throat.

"Irma?"

Her sister stood before her, dressed more casually than usual, her hair pulled back and up with a clip. Trudy's mind raced back to the day at the funeral home when her sister showed up in workout clothes. Both versions so unlike Irma.

"Hey, Trudy."

"I didn't expect you. Are you alright?"

"Yeah. Mr. Bastian said I should be here for the reading of the will. Though I can't imagine Aunt Gertrude leaving me anything."

"Don't be so sure about that, Irma. One of her friends mentioned how proud she was of us both."

"Really?"

"Yeah. Wish she told us."

"I know. She didn't hand out compliments. Not even with Daddy."

"That's true."

The receptionist returned. "Good. You're both here. Follow me, please." She led them down a short hallway into a conference room. "Can I get you anything? Coffee? Tea?"

Both women shook their heads.

"OK. If you change your minds, let me know. Mr. Bastian will be only a moment longer."

After a minute, Trudy stood and ventured over to the credenza with water and ice in a pitcher and glasses beside it. Her mouth dry, she glanced at Irma. "Want some?"

"No. I just wish he'd get this done." She chewed on a fingernail—something she stopped before high school.

"You look nervous, Irma. Why are you wound like Gertrude's ancient clock?"

Her sister's gaze darted to the door. "Do you think she had money? Real money, I mean."

"Who knows. She accused me of trying to steal her money, but that's common for Alzheimer's patients."

"But you paid her bills."

"She had a sizable bank account, but not millions or anything. Without a mortgage, she socked away most of her paychecks. But whether she had any investments? I suppose that's for Mr. Bastian to reveal."

As Trudy retook her seat, she placed the water glass on the table, sloshing some over the sides. "Oh my gosh. I'm so clumsy today." She jumped up, retrieved several napkins and cleaned up her mess before taking her seat again.

Irma giggled. "Guess I'm not the only nervous one."

Trudy took a deep breath and released it. "You got me. I don't know what to expect, but I have a sinking feeling I have a long road ahead cleaning out that massive house. I wonder how much she stipulated in the will? Some people try to keep control from the grave."

"Guess we'll see."

The door swung open, capturing their attention. "Good morning, ladies. I'm sorry to keep you waiting. Can I have my assistant get you some coffee?"

"No." Trudy shook her head. "I already managed to spill water. I don't trust myself with coffee."

He laughed. "Nothing to be nervous about. Gertrude's will—straightforward, short, and sweet. You are the only two named to inherit anything, and I don't anticipate anyone else coming forward to stake a claim. Do you?"

Tiny footprints crawled over Trudy's consciousness. Could there be someone else with a stronger claim to Gertrude's estate? She had no way of knowing. Maybe Gertrude left the safe combination in the will. She hoped for such a simple resolution. If not, she might need a locksmith capable of cracking it. But if Gertrude had a child, surely, she put him or her in the will. If she knew the child's whereabouts. If the baby survived.

Still so many unanswered questions.

Trudy pressed her arms against her stomach.

I should've tried harder to learn the truth.

No time for guilt. Mr. Bastian's voice broke into her wayward thoughts, bringing her back to the moment.

"To Irma. Your mother coddled you too much, I fear, making you weak. And that controlling husband of yours did not help. He kept a close thumb on you most of the time, although he managed to do it from a distance. I detest the idea of him receiving a dime—even a penny—of my money. You may someday come to your senses and break free from him. If you do, I'm leaving $250,000 in a trust fund for you. Mr. Bastian, as the trustee, can release any amount to you for stated purposes that do not include access by Zane or your disrespectful children. Stand up, find your strength, and become the beautiful woman I always admired. You have it in you." The attorney paused. "Do you have questions, Irma?"

Wild eyes blazing, she licked her lips. "Is this real? She left me a lot."

"Yes. But it has tight stipulations about withdrawals. She wanted to provide for and protect you. Zane can't touch it. You might be wise not to share the amount with him."

A quarter million dollars? Gertrude had that kind of money? Wow. Who knew?

Irma nodded. "I agree. Not telling him anything about it."

Mr. Bastian smiled and turned back to the will. "My dear namesake we call Trudy. You always put up with me, but after Ben died, you became more than a caregiver. You befriended me, enduring the many tirades about government, life, neighbors. More than once, I lashed out at you, grieving over your father. And for that, I am sorry. You went through tough times and stood firm. I am proud of the strong, beautiful woman you became."

The attorney took a sip of his coffee and proceeded. "Everything I own belongs to you now. Do with them as you will, although I always hoped you might one day choose to live in my childhood home, maybe pass it down to future generations. You may give the antique furniture to your mother, if you wish. She always had an eye on Mama's things. But keep the trunk. You will find the key in my secret key-hiding plaque. It contains memories only you could treasure. Look behind the quilt, unless you already sneaked up there and did it. All in the closet, keep close to your heart."

Mr. Bastian looked up. "Trudy, the market value on that house itself—I haven't had time to get an assessment, but I suspect well over a million dollars—maybe closer to two. Plus, investments, bank accounts, all that—another $500,000 give or take."

Trudy grabbed Irma's hand. Spots danced before her, muscles refusing to make her arms or legs move. "She used to tell me she had plenty to take care of us—that I could forget my job. I... I... I thought the dementia had her imagining things. It wasn't a delusion?"

Mr. Bastian laughed. "No. A very wise woman, she took out a massive life insurance policy on her mama before her father died. Then she came to me when she moved back in after his death. No mortgage or car payment, she kept her job for a time. Then after her mama passed, Ben grew up, and she went back to work, making a nice salary. With my help, she made wise investment choices. I hope you'll let me continue advising you."

"Absolutely." Trudy cocked her head at Irma. "You believing this?"

Irma shook her head. "Too much to comprehend."

Mr. Bastian smiled. "I'll take care of title transfers for the car and house. I suggest you not rush to any decisions though. Let yourself grieve and consider all options." He stood. "One more thing. Gertrude called me several months ago. She wrote a letter for you, Trudy, but I never received it. Do you know anything about that?"

Trudy scratched her head. "I remember one night—she seemed secretive. But I never saw a letter. She certainly didn't ask me to mail it."

"Well, look around. She insisted I get it to you when she passed. I didn't expect that to happen so soon. If it isn't in her desk, check her Bible—or the pantry, or freezer… With dementia, she might have put it anywhere. Let me know when you find it."

"I will. Any idea what she wrote?"

"Something about secrets, but she went chasing a rabbit all the way down its hole and out the other side after that." He shrugged and shook both their hands. "I'll talk to you both when you're ready."

The women shook as they held each other up and exited the office.

Irma spoke first. "Lunch?"

"Nah. I'm not that hungry. Later this week, and I'm buying this time."

In her car, Trudy threw back her head, willing the spinning to stop.

Gotta go to Gertrude's and find that letter. Secrets? Hopefully she gave me the answers too.

The Letter

When Trudy stepped into the dark interior of the house, silence deafened her. No TV, no soft music—nothing. She listened in the stillness, half expecting Gertrude to call her name. But the silence remained, a lonely reminder of a life lived and lost.

She swallowed and headed to the study. Searching through the desk, she found nothing unexpected.

From the moment she found Gertrude, she avoided the bedroom. Never considered going back for the Bible her great aunt adored. She hesitated at the door, dreading the memories of that night.

With a deep sigh, she pushed the door open and stepped inside. The Bible lay on the bedside table where someone put it before removing the corpse.

She picked it up and sank into the creaky rocking chair—Gertrude's last place in the home.

Creepy.

Get a grip, Trudy. It's not like she wanted to haunt this place. The gardens maybe, but not the house.

With trembling hands, Trudy peeked through the Bible and finally found an envelope—her name written across the front. Drawing in a sharp breath, she looked around the room before retreating to her haven, the study. Safely tucked on the sofa, she carefully broke the seal and pulled out a single sheet of paper. Shaky, but Gertrude's handwriting.

My dearest Trudy,

My hands shake as I write this letter. An evening when my mind works. I think. I vaguely remember you mentioning something you found in my closet.

No one was supposed to find those secrets until after I died. It is why I never let you and Irma play in the closet. The adventurous one, Irma, would find my little box. You would scour every inch, driven by curiosity.

You already know about Will, then. I loved him with all my heart. Even now, I cannot bear thinking of my handsome young love. My Father did not like him, but he liked no one who might take me from him. Such a sick, evil man. Rather than include all the secrets and details here, I plan on giving you a key to the answers.

Under the pearls in my jewelry box, the key to the lock-box in my closet. The documents there explain a little. Upstairs in the "forbidden" room, you will treasure everything in the ancient trunk. Mama brought that with her when she married. It belonged to her grandmother. She brought it when they immag—came to America. The key holder on the back porch holds a small key with hearts. A replica. I do not remember where I hid the original one.

Behind that trunk, you may notice the quilt on the wall. Mama made that with her mother not long after she married my father. She loved quilts. The old wardrobe up there holds many more. But behind the one hanging, you will find a closet. Everything inside belongs to you now. Treasure it all.

Irene would have loved you. I barely believed you arrived on what would have been her 44th birthday. What a perfect combination.

With all my love,
Gertrude

Trudy finished the letter, frustrated. "No mention of the safe or the combination! Gertrude! How could you forget that most important part?"

The last line of the letter glared at her. "Wait. A perfect combination? Could it be that simple? My birthday but the year of Irene's birth? No way."

She pounded up the stairs and pulled down the quilt. Light flooded the small closet as she yanked the string attached to the lone, naked bulb. She tiptoed through the closet and kneeled before the safe. Turning the dial a couple times to the right, she stopped on her month, all the way to the left and beyond to the correct day. Once more to the left, stopping at 36. She pulled the lever.

Nothing.

"Noooooo."

Trudy raced to her bedroom, retrieved a flashlight, and returned. She tried again, this time paying closer attention. Still nothing.

What if it has four numbers? Not usual, but Gertrude never did the expected.

She tried again, using several spin combinations.

Still nothing.

Lord, a little help here? I'm so close I can feel the answers screaming at me.

She froze. Of course. Not a simple, modern lock. Pulling her phone from a pocket, she searched for how to open an old safe. Following the directions, she started at the top. Spun the dial to the right four times, then carefully stopped on the first number. Three times to the left, then stopped at the second number. Two full turns back to the right. Third number—first half of the year. Then back to the left without a full turn, stopping at Irene's birth year.

She pushed the lever, holding her breath.

The door swung open.

Peeping inside, her eyes widened. Volumes of journals. Various sizes, shapes, colors. She pulled out a stack. So many. Gertrude's entire life, written between covers and hidden from anyone's prying eyes. On the bottom shelf, an old brown grocery bag caught her eye. Inside, green bills peeked back at her.

"Cash? Oh, Lord."

Squeezing her eyes shut, dizziness swept over her for a moment. When her hands quit shaking, Trudy opened her eyes again, and peeked in the grocery bag. Cash. Lots of cash.

Returning her attention to the safe, she retrieved a metal box and opened it. Gold and silver coins filled the box—more than she wanted to count. Beneath them, a fat envelope. Hands trembling, she moved it to the top. No writing. Plain, brown envelope.

The round clasp held by thin twine quivered as she fingered it. Did she want to look inside?

She hesitated—for a moment and then unwound the twine. When she pulled out the documents, she gasped. The very ones she hoped to find.

The flashlight flickered. Leaving the cash and coins inside the safe, she pulled out the journals and closed the door. Making several trips, she took the new treasure to her bedroom.

Curled up on the bed, she perused the documents. Certificates of achievement, awards, multiple admirable documents that meant little and answered no questions. Frustration seeped into her soul as she neared the bottom of the stack.

She huffed, studying one of the last documents. Adoption papers.

Hmmm. Maybe she adopted dad after all.

The words swam as Trudy read them. Birth mother: Gertrude Anne Ryan. Trudy gasped. Birth father: William Ryan Dade, deceased. Baby's name: Benjamin William Dade. Blood raced to her head, dizziness consuming her.

Daddy? No way.

She scanned the rest of the document. Adoptive mother: Irene Cathleen Franklin.

The paper fluttered to the bed.

The Journals

Gertrude. My grandmother—not my great aunt.

As Trudy let the thoughts play, she kept shaking her head. Impossible. But the papers didn't lie. Curled on the bed, she hugged a pillow, realization pummeling her logic.

The clock downstairs bonged twice.

With half her day gone, she stared at the journals.

More answers? Maybe.

Lead-filled legs barely obeying, she took the stairs, clinging to the banister. Her stomach grumbled, a reminder she had eaten nothing all day. After finding adhesive file stickers from the study, she detoured to the kitchen, selecting cheese, grapes and crackers to sustain her. Filling a glass with iced tea, she headed back upstairs.

First, identify dates of journals. Looking at the first and last entries, she wrote dates on the stickers and pressed them to the front of each book. Opening the oldest, she discovered a troubled young girl. Never allowed sleepovers at home or someone else's house. Few friends visited after school. Even babysitting Kit only served as a momentary reprieve, and her father kept half of any money she earned. The least infraction of the old man's rules met with swift and harsh punishment.

As Gertrude aged, the journal entries grew darker. She detailed nightly visits from her father. Trudy gagged, almost throwing up as she read. One entry stood out.

I finally confided in Irene. Father never 'loved' her the way he did me. Already married, she told me to come live with her. But Father... He'd never allow that. I mentioned it. He answered with his fist. I hate that man.

Unable to stand more, Trudy searched for the journals from 1956 and 1957. Those surely held the truth about Will. Flipping through pages, she scanned the words, searching for the name until she found it.

Will came to the house today. I wanted to run away—elope. But he wanted my father's blessing. Bad idea. I threw myself between them and caught the blow meant for my beloved. Now maybe he'll listen.

Bile rose in Trudy's throat again as she pictured Gertrude enduring a beating. She scanned a few more pages and stopped at an entry.

We did it! Will and I eloped. I lied about my age. I had to. I couldn't stay in that house one more day. We spent the night at an inn a few towns over. For the first time in my life, I understood what people meant when they said making love. So gentle and sweet. We both cried afterward.

Trudy sighed. An entry two months later.

I'm pregnant and scared. Will's off with the military. No one to protect me. I told Irene. She's pregnant too. I'm hiding it, but Mama knows. She can tell. I worry about her. She doesn't seem herself. I think my father's beatings damaged her brain. I know they almost destroyed her body.

Two days later. The words in the journal curdled Trudy's blood.

Father found out. About the pregnancy and the elopement. He says he's having it annulled, then he'll figure out what to do about the 'bastard'. But it isn't a bastard. Will married me before he touched me like that. He's a man of honor. I'm at Irene's now. Last night, the old man locked me in the shed. He left me there overnight, without a light. All night long, rats scuttled around the shed. I heard them squeaking. I climbed up on the worktable, trying to protect myself and the baby. Just before dawn, I dozed off, waking to a rat staring at me. I screamed. The rodent ran.

Mama unlocked the shed, knowing she'll probably meet with the old man's fists tonight. She helped me pack, gave me a few dollars, and called a cab. When Fred heard about everything, he insisted I stay, promising the old man won't get near me. I don't know if he can really annul the marriage, but I don't care. In my mind, I'll always be Will's wife.

Trudy placed the journal on the bed, grief covering her with icy fingers. She didn't want to read more. She had to read more. But only after a visit to the garden. She wanted to process all she knew so far—more terror than she ever imagined.

Upstairs again, she read every page of Gertrude's journals after she went to live with Irene. Days of them shopping for babies, a job, happiness for the sisters. Both babies due around the same time, they planned a future of precious cousins, raised more like siblings.

The day came when Gertrude learned of Will's death.

I cannot bear this pain. My heart—ripped from my chest. My beloved. Gone. How can I survive?

Trudy blinked back tears, refusing to read the rest of that entry. Sorrow too deep to carry, especially after Gertrude's death and learning the truth. She pushed past looming sadness and read more. Two months before the babies' due dates, Irene went into labor. She delivered, but the little girl died within 24 hours. Too tiny to survive, the sisters grieved together.

My heart hurts for Irene. She's broken, and nothing can fix her. Unless… I love this baby—Will's gift to me. But I can't raise him alone. Last week, a woman called me a whore. Because of the old man, no one knows I got married. What kind of life will this child have? No one knows about Irene's baby. We kept the death secret, mostly because Irene didn't want anyone to discuss her pain.

What if…? I can barely stand the thought, but I must do what is best for everyone. I will give my baby to my sister. I know it's a boy. Somehow, I know. He needs a daddy. Irene and Fred can adopt him—give him a proper home. I will still live here, be part of his life.

Spots dotted the page, splashes from a grieving heart that wanted the best for her son and to ease her sister's suffering.

Trudy searched for one last entry. She needed to know. The days around Gertrude's father's death.

I found Mama today. Tied up, starving, filthy. Never so mad. No matter what Father did to me, how dare he treat her like that? I wanted to beat him.

But I had Ben with me, and I knew that man would hurt me, then maybe kill Mama and my baby. I could never let that happen. I locked him in the shed, and I do not regret it for one second. I hope the rats taunt him all night long.

Two days later.

I found the old man yesterday, dead. When I opened the door, rats scurried away, leaving their poop beside his ice-cold body. I do not care if they ate their fill. He deserved it. The police suspect a heart attack. Not sure a man without a heart can have an attack. I thank God for setting us free from pure evil.

The words blurred. Trudy pulled a quilt over herself.

Exhausted, she fell asleep and dreamed of nothing.

Moving Forward

At the entrance to the restaurant, Trudy checked her image in the front window.

Not bad.

She smiled and pushed the door open. Glancing around, she expected to see Irma. The hostess approached. "I'm meeting my sister here, but I don't see her anywhere. We usually sit on the patio."

"No problem. We have plenty of tables out there. Bit windy for most folks today."

"We don't care. We prefer the quiet out there—easier to talk." Trudy smiled.

"Right this way."

After ordering iced tea for both of them, Trudy relaxed into her chair. A cardinal perched on the rail. "Oh, hello little friend. It's been a while since I last saw you."

The bird chirped a few times, cocked his head, and flew to a nearby tree.

No wonder Gertrude loved them so much. Sweet little birds.

A tall, short-haired blond in workout clothes plopped into the chair across from Trudy. She started to reprimand the woman. Drawing in a quick breath, she stared at her. "Irma?"

"Were you expecting someone else? You asked for this lunch meeting. Something important."

"I... I just didn't recognize you at first. The haircut. I... I never expected that. It's cute."

"Zane likes long hair. He never wanted me to cut it. So guess what? I showed him. I like it this way."

"Yeah. It looks amazing on you." Trudy didn't mention the dark circles under her sister's eyes.

"So, how is Zane?"

"Gone. Apparently, his mistress got pregnant and 'she needs him so much.' Makes me want to puke. Like the kids and I don't need him?"

"Actually. You don't, Irma. You will be fine without him. Good riddance. Let the slut have him. Matter of time before he cheats on her. By then, you will be over him and on to a better life."

Irma looked into the distance. "Do you think Mr. Bastian will release enough money for me to buy a house?"

"I'm sure he'll at least make sure you have a good down payment. If not, let me know. I happen to have two houses. I might sell one."

"No, Trudy. You can't let that cottage go. It's perfect for you."

"I know. But I love that old Victorian too."

"Rent one out."

"Maybe. The historical society called me. They want to have the house declared a historical landmark. Would I be crazy to do that and turn it into an art gallery?"

Irma brightened. "What a fantastic idea. I think even old Gertrude might like that idea."

"I could keep a couple of the bedrooms separate and have artists in residence at times."

"I love it. You should do it. Are you thinking of pursuing an art career yourself?"

"Already registered for a couple classes. I quit my job, too."

"No! What did Peter say?"

"Quote; 'I'm disappointed to see you leave, but if it's your dream, go for it.' Then he asked me out for dinner Friday night."

"He what?"

"Yep. He's not my boss anymore. We can date if we want."

"That rocks! See what happens when you look good? And you

do, by the way."

"Except for the puffiness under my eyes?"

"Well, I ignored that. Figured you ignored my dark circles."

"We know each other too well."

"With Gertrude gone, what keeps you up at night? Habit?"

"No. She had a safe, Irma. And she left the combination for me in that letter the attorney mentioned."

"Let me guess. Cash, gold, silver. You're a multi-millionaire, but you don't know what to do with it all."

Trudy laughed. "Not that much, but yes, a little cash stuffed away. I suspect she considered it her emergency fund. But it gets better."

"Better than money? Oh, no. That senility stuff's contagious, and you caught it from her. Forget lunch. Let's get you to the ER."

After a good laugh, Trudy took a sip of tea. "That feels so amazing."

"What?"

"Laughing. Seriously, though, I gotta tell you something unbelievable. Irene—our 'grandmother'—adopted Daddy."

"What? No way."

"Yes. You'll never guess his mother."

"You are not gonna tell me Gertrude."

Trudy nodded. "She was our grandmother, Irma."

"But she never got married. Scandalous!"

"She did. Will and she eloped, but then he went off into the military and died from some stupid infection. Her father annulled the marriage because Gertrude lied about her age. She lived with Irene, also pregnant. Irene's baby girl died, so Gertrude insisted she adopt Daddy."

"How do you know all this?"

"The safe held secrets. Years of journals. I read all day and night, finally falling asleep not long before dawn today. Irma, our grandmother had far too many secrets, and I understand where the bitterness originated. I wish she'd been able to forgive people who hurt her."

"Do you think Daddy knew?"

"No. Back then—too hard for unwed mothers. And the children caught the brunt of it. She protected him."

"Unbelievable."

"My thoughts exactly."

"So does any of this matter?"

"No. But I suspected Gertrude had a baby from something I found months ago. I worried that child might find out, come back, and want all her money. Not that we couldn't survive without it, but it sure makes our lives easier." Trudy sipped her tea. "You know, that Victorian has lots of space. If you need a place to stay, away from Zane, you're welcome."

"Maybe. I'm fighting him, Trudy. If he thinks I will lie down and let him bring his mistress into my house, he's more senile than Gertrude ever was."

"Good for you." Trudy raised her glass. "To moving forward. I'm so done with this journey to senility. I don't plan on ever going there again."

"Agreed." Irma clinked glasses. "To us. I look forward to a return to the closeness we had as kids. No Zane. Little Mom. And kids… well, I have a few more years, but it's time they learn some respect and responsibility. Don't you need help at the old house? I know a couple of teenagers who could use some off-screen time."

"I like that idea. Now, I'm starving. How 'bout I buy your lunch?"

An Afterword from the Author

Not all dementia comes from Alzheimer's, but all Alzheimer's is a form of dementia.

For a brief time, my mother and stepfather suffered from dementia. As he experienced a fourth round of cancer with no confirmation for the source, they made a decision to move into a local rehab and nursing facility. While we already saw hints of his dementia, he still had enough mental presence to realize he could no longer take care of Mom. Her waning health led to the decision. Part of him I never saw emerged after they moved. My siblings knew that piece well, but as the youngest, favored one, he never let me see it—until he did. Like Trudy, I faced cold facts I didn't like. For a moment, we thought Mom had dementia, too. After his death, she became more social and her mind improved.

Watching my stepmother and my brother-in-law's mom later, gave me another view of the harshness of dementia. The bitterness that arose from these people I loved troubled me. When I looked closer, it always existed, well hidden beneath the surface of people "blessed by God." The idea for this novel took root in my imagination.

In talking with others who served as caregivers, I came to realize not everyone yells and accuses and curses loved ones. Some told me their loved one never acted mean. Frustration and irritation, yes. But not what I experienced.

My observed conclusion—those who suppress anger and let it grow into bitterness become the mean old crazy person. Those without buried bitterness, suffer effects of dementia, but they don't necessarily become unbearable.

While many things can cause various types of dementia, Alzheimer's is the most common type. When it first develops, the person may hide the symptoms. In the mild stage, the person knows something's off, but others remain clueless. As the disease progresses, others see the signs. Everyone sees the changes. In the final stages, others know the person has Alzheimer's, but he or she no longer realize they have it.

A heartbreaking disease, the best defenses come from healthy nutrition, physical exercise, keeping the mind active, and remaining socially active. With no cure and no guarantee, the disease can attack anyone. Although research continues, we still have no cure for Alzheimer's, but with early diagnosis, potential medications, understanding, and a support group, those affected by the disease can enjoy a better quality of life.

For more information visit www.alz.org. The Alzheimer's Association provides classes, support groups, and local resources to join you on the journey—and it *is* a journey.

If the bitterness that runs rampant in this book struck a chord within you, let me encourage you to take a moment and look deeper within. While we may not choose whether to take a Journey to Senility, we can choose how deeply our journey wounds others.

Jesus didn't tell us to forgive because the offender needed our forgiveness, although they do. He told us to forgive, so we let go of anger and bitterness before it becomes a festering wound that spews gunk on everyone around us. Even the most sane person in the world can puke bitterness.

Forgiveness doesn't come easy. Can we forgive others without knowing God intimately through Jesus Christ? Perhaps. I never could. Without experiencing His love and forgiveness, I do not have the capacity to forgive others.

He waits for us to ask, but when we do, He forgives us and helps us forgive others, so we can experience a peace beyond comprehension. Today is a good day to forgive and receive forgiveness.

So, you will be saved, if you honestly say, "Jesus is Lord," and if you believe with all your heart that God raised him from death.

Romans 10:9 CEV

To learn more about a relationship with Jesus and walking in His forgiveness, you may want to read "Becoming a Disciple of Jesus," William L. Kynes, March 3, 2011, www.cslewisinstitute.org/resources/become-a-disciple-of-jesus-he-demands-our-all/

You may contact Lisa Bell through her website or by emailing LisaBell@bylisabell.com.

About the Author

Lisa Bell is a published author of fiction and non-fiction books. As a community editor for NOW Magazines LLC (*BurlesonNOW* and *WeatherfordNOW*), she has published hundreds of articles. Besides personal publications, she also has stories in several Chicken Soup for the Soul titles and other anthologies alongside developmental editing for numerous clients.

Lisa works with writers to encourage and help improve their skills. She offers her expertise to those who desire to pursue independent publishing. Providing coaching, editing, formatting, and cover design as well as assistance with uploading documents to chosen platforms, she supports writers who want to use cost-effective publishing options while creating quality products.

Lisa leads two writing groups that fall under the umbrella of Radical Writers (www.texasradicalwriters.com) and speaks or teaches whenever the opportunity arises. She holds a BS in Business Management from University of Phoenix, is a CLASS alumni, Editorial Freelance Association member, and active member of multiple writing groups. Single mother and grandmother, she lives southwest of Fort Worth, Texas.

For more information about the author, please visit www.bylisabell.com. You may email Lisa at LisaBell@bylisabell.com.
Lisa Bell (@lisa.bell.5249349) • Instagram photos and videos
Amazon Author Page: www.amazon.com/author/bylisabell

Other Books by Lisa Bell

Non-Fiction Titles

- ❖ *Littleness of Faith,* May 9, 2012, Radical Women
- ❖ *The Third Step,* August 28, 2012, CreateSpace Independent Publishing Platform
- ❖ *Homeless Hearts: A Journey of Spiritual and Emotional Healing,* October 30, 2019, Radical Women
- ❖ *My Inner Nemesis: A Journal Designed for Writers,* April 7, 2019, Radical Women
- ❖ *A Day in a Writer's World: Daily Planner for Writers,* December 29, 2020, Radical Women
- ❖ *Unwavering Honor,* with Jim Calams,

Fiction Titles

- ❖ *Out of the Dungeon,* February 15, 2013
- ❖ *Journey to Senility,* August 2022

UP Next?

Returning to the women introduced in *Out of the Dungeon,* the five-book *Walking in Freedom* series revisits each of the women confined in the dungeon with Charissa. A decade later, where are the women? Are they walking in freedom, or do they still have chains holding them back?